# Praise for the Violet Brewster Mystery series

'If it's cosy crime you're after, this has
all the essential ingredients'
***Daily Mail***

'An entertaining and engaging cozy mystery
set against a beautiful backdrop.'
**Clare Chase**

'Jane Bettany delivers cosy with a dash of sass –
thoroughly enjoyable and utterly irresistible'
**Peter Boland**

'A murder mystery with a blossoming romance . . .
what more could one ask for? Delicious!'
**Katie Gayle**

'Completely compelling from the get-go, I didn't want to put
it down! Brilliant cosy mystery at its most charming best.'
**Jonathan Whitelaw**

'A perfect cosy mystery with an engaging cast of
characters and a beautifully drawn setting'
**Roz Watkins**

'If you love cozy crime/mystery books then you
will not be disappointed . . . A book to put to
the top of your "must read now" pile!'
**C.L. Peache**

'Violet Brewster is everything you could want in
an amateur sleuth: empathetic, determined, and
ruthless in her quest for truth . . . A must read!'
**Charlotte Baker**

**JANE BETTANY** is the author of the DI Isabel Blood crime series, set in the fictional Derbyshire town of Bainbridge, and the cosy crime series featuring amateur sleuth Violet Brewster, which is set in the Peak District.

Jane's debut novel – *In Cold Blood* – won the 2019 Gransnet and HQ writing competition, which was for women writers over the age of 40 who had written a novel with a protagonist in the same age range.

Before turning to novel writing, Jane had been writing short stories and non-fiction articles for over twenty years, many of which have appeared in women's magazines, literary magazines, newspapers and online.

Jane has an MA in Creative Writing and lives in Derby.

## Also by Jane Bettany

The Violet Brewster Mystery Series
*Murder in Merrywell*
*Murder at the Book Festival*
*Murder at Maple Grange*
*Murder on Bluebell Hill*

The Detective Isabel Blood Series
*In Cold Blood*
*Without a Trace*
*Last Seen Alive*

# A Christmas Murder in Merrywell

## JANE BETTANY

ONE PLACE. MANY STORIES

HQ
An imprint of HarperCollins*Publishers* Ltd
1 London Bridge Street
London SE1 9GF

www.harpercollins.co.uk

HarperCollins*Publishers*
Macken House, 39/40 Mayor Street Upper,
Dublin 1 D01 C9W8
This edition 2025

1

First published in Great Britain by HQ,
an imprint of HarperCollins*Publishers* Ltd 2025

Copyright © Jane Bettany 2025
Emoji(s) © Shutterstock.com

Jane Bettany asserts the moral right to be identified as the author of this work.
A catalogue record for this book is available from the British Library.

ISBN: 9780008714833

This novel is entirely a work of fiction. The names, characters and incidents portrayed in it are the work of the author's imagination. Any resemblance to actual persons, living or dead, events or localities is entirely coincidental.

All rights reserved. No part of this publication may be reproduced, stored in a retrieval system, or transmitted, in any form or by any means, electronic, mechanical, photocopying, recording or otherwise, without the prior permission of the publishers.

Without limiting the exclusive rights of any author, contributor or the publisher of this publication, any unauthorized use of this publication to train generative artificial intelligence (AI) technologies is expressly prohibited. HarperCollins also exercise their rights under Article 4(3) of the Digital Single Market Directive 2019/790 and expressly reserve this publication from the text and data mining exception.

Printed and bound in the UK using 100% Renewable
Electricity by CPI Group (UK) Ltd

This book contains FSC™ certified paper and other controlled sources
to ensure responsible forest management.

For more information visit: www.harpercollins.co.uk/green

*For Sam and Janet
with love*

# Chapter 1

On a frosty Friday evening twelve days before Christmas, seven people had gathered in the bookshop at Merrywell Shopping Village. Raising glasses of hot cider, they were toasting the end of a successful first day for the much-anticipated Merrywell Christmas market.

After months of careful planning and preparation, the event had got off to a flying start. Throughout the day, crowds had milled around the craft stalls, buying handmade gifts and ornaments and enjoying the culinary offerings from a variety of street food vendors. The shopping village's deli, *The Epicurious*, had been doing a brisk trade in Stilton cheese and locally produced jars of preserves, and in the bakery, Fiona Nash had completely sold out of her festive mince pies and stollen bread. Inside the bookshop, the till had been ringing almost constantly, thanks mainly to the enormous and very eye-catching display of new releases just inside the door. Overall, it had been a hugely rewarding day for the traders, but also a long and tiring one. It was now a quarter to nine, and the shops and stalls had closed for the evening in anticipation of another early start the following morning.

At the bookshop counter, Judith Talbot clapped her hands

in a call for silence. As leader of Merrywell Parish Council, she considered it her civic duty to make a speech on such occasions.

'Congratulations, everyone,' she said, beaming happily. 'Thanks to your valiant efforts, today has been a resounding success, and I'm sure we can expect more of the same over the coming week. You've all worked jolly hard to pull this off, and on behalf of the parish council and the village, I'd like to thank you and say "well done" on delivering such a super event.'

She took another swig of hot cider and raised her glass again.

'Thank you, Judith,' said Eric Nash, the owner of the bookshop and chair of the local traders' association. 'I think I speak for the whole organising committee when I say the last few weeks have been extremely hectic. Putting on a Christmas market is no mean feat – but, miraculously, everything seems to have come together beautifully, and watching people enjoying themselves today has made all the hard work worthwhile. As you're aware, we have quite a few extra activities lined up for the week ahead. The local choir is coming over in the morning to sing carols, and Father Christmas will be putting in an appearance at three o'clock sharp both tomorrow and on Sunday.'

'Providing he can still fit into the suit,' said Matthew Collis, leaning in to whisper into Violet Brewster's ear. 'Dad's been Father Christmas at every local event for the last five years. The first time he volunteered, he needed extra padding to widen his girth. This year, Mum's had to let out the waistband on his red Santa trousers. She's putting him on a strict diet in the new year.'

Violet giggled. 'It's her own fault. Your mum's puddings are irresistible and highly calorific. She'll have to stop making them if she wants your dad to lose weight.'

Outside, the flashing, coloured lights on the huge Christmas tree went out suddenly, plunging the far corner of the courtyard into darkness, leaving only the strings of lights between the stalls to illuminate the cobbled square. Violet glanced towards the window, watching as Tim Waldron crossed in front of the bookshop in his high-visibility gilet. He was the caretaker at Merrywell Primary School, but had agreed to step in as a security guard for the week-long Christmas market.

'It looks like Tim's switching things off and doing his final rounds,' Eric said, bringing his short speech to an end and tilting his head towards the window. 'Now that everything's closed down for the evening, we should probably go home and get some sleep. In less than twelve hours we'll be back here getting ready to do it all over again.'

Violet had spent the day running a pop-up 'Christmas Past' booth at her videography business, *The Memory Box*, which was located in a small office in the shopping village. In exchange for a nominal donation to a local children's charity, she and her assistant, Molly Gee, had been offering visitors the opportunity to record a short video of their happiest or funniest Christmas memories. The booth had proved surprisingly popular, especially among the older generation, who'd relished the chance to appear on camera and reminisce about their festive antics from earlier decades.

'Unfortunately, it'll be another hour before I can go home,' said Fiona, with a heavy sigh. 'I need to go into the bakery to prepare six dozen mince pies and some more gingerbread people, ready for tomorrow.'

'I'll stay on and help you, love,' Eric said. 'I'll join you in a minute, once I've closed up the shop.'

'Go now if you like, Eric,' said Jill Atherstone, who was the bookshop's assistant manager. 'I can lock up here.'

Smiling gratefully, Eric thanked Jill and followed his wife through the side exit, which led directly into the bakery.

Taking the departure of the Nashes as their cue to leave, the rest of the group drained their glasses and put on their coats.

'I'll see you tomorrow then, Violet,' said Molly, as she wound a long woollen scarf around her neck. 'What time do you want me to come in?'

'How does ten o'clock sound? Things will be starting to get busy by then.'

'OK.' Molly gave her a double thumbs-up. 'Ten o'clock it is.'

'Are you going to be all right getting home, Molly?' said Matthew. 'It's late and it's dark out there.'

Molly smiled. 'Don't worry about me. Robert's still in his shop. I'm going over there now . . . He's promised to walk me home.'

Robert Dorman was the proprietor of the shopping village's *Antiques Emporium*, and also Molly's boyfriend.

'What about you, Jill?' Matthew said. 'Violet and I can wait while you lock up if you want some company walking into the village.'

Jill glanced at her watch. 'Thanks for the offer, but I'll be OK. Adrian said he'd come over to meet me. He'll be here in a minute, so no need for you to wait.'

As Jill began a final inspection of the shop, Violet, Matthew, Judith and Molly gathered their belongings and prepared to leave. As they reached the door, Tim Waldron burst in, bringing with him the distinctive, woody smell of winter air. Despite the padded coat he was wearing under his hi-vis gilet, he looked pale and cold.

'Goodness me, Tim, it must be awfully nippy out there,' said Judith. 'Look at you . . . you're shivering.'

Tim shook his head. 'It's not the cold making me shiver. I've just finished my last rounds. You're not going to believe this, but I've found a body.'

# Chapter 2

The recipients of this shocking and unwelcome piece of news gave a sharp, collective intake of breath.

'A body?' Judith said, sounding utterly horrified. 'What do you mean?'

'A body,' Tim repeated. 'A dead person. What's not to understand?'

'All right,' Judith snapped. 'There's no need to be flippant. If I'm failing to grasp what you're saying, it's because I'm in shock.'

'*You're* in shock?' Tim puffed up his cheeks and shook his head. 'Imagine how I'm feeling. I tell you . . . I wasn't anticipating this when I volunteered to help out at the Christmas market.'

'Are you absolutely certain the person you've found is dead?' Violet said, her heart racing as a rush of adrenaline kicked in.

'No doubt about it. As well as being the school's caretaker, I'm also one of its first-aiders. He's a goner all right. I've checked. There's no pulse and he's not breathing.'

'He?' said Judith, a sudden note of panic in her voice. 'It's not Andrew, is it?'

Judith's husband, Andrew, had texted her a few minutes earlier to say he was on his way over to meet her.

Tim screwed up his face. 'No, of course it's not. Do you really think I'd be talking to you like this if it was Andrew? I've no idea who the poor fella is. I've never seen him before in my life.'

'Have you rung the police?' Violet asked.

'Yep, they're on their way. Hopefully, they'll be able to work out who this guy is when they get here.'

'Is he out in the courtyard?' Matthew said, stretching his neck to look out of the window.

'No, he's round the back, at the far end of the alley,' Tim replied. 'Unfortunately, the big sensor light's packed up, so it's as black as a coal mine in there. Maybe whoever it is had one too many glasses of mulled wine, fell over in the dark and bashed his head.'

Judith released a long, shaky breath. 'We can't just leave him out there. Even if the poor man *is* beyond help, someone should stay with him until the police arrive. I think you're the best person for the job, Violet.'

'Me?' Violet shuddered, her blood running cold at the thought of standing guard over a dead body in a dark alleyway.

'As our local sleuth, you have experience of these things,' Judith said. 'And while you wait with the body, perhaps you could give the scene the once-over . . . look for clues as to what's happened.'

'Now hang on a minute, Judith,' Matthew said, raising a cautionary hand. 'Looking for clues and evidence is the police's job.'

'I'm well aware of that, but don't you think someone from the traders' association should check the area as well?' Judith said. 'If there's been a fatal accident because of inadequate lighting, there's every chance the man's family will want to sue. That could be bad news for the shopping village.'

'It's far more likely the poor bloke has taken ill, become disorientated, wandered off and collapsed,' Matthew said. 'Why else would he be in the alley? It's clearly marked, *no public access*.'

Judith flapped her fingers. 'We all know what the sign says, but like it or not, this guy *has* ended up in the alley. The question of liability is bound to raise its head.'

Violet held up her hands and waved them either side of her ears. 'Sorry . . . but do we have to have this conversation now? This is hardly the time to be worrying about liability. A man has died. Let's show him some respect, shall we?'

Judith sucked in a breath. 'My suggestion that someone stay with him was made out of respect,' she said, clearly unhappy about being taken to task.

Violet was willing to concede the point in order to keep the peace. 'I'm sure it was,' she said, 'and, on reflection, maybe you're right. Perhaps someone *should* wait with the body – but out of concern for the victim's dignity, rather than any possibility of legal action. If no one else is willing to volunteer, I *will* go and wait in the alley, providing Tim comes with me. I take it you have a torch with you, Tim?'

'Aye, I do,' Tim replied, tapping the pocket of his cargo pants. 'It's a good 'un too. Very heavy. Even so, it might be worth Matthew coming along as well. He's younger than I am.'

'What's age got to do with anything?' said Judith, her face puckering into a frown.

'You can't be too careful in these situations,' Tim said, sounding slightly embarrassed. 'I'm sure this poor chap died of natural causes, or as a result of an accident. However, it's also possible there's been some kind of jiggery-pokery out there in the alley – and if that's the case, someone might still be lurking around.'

Judith screwed up her nose. '*Jiggery-pokery!?*'

Matthew opened his mouth to say something, but Violet silenced him with a quick shake of her head.

'Come on, Matthew,' she said, resigning herself to the inevitable. 'Let's just go and take a look, shall we?'

'What about the rest of us?' said Molly. 'Can we go home, or do we need to wait here until the police arrive?'

Violet shrugged. 'None of us saw what happened, so it's not as if we're material witnesses. Even so, it might be worth sticking around for a while. Why don't you go over and tell Robert what's happened? You can wait with him until the police say it's OK to leave.'

Giving Molly and Judith a single brief nod, Violet zipped up her coat and took a deep, fortifying breath. Then, clutching Matthew's hand, she followed Tim out of the bookshop and into the courtyard.

Outside, the temperature was dropping rapidly and frost was glistening on the uneven cobbles. With its lights switched off, the Christmas tree looked dreary and forlorn – and although the multi-coloured lanterns strung between the empty stalls were still glowing brightly, they now seemed garish and incongruous.

'Wait here for a sec, would you?' Tim said, as he peeled off to the right and entered the small, windowless plant room that contained the shopping village's boiler, electricity meters and control switches. Seconds later, the coloured lanterns went out and Tim reappeared, eager to explain his actions.

'Didn't seem right,' he said. 'Festive lights blazing away when there's a man lying dead a few yards from here.'

Sticking close together, the trio traversed the courtyard, heading towards the alleyway in the corner. It was a narrow entry, roughly the width of an old-fashioned horse and carriage – a throwback to the nineteenth and early twentieth centuries, when the courtyard area had formed the busy stable block and workshops of the local manor house.

In the 1990s, when the complex of buildings had been converted into a shopping village, the alleyway had been deemed too narrow for modern cars, and a decision had been made to mark it 'out of bounds'. A large sign had been fixed to the wall inside the courtyard that said: 'NO ACCESS FOR VEHICLES OR THE GENERAL PUBLIC'. To dissuade anyone from accessing the alley from the outside, the opposite end was blocked off by a heavy-duty chain barrier, which had a NO ENTRY sign hanging from its centre.

That said, despite it being strictly off limits to the shoppers, staff working in the shops and businesses regularly walked through the alleyway as a shortcut to and from the 'staff only' car park at the rear of the shopping village. Occasionally, traders would also trundle the communal sack truck through the alley – a harmless bending of the rules that was considered acceptable, as it provided a quick route for traders to transfer boxes of stock and supplies from their vehicles into the retail units.

The general public had complied fully with the restrictions until twelve months ago, when a renegade shopper had decided they didn't apply to her. Having bought a chest of drawers from the *Antiques Emporium*, and determined to avoid a delivery charge, she had disregarded all the signs, lifted off the chain barrier and attempted to drive her estate car through the alleyway. When it became clear the vehicle wouldn't make it through into the courtyard, the driver had quickly reversed – scraping the wing of her car in the process and leaving lasting scars on the alleyway's brickwork. Following that incident, the traders' association had voted to install a retractable, lockable bollard directly in front of the metal chain – a solution that Eric Nash had referred to as a 'belt and braces' approach.

Now, as Violet stood at the entrance to the dark, narrow alley, she braced herself for what was to come. Tim had switched on his torch, but was keeping the beam pointing downwards, towards the steel toecaps of his safety shoes.

'Are you sure you want to do this?' he said, giving her one last chance to change her mind.

Matthew gave Violet's hand a reassuring squeeze.

'I guess someone has to,' she said, keeping her voice steady, even though her heart was thumping. 'I'm not looking forward to it though. It looks awfully dark in there.'

'This will help.' Tim lifted the torch and directed it into the gloomy depths of the entryway.

Gripping Matthew's hand and keeping behind the beam of light, Violet took a tentative step forward.

The man was lying at the far end of the alley. His dark clothing – a charcoal grey winter coat and black jeans – made him hard to spot, despite the intense glare from Tim's torch. It was the reflective logo on the man's trainers that Violet saw first. As her eyes adjusted to the light, she took in the splayed limbs, a head of grey hair and a pale, ungloved hand.

She approached cautiously and bent down. Taking her phone from her pocket, she switched on the torch and checked the body for signs of life.

'You're wasting your time,' Tim said. 'Like I told you, he's a goner.'

The man had fallen onto his front, his head twisted to one side. His pallor and unblinking stare confirmed Tim's verdict, but Violet pressed her fingers against his carotid artery anyway, just to make sure. There was definitely no pulse, and the injury on the man's temple and the congealing pool of blood on the cobbled walkway suggested he'd been dead for several minutes. Violet pointed the beam of her phone towards the retractable metal bollard that stood only inches away. There were traces of blood on its square, top edge.

She shuddered. 'Looks like he's fallen over and hit his head on the bollard.'

'Maybe he tripped over the chain . . . didn't see it in the dark,' said Tim.

'Perhaps,' Violet said. 'Except the chain is unhooked. It's lying *underneath* his legs.'

'He couldn't have tripped over the chain,' Matthew said, sounding very sure of himself. 'When the traders' association decided to hold outdoor events at the shopping village, we had to have a risk assessment done. The chain barrier was one of the things flagged up in the health and safety report. We were told it was hanging too low, and that it was considered a trip hazard. Even though the alley was off limits to the general public, we were told to raise the chain to above knee height.'

'Maybe that change never happened,' Tim said. 'Little jobs like that are easy to overlook.'

'Oh, it definitely happened,' Matthew said, unwaveringly. 'The risk assessment certificate couldn't be issued until the adjustment had been made. The height of the chain was reconfigured – so even if this guy *did* walk into it in the dark, it would have been at waist height, or thereabouts. It certainly wouldn't have tripped him up.'

'Maybe someone unhooked the chain and forgot to put it back,' Violet said. 'He's lying on top of it, which suggests it was already on the ground when he fell.'

'He must have got his foot tangled up in it,' said Tim. 'Poor sod. I wonder what he was doing down here?'

'I expect the police will ask the same question,' Violet said. 'Hopefully, the CCTV cameras in the courtyard will tell them what they need to know. Will you be able to download the footage, Tim, ready for when they arrive?'

Tim rubbed his chin. 'They've given me a login, but I'm not sure I'd know how to access the files. I'll give it a go, but it's a totally different system to the one we use at the school.'

Matthew patted Tim's shoulder. 'I can help. Between us, we should be able to work it out. If not, we'll get Eric involved. He's a whizz with technology. Failing that, the police will have to wait until tomorrow, when the facilities manager is on site.'

'Righto,' said Tim. 'For now, why don't the three of us step aside while we wait for the coppers to get here?'

Matthew and Tim spun on their heels and returned to the courtyard end of the alleyway. Before joining them, Violet took a last look at the body, trying to understand what had happened.

She glanced briefly at the head wound, and then swept the torch from her phone along the man's legs, down towards his trainers. When the beam of light reached his right ankle, she noticed something odd – an orangey-red mark on the front hem of his jeans. Violet tugged gently at the front hem to get a better look, and then angled the torch along the ground, studying the metal chain that was lying on the cobbles. Even in such poor light, she could see that some of the links were rusted. Was this the source of the orangey-red mark on the dead man's trouser leg? If it was, then maybe his ankle *had* come into contact with the chain barrier.

Violet was tempted to inspect the mark more closely, and check whether there was a similar smudge on the other leg, but she knew better than to touch or move a body. This death had all the hallmarks of a tragic accident, but if there was something more sinister at play here, the last thing she wanted was to be accused of interfering with a crime scene.

# Chapter 3

Within a few minutes, two police officers had arrived, escorted to the scene by a nervous-looking Judith Talbot.

'I've told them everything I know,' Judith said, as she waited with Violet, Matthew and Tim while the police officers checked the body. 'Not that there was much I could say, of course – although I did mention we don't know who this gentleman is. I take it that's still the case?'

'It's not anyone I recognise,' said Matthew.

'Me neither,' said Violet. 'But don't worry, the police will check for ID.'

'Now they're here, why don't we go and wait inside the bookshop?' Judith said. 'It's awfully dark and cold out here, and I don't know about you, but this whole situation has shaken me up. I could do with a hot drink.'

Tim nodded eagerly. 'Good idea, Judy. I'll just let the officers know where we're going, in case they need to ask any questions.'

'It's all right, I can do that,' Violet said. 'You three go on ahead. I'll join you in a minute.'

Tim and Judith hurried away, eager to return to the warmth of the bookshop, but Matthew folded his arms and remained where he was.

'I hope you're not looking for a mystery to solve, Violet. It seems obvious to me this was an accident. Nothing more.'

'I'm sure you're right, but I did spot something strange . . . a mark on the man's jeans. It might be nothing, but I think I ought to mention it to the police.'

'Violet . . .' There was a note of warning in Matthew's tone. 'They're trained officers. If you noticed the mark, we can safely assume they will have spotted it as well.'

Violet huffed. 'OK, but I still need to let them know where we'll be, in case they want to talk to us. I'll be a couple of minutes at the most. Why don't you go and speak to Tim and Eric about downloading the security footage?'

Matthew gave a reluctant nod. 'All right, but don't be long. I'll see you shortly, yeah?'

He went into the courtyard and turned left, cutting across towards the bookshop. Violet couldn't see the shopfront from where she was standing, but she knew the window would be blazing with golden light, and the heated interior would be cosy and welcoming, filled with the wonderful smell of new and second-hand books. The reassuringly safe environs of *Books, Bakes and Cakes* held far more appeal than returning to the dingy depths of the alleyway.

'Excuse me,' Violet said, raising her voice to catch the attention of the young female officer who was standing guard a few yards from the body. 'If you need us, we'll be in the bookshop. We're going to try and get the CCTV footage downloaded. I'm sure you'll want to see it.'

The officer raised a hand to acknowledge the offer. 'Thanks. That's really helpful.'

The other police officer was kneeling next to the body, checking the inside pocket of the charcoal grey coat. When he stood up, he was holding a wallet in his hand.

'Actually . . .' Violet made up her mind to say something about the rusty-red mark. 'There is one thing I should tell you about.'

'What's that, then?' the female officer said, strolling over to meet Violet at the midpoint of the alleyway. 'Are you acquainted with the deceased? Is that it?'

'No . . . sorry, I honestly don't know who he is,' Violet replied. 'But when I checked for a pulse, I did notice a lopsided mark on his jeans. It was a centimetre or so above the right hem.'

'What kind of mark?'

'I couldn't be certain, but it was rusty-red – and I noticed some of the links on the chain barrier are rusty.'

'You think he tripped over the chain?'

Violet frowned. 'That's what it looks like . . . but that doesn't make any sense. When the chain is hooked in place, it hangs at waist height – so if he ran into it in the dark, he wouldn't have tripped over it.'

'Yes, but the chain's lying on the ground. Maybe someone unhooked it and forgot to put it back. Leave it with me. I'll check it out, and I'll also have a look at this red mark you mentioned.'

The other officer wandered over to join them. He was pointing his torch at a credit card in his left hand, which he'd presumably found in the wallet.

'It's Ms Brewster, isn't it?' he said.

'That's right . . .'

'I think we've met before. I'm PC Turner. You were there when we had that suspicious death at the garden centre on Bluebell Hill, earlier in the year.'

Violet nodded. 'Yes, unfortunately I was,' she said, recalling the incident only too vividly.

PC Turner glanced at the credit card again. 'Can I ask whether the name Daniel Midship means anything to you?'

Violet thought carefully before replying. 'No, I'm sorry, it doesn't. It's an unusual surname, so I'd remember if I'd heard it before. I take it Daniel Midship is the name of . . .' She nodded in the general direction of the body.

'Yes, assuming the bank card in his wallet belonged to

him – and I've no reason to think that wouldn't be the case. If the name's not familiar to you, it's possible this guy wasn't from around here.'

'I've definitely not seen him in Merrywell, but he might live in one of the outlying villages or towns. He could even be from much further afield. Today has been the first day of our Christmas market, and it's attracted visitors and tourists from all over the place.'

'OK,' PC Turner said. 'Don't worry, we can check with the bank and run the name through the police national computer. Once we have more information, we'll get in touch with the deceased's family to let them know what's happened.'

'My heart goes out to them,' Violet said. 'It's awful losing someone so suddenly – and right before Christmas too.'

PC Turner gave a slow shake of his head. 'Breaking bad news to relatives is the part of this job I dread the most. It never gets any easier. It would help if we could tell the family exactly what happened, but unfortunately, we haven't worked that out yet. I'll need to have a word with the security guard. Do you know where he is?'

'Tim's in the bookshop, waiting with those of us who were at the shopping village when the body was found. Most of the traders and shopkeepers closed up and went home at eight o'clock when the market finished, but a few of us stayed behind for a celebratory drink. None of us saw what happened to Daniel Midship though, so there's not really a lot we can tell you.'

'I'll still need to ask a few routine questions,' PC Turner said. 'Go to the bookshop, and I'll join you there in a little while. I'll take a formal statement from the security guard, but I won't keep the rest of you any longer than I have to.'

'And you mentioned CCTV footage?' said the other officer. 'If you can let us have that, it would be very useful.'

'Of course,' Violet said. 'I'll see you in a few minutes then.'

She returned to the bookshop to find that three new faces had joined the assembled group. Judith's husband, Andrew, had arrived. He was a tall, distinguished-looking man – a retired accountant, with white hair and a slightly florid complexion, and the apple of Judith's eye. Her relief that he had turned up safe and well was apparent in her beaming smile and the way she was fussing around him.

Jill's partner, Adrian Billings, had arrived too. Jill was leaning into him, looking pale, clearly shaken by the evening's turn of events. Molly and Robert had also gravitated to the bookshop. Robert was helping himself to coffee from a pump flask which had, Violet assumed, been provided by Fiona, who had returned with Eric from the bakery.

All eyes turned in Violet's direction as she rejoined the group, slipping in next to Matthew.

'What's happening out there?' Fiona said.

'Not a lot,' Violet replied. 'The police will be joining us in a few minutes. They need to ask some questions, and take a statement from Tim.'

'That's fine with me,' Tim said. 'As long as they don't keep me waiting too long. It's getting late, and I need my kip if I'm going to be back here again first thing in the morning.'

'Depending on what the police say, you might not need to come in tomorrow, Tim,' said Eric, who looked exhausted and thoroughly deflated. 'In light of what's happened, we might have to cancel the market.'

'Seriously?' Fiona gave her husband an old-fashioned look. 'Let's not assume the worst, love. Someone has died . . . and that's awful . . . but sudden deaths like this can't be that uncommon. The police won't close us down, surely? I'm obviously no expert in these matters, but I imagine the body will be taken away soon. You just wait and see . . . by morning everything will have returned to normal.'

'Normal?' Eric blew air through his mouth. 'It won't be normal for that poor man's family, will it? Imagine how they'll feel when they hear the news.'

'You're absolutely right, Eric,' said Judith. 'Of course you are. It's tragic, and I'm sure all our thoughts and prayers are with the dead man's family. However, cancelling the market at this late hour simply isn't practical. Most of the stallholders will be tucked up in bed by now, getting some much-needed rest for tomorrow. They'll be back here first thing in the morning, keen as mustard – as will the shoppers. I don't think we could keep them away now, even if we tried.'

Adrian Billings cleared his throat and placed a comforting arm around Jill's shoulder. 'I realise I'm a relative newcomer to Merrywell, but can I just say that I've seen first-hand how much work has gone into organising this event. It would be a shame not to go ahead with the market, now that everything's in place.'

Andrew Talbot nodded vigorously. 'Adrian's right. Today has been a runaway success, and a real boost for trade in the shopping village. And let's not forget, as well as benefiting the local businesses, the Christmas market is good for Merrywell as a whole.'

'I agree,' said Judith. 'Providing the police have no objections, I think the week's festivities should go ahead as planned.'

Eric sighed. 'If you're all of the same opinion, then I'll obviously have to go with the consensus.'

Violet unzipped her coat and ran her fingers through her fringe. 'Ultimately, it's the police who'll get to decide. They'll be here in a minute, so let's wait and see what they say. They've asked to see the CCTV footage. Have you had any luck downloading it?'

Matthew shrugged, and Eric shook his head distractedly.

'No, sorry,' he said. 'Matthew said they'd asked about it, but I've only just finished in the bakery and I haven't had chance to access the system yet. Give me a minute to finish my coffee and I'll see what I can do.'

'Why don't you let Adrian do it?' said Jill. 'He's brilliant with computers.'

Adrian smiled modestly. 'I wouldn't go that far, although I am familiar with quite a few different software packages. I'm happy to give it a go, if you want me to.'

'It's kind of you, Adrian, but before I can access the system, I'll need to log in.' Eric opened a drawer beneath the counter and took out a notebook. 'To be honest, I'm hoping the police can wait until the morning. It's getting late, and we've all had a long day . . .'

His words tailed away as the bell jangled over the door and PC Turner entered the bookshop.

'Thanks for waiting, everyone,' he said. 'I appreciate you want to get home, so I won't keep you long, but I do need to ascertain whether anyone saw what happened out there this evening?'

There was a unanimous shaking of heads.

'Most of us were here in the bookshop when Tim found the body,' said Matthew. 'We met up at about ten past eight for a drink, after the market had finished.'

Robert ran a hand through his mousy brown hair. 'I've been in my own shop, cashing up and pricing some new stock,' he said, clearing his throat before continuing. 'I run the *Antiques Emporium* on the other side of the courtyard. I've been there all day, but I haven't spotted anything out of the ordinary.'

Andrew Talbot spoke next. 'Adrian and I only arrived at the shopping village a few minutes ago. I paid a brief visit to the market this morning, but I've spent the rest of the day at home. I came here this evening to meet my wife. I bumped into Adrian on the way, and we walked over here together.'

Adrian backed him up with a nod. 'I'm Jill's partner. I'm here to walk her home. Andrew and I only found out someone had died when we arrived.'

'OK,' PC Turner said, looking disappointed that no one was able to shed any light on what had occurred. 'What about the CCTV cameras? Can we see the footage?'

'Sorry, I'm afraid I haven't downloaded the file yet,' Eric said, as he drained his coffee cup. 'I'll get on to it now.'

PC Turner held up a hand. 'It's OK. I appreciate you've had a long day. The footage can wait until the morning. We'll take a look at it then.'

Relief smoothed away the lines around Eric's tired eyes, as he shoved the notebook back into his desk. 'I'll get Nick Penfold onto it first thing tomorrow.'

'Nick Penfold?' PC Turner made a note of the name. 'Who's that then?'

'He's the facilities manager,' Eric said. 'He's responsible for overall maintenance and security of the shopping village, so he's a lot more familiar with the CCTV system than I am. I thought about asking him to come and sort it out tonight, but he lives on the other side of Chesterfield and he didn't leave the shopping village until eight o'clock. I didn't want to drag him all the way back here again unless it was absolutely essential.'

'Like I say, it'll do in the morning,' PC Turner said. 'We'll need to come and talk to the stallholders anyway.'

Judith's face brightened. 'Does that mean we can go ahead with the market tomorrow? We were worried you might close us down.'

'That won't be necessary,' PC Turner replied. 'As far as we can tell, the man in the alley died as the result of an accident, although we won't know for certain until after the post-mortem. The body will be taken away shortly, and by tomorrow morning, everything will be back to how it was, ready for the market to reopen.'

Judith smiled gratefully. 'Thank you, officer. That is very much appreciated.'

'Can we go home now, then?' said Molly. 'Only it's getting late and my mum's looking after my little boy. I need to go and pick him up.'

'One final question, and then you can be on your way. Do any of you know anyone by the name of Daniel Midship?'

PC Turner's question was met with shaking heads and blank faces.

'I'll take that as a "no" then,' he said, as he took in their expressions. 'As I said, we'll be back tomorrow – so if you do think of anything, or the name Daniel Midship starts to ring even the faintest of bells, please speak to me or one of my colleagues in the morning.'

# Chapter 4

Violet slept fitfully, her dreams plagued by flashbacks to the damp, dark alleyway. At 5.30 a.m., she was jolted awake by a particularly unsettling nightmare, in which Daniel Midship had come back to life, grabbing her wrist as she rechecked his pulse.

Knowing that any attempt to go back to sleep would be futile, she pushed the bed covers aside and went downstairs to make herself an early breakfast. An hour and a half later, after a refreshing shower and several cups of strong black coffee, she set off for work.

The weather was cold and nippy, and Merrywell was bathed in a quiet Saturday morning calm. The upstairs curtains at most of the properties were still drawn, but there were lights on in the village shop. As Violet strolled past, she waved to the shopkeeper, Will, who was stacking newspapers onto the shelves by the door.

When she got to the shopping village, she bypassed the front entrance and made her way along the rear driveway to the staff car park. She was determined to enter the courtyard through the alleyway – partly to chase away the bad dreams from the previous night, but mainly because she wanted to check that normality really had been restored.

As it was still early, it came as no surprise to find the car park empty. In half an hour, the market traders would begin to arrive – but for now, it looked as though she had the entire shopping village to herself. Sucking in a deep breath, she went to stand in front of the narrow entryway. The bollard was securely in position, standing a couple of feet in front of the chain barrier, which was now hanging in its proper place. When Violet peered through the half-light at the bollard, she could make out minute specks of dark, dried blood on its sharp, top edge. Behind it, the chain barrier hung across the entrance, cutting off access to the alleyway. The yellow plastic NO ENTRY sign at its centre was swinging slightly in the morning breeze.

Violet moved closer, positioning herself between the bollard and the chain. At its midpoint, the heavy metal links hung at the same height as her midriff, curving gradually upwards towards the walls on either side of the entrance. On the left-hand wall, the chain was fixed to the brickwork with a strong metal plate. She wandered over and gave it a tug, checking it was securely fitted before moving across to the other side, where the end of the chain was attached to a hook on the wall. It was easy enough to lift off, allowing access for the staff walking in from the car park, or wheeling the sack truck into the courtyard.

*What happened to you last night, Daniel Midship?* Violet wondered, as she stared into the covered alleyway. *From what I saw of the wound on your head, I'd say you crashed into the bollard with a great deal of force.*

Giving free rein to her imagination, Violet conjured up a few possible scenarios. Ducking under the barrier, she entered the covered alleyway and turned back, in the direction of the staff car park. It was almost daylight now, and the chain was clearly visible – but that might not have been the case last night. There had been a full moon, but its light wouldn't necessarily have penetrated the depths of the alley – and the broken sensor light had also failed to provide any illumination.

Violet tried to picture Daniel Midship striding through the

gloomy alleyway and careering over the chain barrier – and the more she thought about it, the more convinced she was that the chain must have been unhooked. He wouldn't have acquired a rust mark on his ankle if he'd crashed into the chain at waist height.

She went over and lifted the metal chain off the wall, testing its weight in her hand before lowering it to the ground, where it lay coiled like a snake. She took a step back and purposely walked towards it, checking how easy it would have been to stumble over the chain in the dark – but when the toe of her boot made contact, the chain barely moved. Given its weight, it was more likely to have stubbed Daniel Midship's toe, rather than trip him over. There was certainly no possibility of it having become tangled around his foot.

Violet crouched down and studied the traces of rust on the links, certain now that the orangey-red iron oxide matched the mark she'd seen on Daniel Midship's jeans.

'So, how did that mark get there?' she said aloud. 'It doesn't make any sense.'

'Hello, Violet. I might have known I'd find you here.'

The deep, male voice startled her, and – as she attempted to jump up – she lost her balance and landed in a heap on the cold, damp cobbles.

DS Charlie Winterton looked down at her with a mischievous smile on his face. 'Sorry, I didn't mean to startle you.'

'Bloomin' heck, Charlie.' Violet scrabbled to her feet. 'You shouldn't creep up on people like that.'

'I wasn't creeping,' he said, holding out a hand to help her up. 'If you hadn't been so fixated on that chain, you'd have seen me coming towards you.'

Violet dusted the back of her coat. 'What are you doing here anyway?' she said.

'I could ask you the same question, but I think I already know the answer. You're investigating again, aren't you?'

'Not exactly,' Violet said, trying to bluff her way out of a potentially tricky situation. 'I'm on my way to work. This is the quickest way into the courtyard from the staff car park.'

Charlie spun around, and then turned back, frowning.

'There are no cars in the car park, so I can only assume you walked to work? Wouldn't it have been quicker for you to use the front entrance?'

Violet held up her hands in surrender. 'All right . . . you got me. I wanted to have another look around. I was at the shopping village last night when the security guard found the body. I kept watch with him in the alleyway until the police arrived.'

'Why am I not surprised?' Charlie said, rolling his eyes and shaking his head.

'So, what are *you* doing here?' Violet said, ignoring his sarcastic tone. 'Last night, PC Turner said this had all the hallmarks of an accident. I wouldn't have thought that would warrant the presence of a detective sergeant.'

DS Winterton folded his arms. 'Actually, I'm not here in an official capacity. It just so happens I've got a rare weekend off to do some Christmas shopping with my missus.'

'Oh, right,' said Violet. 'Well, if you're here for the Christmas market, you're a couple of hours too early. It doesn't open until nine o'clock.'

'I'm not here for the market. The wife's taking me to the shopping centre at Meadowhall — which, quite frankly, is likely to be Meadow*hell* at this time of year.'

Violet gave him a sympathetic smile. 'If you've not come to Merrywell for the shopping, then you must be here because of the incident last night.'

Charlie nodded. 'I am. Curiosity got the better of me. My wife's still in bed and won't be up for at least another hour, so I thought I'd drive over and take a look at where Daniel Midship died.'

'Are you taking an interest because you're worried it wasn't an accident?'

'Something like that. I'm guessing you must be thinking the same thing yourself. Why else would you be on your knees, examining the chain barrier?'

Violet shrugged. 'I was trying to make sense of something that's been bothering me.'

Charlie gave a half-smile. 'Go on, then. Enlighten me.'

She pushed her hands into her pockets and studied Charlie's face, trying to work out whether he was genuinely interested or hoping to wind her up.

'There was a mark on Daniel Midship's jeans. It was on the right leg, just above the hem, and I think it was rust . . . from this.' She picked up the end of the metal chain, walked over to the wall, and dropped it onto the hook.

'As you can see,' she said, pointing out the height of the chain's central section, 'if this had been hanging in its proper place last night, there's no way Daniel Midship could have tripped over it.'

'According to PC Turner's report, the chain was lying *underneath* the deceased's legs,' Charlie said.

'It was. Which suggests it was already unhooked when he fell. However, in my opinion, the chain is too heavy and bulky to have tripped him up. If he banged his foot against it, it's more likely to have stopped him in his tracks.'

'Depends how fast he was moving, I suppose.'

Charlie lifted the chain, feeling its weight and examining the rusted links.

'It's puzzling, isn't it,' Violet said. 'Although not quite as baffling as you being here on your day off. I've known you long enough now to know you never do anything without a good reason. So, why *are* you here, Charlie? Tell me the truth.'

The detective rubbed a hand across his jawline as he considered his reply.

'It turns out Daniel Midship is an ex-copper,' he said, eventually. 'He worked for the West Yorkshire Constabulary, based in Leeds. Took early retirement five months ago.'

'Did you know him?'

'We'd met a couple of times, but I didn't know him well. Our paths crossed only briefly – once in the course of an investigation, and another time when we were on the same training course.'

'So, you're here to pay your respects to an old colleague – is that it?'

Charlie shook his head. 'Even if Dan and I had never met, I'd still have come. Although I am here mainly because he was ex police. The thing is, Violet, when you're in my line of work, you encounter some rum people – and it's not unheard of for some of them to bear grudges. So . . . when a police officer – serving or retired – dies suddenly, I get the jitters. The officers who came here last night are of the opinion this was an accidental death, but I wanted to come and check it out for myself. I'm going to have a scout round and I want to view the CCTV footage as well, just to make absolutely sure there are no suspicious circumstances.'

'Nick, the facilities manager, is due in at eight,' Violet said. 'He'll be able to download the security camera files for you.'

'Perfect. I'll take a proper look at the scene, and then I'll go and wait in the café until he arrives.'

'Sorry to disappoint you, Charlie, but the café doesn't open until nine o'clock on Saturdays. You're more than welcome to come and wait in my office though. I can rustle up a cup of tea for you, or coffee . . . maybe even a few biscuits if you play your cards right.'

Charlie smiled. 'Thanks. I'll take you up on that offer. I'll have a gander out here first, and I'll be with you shortly. Get the kettle on.'

Violet ran her videography business, *The Memory Box*, from the smallest unit in the shopping village. Her office was large enough to accommodate two desks and a filing cabinet, but very little else. There was another tiny room at the rear – more of a storeroom really. It had a sink, and space for what Molly referred to as the 'mashing tackle' – a kettle, a random collection of mugs, a cafetière, three canisters containing tea, coffee and sugar, and a miniature fridge for storing milk. As she filled the kettle, Violet wondered again about Charlie Winterton's presence in the shopping village. Would he have bothered coming here if Daniel Midship had been an ordinary citizen, instead of a retired police officer?

Leaving the kettle to boil, she retrieved *The Memory Box*'s promotional pull-up banner, carried it outside into the courtyard and set it up outside the door. Next, she unlocked the cupboard, got out her Canon camera, and attached it to a tripod, which she placed in front of the visitor's chair that had been commandeered to serve as the temporary 'pop-up' booth. It was positioned against a festively decorated backboard in the only spare corner available. Later, when the shoppers arrived, she and Molly would stand outside and entice people into the office to record their recollections of Christmases past.

With the camera in place, Violet turned her attention to making coffee. Charlie arrived just as she was pouring hot water into the cafetière.

'You timed that well,' she said, as she emerged from the back room. 'I've made coffee, but I can do you a tea, if you prefer?'

'No, coffee's fine. It smells great, actually. Thanks, Violet. A hot drink is just what I need. It's parky out there this morning.'

'Have you finished your recce of the alleyway?'

Charlie side-stepped the legs of the tripod, and sat down at Molly's desk.

'Yeah, but I couldn't see anything untoward or suspicious. It seems like Daniel Midship must have stumbled in the dark, fallen over, and smashed into the sharp end of the bollard. It certainly looks like an accident – a slightly bizarre and unfortunate one – but an accident nevertheless.'

'I suppose that's good news, then,' Violet said, as she placed a mug of steaming coffee on the desk. 'Although the scenario with the chain still doesn't make sense to me. If it was lying on the cobbles, it might have thrown him off balance . . . he might even have stumbled, but I don't believe it would have caused him to fall quite so heavily, or catastrophically.'

'It could have been some kind of fluke. Or sheer bad luck. These things do happen. Hopefully, we'll get a better idea of the circumstances when we check the security cameras.'

Violet smiled, pleased that he'd said *we*. 'Does that mean you're going to allow me to view the CCTV footage with you?'

Charlie picked up his coffee and blew on it. 'I don't see why not. It's not as if I'm here in an official capacity. If you introduce me to the facilities manager when he arrives, I won't object if you want to stick around and look over my shoulder while I watch the footage. You're one of the traders, so I'm guessing you can request to see it at any time anyway.'

Violet nodded. 'Thankfully, the shopping village doesn't have too many problems with security, so it's not often anyone has reason to do that; but you're right – any of the traders can ask to view the footage. Unfortunately, in this instance, I'm not sure how much help it's going to be. The alleyway is off limits to the general public, so there are no cameras in that area.'

Charlie curled his lip. 'That's a shame. What about on the other side, where the bollard is? Are there cameras covering the traders' car park?'

Violet shook her head. 'Sorry, I don't think there's anything there either. But there's a camera covering the customer car park, and two more in the central courtyard. Hopefully, one or both of those will have picked up Daniel Midship's movements before he went into the alley.'

Charlie sipped his coffee and winced. 'Ergh . . . have you put any sugar in this?'

Violet laughed. 'I'd forgotten you were a sweet tooth. Hang on, I'll go and get you some.'

\*

After Charlie had stirred four teaspoons of sugar into his coffee, he pulled out his phone, stared briefly at the screen, and then slipped it back into his pocket.

'Doing anything nice for Christmas?' he said, making polite chitchat as they awaited the arrival of the facilities manager.

'Just a quiet, family Christmas at my place. My daughter's coming over for a few days, and my mother's staying for a couple of weeks. As a matter of fact, Mum's due to arrive this evening. When I told her about the Christmas market, she decided to get here in time to do some last-minute gift shopping.'

'It doesn't sound like you'll get much of a break if you've got people staying over for the duration.'

Violet smiled. 'Probably not, but it should be fun. We're teaming up with Matthew Collis and his family on Christmas Day. I've agreed to do the cooking – but I'm hoping everyone will pitch in and help.'

'You make sure they do. If your lot are anything like mine, they'll try and wriggle out of doing any work at all. Our kids will be staying with us for three days and, given half a chance, they'll spend most of that time sprawled out in front of the television. We love 'em to bits, but I must admit, the missus and I are glad to wave 'em goodbye when Christmas is over.'

Out of the corner of her eye, Violet caught sight of Nick Penfold scurrying past the window, heading towards his first-floor office on the western side of the courtyard.

'There's Nick,' she said, nodding towards the window. 'Let's give him a minute to take his cap and his coat off, and then I'll take you over to see him.'

# Chapter 5

'Do you know roughly what time the accident happened?' Nick said, as he sat down and logged into the shopping village's security system.

Eric had already messaged him with the news of Daniel Midship's death and given him a heads-up that the police would need to see the video surveillance footage.

'It was just before 9 p.m. when Tim found the body,' Violet said. 'The market closed at eight, and most of the traders had gone by ten past. A lot of them would have used the alleyway to get to the car park, so I'm guessing the accident must have happened after they'd all gone home.'

Nick tapped the keyboard and opened up a couple of video files, homing in on the activity from 8.10 p.m. onwards. DS Winterton peered at the computer screen, one hand resting on the back of Nick's chair. Violet stood to one side, but her gaze was fixed firmly on the unfolding footage, eyes peeled for any sign of activity.

The main security camera in the courtyard was located at first-floor level, close to the main entrance. It pointed along the front of *Books, Bakes and Cakes*, over towards *The Epicurious* deli on the western side of the courtyard. The second camera was situated between *The Memory Box* and a shop that sold arts and craft supplies. It covered the area around the main entrance (to the left of the bookshop), and the eastern side of the courtyard, which housed Matthew's furniture workshop, an outdoor clothing outlet and a wool and fabric shop called *Sew Into Knitting*. There was no camera directly facing the *Antiques Emporium*, *The Memory Box* or the arts and crafts shop, and – more significantly – no coverage of the rear exit and alleyway.

'The focus of the cameras is towards the main entrance and the courtyard,' Nick said. 'Unfortunately, the images aren't the highest resolution and, sadly, there are no cameras pointing into or towards the alleyway.'

DS Winterton curled his top lip again. 'So I've been told. It was ever thus. Show me what you've got anyway. Let's start with the footage from camera one.'

Nick clicked his mouse, tapped the keyboard, and nodded to the screen, which had a timestamp in the top right-hand corner. A grainy black-and-white image showed a side view across the front of *Books, Bakes and Cakes*. The lights were on in the bookshop and café, but the bakery in the central section was in darkness, and the market stalls dotted around the courtyard were empty. Nick increased the playback speed, fast-forwarding to a flurry of movement at quarter past eight, when a group of four laughing women emerged from the café and made their way between the empty stalls towards the main exit.

'The market and the shops closed at eight o'clock.' Nick paused the footage. 'I clocked off a few minutes after that, but it looks as though the café stayed open for a while longer.'

'Fiona told me that last orders for food at the café would be at half past seven,' Violet said. 'Obviously, the staff would have had to wait for the customers to finish their meals and drinks . . . and it looks like some of them lingered for a while. Chivvying people along isn't always easy when they're deep in conversation and having a good time.'

'Do you know who these women are?' DS Winterton said, pointing to the screen. 'It's possible they may have seen something as they left.'

'I don't recognise them,' Violet said, as she squinted at the image frozen on the screen.

'Me neither,' said Nick. 'Shall I take a screenshot?'

'Please.' DS Winterton nodded.

Once Nick had captured the screen image, he pressed 'play' once again, and they watched as the four women walked to the main entrance/exit and then disappeared from view. A few minutes of inactivity whizzed by on the screen, and then – at 8.22 p.m. – someone else emerged from the café.

Daniel Midship.

Violet moved closer to get a better look, watching as he stopped to button his coat and pull his collar up around his ears. It felt odd and very sad, watching someone so full of energy and vigour, knowing their life was about to come to an abrupt end.

On screen, Daniel Midship fished a glove from his left pocket. As he began to pull it onto his fingers, his gaze flicked to the corner of the courtyard and he became instantly alert. He gave a shout, pushed the glove back into his pocket, and broke into a run, swerving around the empty stalls towards the alleyway.

'He's seen something,' Violet said. 'Or someone.'

'I don't suppose this footage comes with any sound?' DS Winterton said.

'No, sorry. Images only,' said Nick. 'But it looks to me like he shouted *hey*, or maybe *oi*.'

'Can we take a look from the other camera?' DS Winterton said.

Nick switched to camera two, found the relevant section of video and pressed play. Daniel Midship appeared on the far right of the screen this time. They watched him emerge from the café, go through the same routine with his coat and gloves, and then shoot off towards the alleyway, disappearing out of sight at the bottom right of the screen.

'It looks to me like he's chasing someone,' Nick Penfold said. 'There could have been someone hanging around in the alley.'

'Or coming through it, into the courtyard,' said DS Winterton. 'Are there no cameras at all at the rear of the building?'

Nick shook his head. 'No. Nothing, unfortunately. There's a camera covering the customer car park at the front, but apart from that, what you've seen is all the footage there is. Do you want me to save the files onto a memory stick for you?'

'I'll get someone to come in and transfer the files securely,' Charlie said. 'We'll need everything you have from yesterday, including the footage from the customer car park.'

Violet moved over to the window and gazed down at the stalls in the courtyard below. The first few traders had arrived, and the market was slowly coming to life. Over in the corner, a woman was setting out a collection of handmade soaps, and directly below the window someone else was laying out a display of beautifully made treen objects, including crafted wooden reindeer figures. As the traders waved to each other and exchanged greetings, PC Turner entered the courtyard through the main entrance and engaged the soap seller in conversation.

'PC Turner's here,' said Violet. 'Looks like he's questioning the stallholders.'

Charlie joined her at the window. 'I'd better have a word . . . let him know I'm here.'

'I'll come down with you. There are a couple of things I need to do in the office before the market opens.'

After thanking Nick, they made their way down the steep, twisting staircase. Violet noticed that Charlie's expression was sombre, and he was uncharacteristically silent.

'You're very quiet,' she said. 'What are you thinking?'

Charlie paused on the bottom stair, his hand resting on the banister.

'That there's more to this than meets the eye,' he replied. 'Based on the footage, Daniel Midship looked to be in fine health when he came out of the café, so it's unlikely his fall was caused by an unexpected collapse.'

'Unlikely,' Violet agreed, 'but not impossible.'

'True enough. I'll need to wait for the results of the post-mortem to be sure, of course, but judging by the speed with which he shot into the alleyway, I'd say Dan was fighting fit. He'd spotted something and was going after it. There's no doubt in my mind about that. He must have ended up crashing into the bollard during the pursuit, and if he was moving fast . . . running . . . that would explain the severity of his head injury. The question is, did he fall accidentally, or did someone push him?'

'Or use the chain to trip him up? That would account for the rusty mark on his ankle.'

Charlie grinned. 'You're not going to let that go, are you?'

'Not until I've worked out how it got there,' Violet replied. 'But right now, the priority is to establish *who* Daniel Midship was chasing, or what? I'm going to assume it was a person, but it could have been something else.'

'Like what?'

'An animal of some sort? A stray dog, or a cat. Possibly even a lost child.'

'I think we can rule out the latter. If a child had gone missing during the market, someone would have known about it. The parents would have raised the alarm immediately.'

'OK, so maybe Daniel Midship saw something else happening in the alleyway,' Violet said. 'Someone being attacked or robbed perhaps, or some other crime that was taking place. As an ex-copper, his first instinct would have been to intervene.'

'It's a nice idea in theory, Violet, but again, if that had happened, wouldn't we already know about it? If Daniel Midship stepped in to help someone in trouble, that person would have come forward at the time to get help for Dan, after he fell, and to report the crime.'

Charlie descended the last stair but paused again in the entrance hall.

'Unfortunately, there's a possibility we may never get to the bottom of what happened last night,' he said. 'Maybe it *was* an accident, and I'm worrying over nothing. The truth is, I'm only here on my day off because Dan was a retired detective.' He held up a hand. 'I know how that must sound, and I don't want you thinking we'd have been any less thorough if the deceased had been a civilian – but like I said, I get the jitters when something like this happens to a copper. Police officers encounter rogues on a daily basis – it's an occupational hazard – hence my unofficial involvement. I'm probably being overcautious, but I need to make doubly sure there are no suspicious circumstances.'

'Is there anything I can do to help?'

Charlie smiled gratefully. 'I appreciate the offer, but this isn't your problem. If something has gone awry here, it'll be up to me and my team to get to the bottom of it. You've got a busy day ahead of you, Violet. Go and get set up for the market, and forget about Daniel Midship.'

He opened the door and stood aside to let Violet exit first. As they stepped into the courtyard, PC Turner glanced across and raised a cautious hand in greeting.

'He looks surprised to see you,' Violet said.

'Aye. Surprised and, I suspect, not altogether pleased. I'd better go and unruffle his feathers. Thanks again for the coffee, Violet. I'm hoping that by the end of play today we'll have been able to confirm there was no third party involved in Dan Midship's death. In the meantime, it goes without saying that if you see or hear anything that contradicts that, you should get in touch.'

'Will do,' she said. 'Good luck, Charlie. And if I don't see you before, have a lovely Christmas.'

# Chapter 6

By 9 a.m., the stallholders were greeting their first customers of the day. The lights on the tree had been switched on, loudspeakers were blasting out cheery Christmas songs, and the irresistible smell of mince pies was drifting into the courtyard from the bakery. Violet hadn't been expecting much interest in the 'pop-up' booth until later in the morning, but at nine-fifteen she was approached by a soft-spoken Scottish man, who asked to record his childhood memories of Christmases in the 1950s.

'I'll send you a link to download the video file,' Violet said, once the filming was done and she'd made a note of the man's email address. 'I'll have to do some minor editing first, so it'll be a few days before you hear from me, but I guarantee you'll have the file in time for Christmas.'

'Excellent,' said the man. 'I'm going to send it to my sister. We don't see much of each other now, so she'll get a kick out of watching the video. Knowing her, she'll remember things differently – her version of our childhood is always at odds with mine – but hey! It'll give us something to talk about when I call her on Christmas morning.'

After making a generous donation to the charity collection, the man battled his way out through the courtyard, which was now so packed with shoppers there was barely room to circulate around the stalls. As Violet stepped outside, the loudspeakers were belting out Elton John's 'Step Into Christmas' (given the lack of space, she thought '*Squeeze* Into Christmas' might have been a more appropriate lyric).

'Blimey, it's even busier than yesterday,' Molly said, as she pushed her way through the throng. She was wearing a red knitted hat, a tartan coat and dangly, flashing earrings in the shape of Christmas puddings.

'You're looking very festive,' Violet said. 'I love the outfit. Your coat is *so* stylish.'

'It's an early Christmas present to myself,' Molly said, as she stroked the velvet piping on the collar. 'How are things going here? Have you had many takers for the memory booth?'

'Just the one so far, but I've given out lots of flyers. I'm sure it's only a matter of time before we're inundated with customers.'

'Well before that happens, why don't you go and have a quick mooch around the market?' Molly said. 'It might be the only chance you get.'

'OK, you're on. I'll keep an eye on you, and if things look to be getting busy, I'll come straight back.'

'I'll be fine. There's only one camera, so we can only film one person at a time anyway. People will just have to be patient and wait their turn.'

'I'll buy us some coffees on my way round,' Violet said. 'Shall I get a couple of mince pies as well, or is it too early in the day?'

Molly grinned. 'As far as I'm concerned, it's never too early for a mince pie. Especially one of Fiona's.'

As Violet perused the exquisite handmade jewellery on one of the stalls, she spotted PC Turner out of the corner of her eye. He and another uniformed police officer were talking discreetly to some of the traders, and Violet wondered if any of them had seen anything that might help the inquiry. She hoped the police presence in the courtyard would be reassuring to shoppers, and not off-putting.

A long, retro-style pendant caught her attention and, on impulse, she decided to buy it as an extra surprise Christmas present for her mother, who adored chunky necklaces.

With the pendant neatly gift-wrapped and tucked into her shoulder bag, Violet made her way to the next stall, which was crammed with antiques – mostly jewellery and silver curios displayed in tabletop glass cabinets. The stallholder was dressed for cold weather in a well-worn sheepskin coat and a woolly scarf.

'Mornin', love,' he said, giving her a friendly wink. 'Looking for anything in particular?'

Violet smiled. 'Just browsing,' she said. If she wanted antiques, she would prefer to buy them at the *Antiques Emporium* run by Robert Dorman than from some random bloke on a market stall.

'I'll do you a good price if something catches your eye,' the stallholder said, grinning at her with slightly crooked teeth. 'Never be afraid to ask for a discount on this stall, love. There's always a deal to be done. My name's Frank, by the way. Frank Harper.'

He thrust out a fingerless-gloved hand and Violet shook it.

'Didn't I see you yesterday?' Frank said. 'Have you got a stall here yourself?'

'I own one of the businesses,' Violet replied, pointing in the general direction of *The Memory Box*. 'We've set up a pop-up Christmas video booth to raise money for charity. Things are fairly quiet over there at the moment, so I thought I'd have a quick look around the market while I have the chance.'

'If these crowds are anything to go by, I reckon today's gonna be even busier than yesterday,' Frank Harper said. 'I've done a lot of antique fairs and markets over the years, and I have to say . . . this is one of the best I've been to in terms of organisation and attendance. It's obviously been well advertised. I'll definitely be back next year, if there's another market here again.'

'That's nice to hear,' Violet said. 'And I'm glad the police presence hasn't put anyone's nose out of joint.' She looked to her right, where a uniformed officer was approaching the next stall.

Frank glanced in the same direction and sneered. 'I noticed they were sniffing around,' he said, his cranky expression making it clear he had no time for the police. 'What are they doing here anyway? Do you know?'

'A man died last night,' Violet said, keeping her voice low. 'They're checking to see whether anyone saw him at the market yesterday.'

'Died?' Frank said. 'When did this happen then? It's the first I've heard of it.'

'He was found late yesterday evening, after most of the stall-holders had gone.'

'There you are then.' Frank shrugged his sheepskin-covered shoulders. 'I left at eight, as soon as the market closed. I know nothing about anyone dying.'

'The police will want to talk to you anyway. They're speaking to everyone. It's just routine.'

'They'll get short shrift if they come to my stall,' he said. 'I'm not a fan of the police. Mind you, I'm sure the feeling's mutual.'

'If you didn't see anything, then just tell them that,' Violet said, wondering why Frank Harper seemed so ill at ease. 'It really is nothing to worry about.'

'I'm not worried,' Frank said, full of bravado. 'Coppers don't bother me. Just don't like 'em. That's all there is to it.'

Violet smiled, intrigued and suspicious in equal measure. 'I need to get some coffees to take back to my colleague,' she said. 'It was nice meeting you, Frank. Have a good day.'

She rejoined the swarming crowd, allowing it to carry her in the general direction of *Books, Bakes and Cakes* – but when she stepped inside the café, it was packed to the rafters. The hubbub of voices, the hiss of the coffee machines, and the squeals of excited children were overwhelming, and she quickly side-stepped into the adjacent bakery. It was slightly quieter there, but equally busy, with a long and very slow-moving queue at the counter. Realising she would get served more quickly by one of the catering vendors in the courtyard, Violet pushed her way outside – where, much to her relief, the piped music had been switched off.

Instead, the carol singers were outside *Sew Into Knitting*, launching into the first verse of 'Away in a Manger', singing in perfect harmony.

Positioned between the bakery and the bookshop was the *Books, Bakes and Cakes* mobile coffee truck. It was a compact, vintage-style trailer, and one of the few catering vehicles small enough to have been wheeled through the rear alleyway. The truck was managed on a day-to-day basis by Fiona's daughter, Sophie, who regularly towed it to local foodie events and festivals. Today Sophie was being ably assisted by Darren, her brother's partner, who seemed to be a dab hand with the coffee machine. There was a sizeable queue, but Sophie and Darren were working efficiently as a team and dealing with it quickly.

'Hey, Vi,' Sophie said, when it was Violet's turn to be served. 'What can I get you?'

'A cappuccino and a latte, please. I was going to get them from the café, but it's absolutely rammed in there.'

A stitch of worry appeared on Sophie's forehead. 'Did it look like they were coping OK?'

'Yes, they're just really busy,' Violet said.

Darren turned away from the coffee machine and spoke over his shoulder. 'Don't even think about rushing in there to help out, Soph. You can't be in two places at once. I need you here. I can't cope on my own.'

'The thought never entered my head,' Sophie said, giving Violet a sly, conspiratorial wink.

Laughing, Violet stood aside to wait for her coffees and let the next customer place their order.

'What about last night, then?' Sophie said, as Darren prepared the next batch of drinks. 'Bit of a shocker, wasn't it? Have you heard any more from the police?'

Violet said nothing, loath to discuss the previous evening's tragedy in front of unknowing shoppers, or reveal that DS Winterton had made an unofficial visit to the shopping village.

'They came here earlier,' Sophie said. 'The coppers, I mean. They spoke to us about twenty minutes ago.'

'I think they're talking to all the stallholders,' Violet said.

Sophie nodded. 'Yeah, that's what they said. There wasn't anything we could tell them, unfortunately. Darren wasn't even here yesterday, and I'd closed up and gone home by seven-thirty. The market was still open when I left, but the crowds were thinning and demand for coffee had tailed right off by then, so I decided to shut early.'

'Why are the police asking questions anyway?' Darren said, as he frothed milk for the cappuccino. 'I heard it was an accident.'

'It was, as far as I know,' Violet said, determined not to get drawn into any kind of speculation. 'I suspect they're trying to work out what happened so they can give some information to the man's next of kin.'

Sophie handed over the expertly prepared drinks. 'Whatever the explanation, it's unlikely to be of much comfort to the poor bloke's family,' she said. 'Whoever they are, my heart goes out to them.'

'Can I get you anything else, Violet?' Darren said.

'Actually, if you've got them, I'll have half a dozen mince pies. Two each for me and Molly, and a couple for my mum. She's arriving this evening for her Christmas visit.'

'She's early, isn't she?' Sophie said, as she took the next order. 'Christmas is well over a week away.'

Violet rolled her eyes and laughed. 'Mum said she wanted to make her journey worthwhile, so she's staying for a full fortnight. She's booked a ticket for the "Christmas at Chatsworth" experience, and she's also going to do some Christmas shopping here in Merrywell, and in Bakewell. She's coming to the shopping village tomorrow, so I'm sure she'll stop by and say hello.'

Sophie smiled. 'Tell her she can have a coffee on the house. What time's she arriving this evening? Are you going to have to rush home early?'

'She's due here sometime after seven, but I'm going to finish at six. Molly's offered to stay until the end of the market. I don't like leaving her on her own, but I still have a few things to do at home, so needs must. Hopefully, by the time Mum arrives, I'll be ready and waiting with a pot of tea and a couple of mince pies warming in the oven.'

Violet paid for her items, double-checked that the lids were securely fixed to the takeaway cups, and then prepared to do battle with the crowd.

'Ms Brewster . . . can you spare me a minute?'

PC Turner was shouldering his way towards her, looking cold and bored and slightly despondent.

Violet smiled at him. 'Sure . . . but can I give this to Molly first?' She held up the latte. 'If you follow me over to *The Memory Box*, I'll hand it over and then you and I can talk.'

PC Turner looked longingly at the coffee cup.

'I expect you could do with a drink yourself,' Violet said. 'Here, have this one . . .'

She thrust her own, untouched coffee into PC Turner's hands.

'It's a cappuccino, but there's no sugar in it, I'm afraid.'

PC Turner's face lit up. 'Perfect,' he said. 'Just how I like it.'

Once Violet had handed over the latte and mince pies to Molly, she steered PC Turner by the elbow towards a quieter part of the courtyard, where they could conduct their conversation in relative privacy.

'I noticed you and your colleague have been chatting to the stallholders,' Violet said. 'Has anyone been able to give you any information about Daniel Midship?'

'There's a young lad who works in the café who remembers serving someone matching his description late on in the evening.'

'But no other confirmed sightings?'

'Not yet,' PC Turner said, 'but we've asked Mr Midship's family to let us have a photograph. Once we have that, we'll show it around to see if it jogs any memories.'

He removed the lid from the coffee cup, wafted away the steam, and took a swig.

'The reason I wanted to talk to you is that I'm after some local intelligence,' he continued. 'One of the stallholders spotted a young male hanging around the traders' car park last night, soon after the market closed. He was seen trying a door handle on one of the cars, but he ducked out of sight when he realised someone was coming.'

'Were you able to get a description of this youth?' Violet said.

'Tall . . . well over six feet. White, skinny, with dark hair . . . sound like anyone you know?'

'Quite a few people actually, but there is someone locally who matches the description who also has an unhealthy interest in cars – Zac Wallis. He's been in trouble with the police before.'

'What kind of trouble?'

'Motoring offences.' Violet shrugged. 'Driving without a licence and insurance . . . something like that. Zac lives in Merrywell, but he hangs out with a lad from Matlock who owns an old, souped-up Subaru. They drive it around the village at night sometimes. The pair of them are completely obsessed with cars.'

'Thanks,' PC Turner said. 'He may well be the person I'm looking for. I'll have a word . . . see what this Zac character has to say for himself.'

'If it was him, he's not going to admit to being there,' Violet said. 'Not if he was up to no good.'

'True, but if he saw what happened to Daniel Midship and tells us about it, we might be willing to overlook whatever it was he was doing in the car park.'

At one minute to three, the sound of sleigh bells rang out in the courtyard and, at three o'clock precisely, Father Christmas put in an appearance, heading towards one of the studio spaces directly below Nick Penfold's office, which had been converted into a lavishly decorated grotto. Its door was guarded by two volunteer 'elves', who were organising the queue and handing out candy canes to the children waiting in line to see Santa.

Over at *The Memory Box*, Violet was chatting to someone about producing a video recording of their family history. As she handed over a business card, her phone buzzed insistently in her pocket. The unanswered call was followed up with the ping of a message alert.

A couple of minutes later, when Violet was once again free to check her phone, she opened the message, which was from her mother, Rachel.

Can you give me a quick call please? There's something I need to warn you about before I arrive.

Violet's heart sank. *What now?* she wondered, acutely aware that Rachel Middleton had spent most of her life lurching from one minor crisis to another.

She called the number.

'Hi, Mum. Sorry I couldn't take your call. I was in the middle of something.'

'No problem, darling. Thanks for ringing back.' Rachel's voice was warm and comfortingly familiar. 'I know you're busy with the market, and I don't like disturbing you, but I didn't want to turn up with someone in tow without speaking to you first.'

'Someone in *tow*?' Violet said, sensing that her carefully laid plans were about to come crashing down around her.

'I'm bringing Jacqueline Rheinhart with me,' Rachel said, sounding upbeat and annoyingly unapologetic. 'She was supposed to be spending Christmas on a cruise with her new beau, but everything's gone belly-up at the last minute. She and her "new man" have broken up, and Jacqueline is devastated. When I spoke to her this morning, she said as far as she's concerned, Christmas is cancelled. She was all for spending the festive season on her own – and of course, I couldn't let *that* happen. So, after a lot of cajoling, I've persuaded her to spend Christmas in Merrywell.'

Violet experienced a rush of panic, her heart beating wildly as she reviewed the sleeping arrangements. Her daughter, Amelia, was due to arrive on Christmas Eve. Three people in a two-bedroomed cottage was just about doable, albeit a crush – but how on earth was she going to accommodate four people in a house that only had two beds and one sofa?

'It's kind of you to look out for a friend, Mum, but I'm not sure how this is going to work. I can try and borrow a put-me-up bed, but with the best will in the world, I can't see Jacqueline Rheinhart agreeing to sleep on one of those! The only other alternative is that I move in with Matthew for the duration of Christmas – but to be honest, I was looking forward to spending time with you and Amelia at Greengage Cottage.'

'There's no need to concern yourself about the sleeping arrangements,' Rachel said. 'Jacqueline's staying at the Merrywell Manor Hotel. She called them an hour ago and booked a suite for the next two weeks.'

'A *suite*?' Violet said. 'Good grief. That'll cost her a small fortune. The Merrywell Manor Hotel is expensive at the best of times, and their rates will probably be double over Christmas.'

'A suite was all they had left – but don't worry, Jacqueline can afford it. She's absolutely loaded. However . . . there is one favour I need to ask.'

'Go on,' Violet said, as her heart rate returned to something closer to normal.

'It would appear the hotel restaurant is already fully booked for Christmas dinner, so I told Jacqueline she could eat with us. I hope that's OK, darling. I realise it's an imposition, but I couldn't possibly let her spend Christmas Day on her own with nothing to eat.'

Squeezing an extra chair around her small kitchen table wouldn't be easy, but Violet thought she would manage somehow – and if all else failed, they could decamp to Matthew's house, and she would cook dinner there.

'That's absolutely fine,' she said. 'There's no point Jacqueline coming all the way to Merrywell if she's going to spend Christmas Day alone. And anyway, it's the season of good will. I'm hardly going to turn her away, am I? I'm already cooking for seven people. One more person won't make any difference.'

'Thanks, sweetheart. It's very understanding of you. I'll fill you in on Jacqueline's break-up and her ghastly "boyfriend" when I see you – but please don't say anything to her when we arrive this evening.'

'I'll have to say *something* to her,' Violet said.

'Yes, all right . . . but can you give the impression you think her cruise was cancelled at the last minute? Please don't mention her scoundrel of an ex – unless, of course, she brings the subject up herself.'

*Oh, what a tangled web we weave*, thought Violet. So much for a fun family Christmas.

# Chapter 7

The market was still in full swing when Violet fastened her thick winter coat and prepared to leave for the evening.

'I'm sorry to bail out early,' she said, watching as Molly bit the head off a festive gingerbread man (her third of the day). 'Are you sure you'll be OK on your own?'

'Yes, don't worry,' Molly said, as she munched the biscuit. 'You go and get things ready for your mum's arrival.'

'Thanks, Molly. I don't know what I'd do without you. I'll see you in the morning.'

The central heating had already come on when Violet let herself into Greengage Cottage, but she lit the log burner in the living room anyway, along with a cinnamon-scented candle. As she filled the kettle and placed two of her best china cups on a tray, her cat, Rusty, rubbed against her ankles, demanding to be fed by meowing loudly.

Rather than filling the kitchen with the pungent aroma of wet cat food, Violet tipped a generous helping of dry crunchies into Rusty's bowl. The cat blinked furiously, clearly unimpressed – but when Violet showed no sign of giving in to feline pressure, Rusty curled her tail around her body and tucked in reluctantly to the dry offering.

With everything set for her mother's arrival, Violet sat down and sent a message to Matthew, letting him know there would be an extra person joining them for Christmas dinner. He replied in his usual laid-back way.

The more the merrier. xx

Violet held off from saying they might need to relocate to his house, to eat off the large dining table Matthew had crafted for himself a few months earlier. Christmas was over a week away, so there was plenty of time to broach that possibility in person.

At seven-forty, Violet heard her mother's car roll onto the gravel driveway at the side of the house. Braving the cold, she went outside to greet her, expecting to find Jacqueline Rheinhart in the passenger seat – but her mother was on her own.

'Hi, Mum,' Violet said, as she was enveloped in a tight, perfumed-scented hug. 'Where's Jacqueline?'

'She asked me to drop her off at the hotel. It's been a long journey, and she said she was tired.'

Rachel stood back and studied Violet critically. 'I hope you're going to get your hair cut before Christmas, darling. Your fringe is far too long. It's a wonder you can see where you're going.'

'I've got an appointment at a salon in Bakewell next week,' Violet said, sighing inwardly at the speed at which her mother had found something to complain about. 'Now . . . let me grab your case and we'll go inside, where it's warm.'

'You've not cooked a big meal, have you?' Rachel said, as Violet retrieved a large cherry-red suitcase and a matching holdall from the boot of the car.

'No. You told me you were stopping off for something to eat on the way. I was planning to serve you a light supper of a mince pie and a cup of tea.'

Rachel smiled. 'Sounds heavenly. Come on, let's get inside, and I'll fill you in on Jacqueline's disastrous romance.'

After serving the warm mince pies, Violet settled down at the kitchen table, opposite Rachel.

'What's the story with Jacqueline then?' she said, as she poured tea from a bone china teapot.

Rachel gave a slow shake of her head. 'It's a salutary tale. I did warn her that things would end badly, but she wouldn't listen.'

'Is that why the two of you have been playing it cool recently?'

Rachel pouted. 'We have been seeing less of one another,' she said, sounding defensive, 'but we are still friends. We've had a difference of opinion, nothing more.'

Violet gave her mother a disbelieving frown. 'Come off it, Mum. You and Jacqueline used to be as thick as thieves – but she hasn't warranted a mention for months.'

'All right . . . I admit, I've been annoyed with her,' Rachel said, as she sipped her tea. 'In the spring, she signed up with one of those dating apps for seniors. Why people have to resort to those things is beyond me. Why can't people go *out* and meet someone, like we used to do in the old days? Why does everything have to be done online now, like a transaction?'

'It's the way things work in the twenty-first century, Mum. People lead busy lives, and dating sites save time.'

Rachel harrumphed, clearly unconvinced. 'Well . . . that bally app certainly didn't do Jacqueline any favours. Signing up for it was a foolish thing to have done – and I told her so.'

Violet winced. 'That was harsh. Just because you disapprove of the concept doesn't make it a bad thing, you know. Maybe Jacqueline was lonely and a dating site was her only option. Let's face it, she was never going to meet anyone new at the bridge club, was she?'

'True.' Rachel dipped her head in agreement. 'But why does she need a man in her life anyway? Jacq's been a widow for four years and, as far as I can tell, she's coped admirably on her own. She has plenty of female friends to hang out with.'

'Perhaps she'd prefer some male company for a change,' Violet said.

Rachel wrinkled her nose. 'Whatever her reasons, she was definitely on a mission to find romance. I told her she was going the wrong way about it, but there was no deterring her. One hears of so many horror stories . . . people turning up for dates with someone who looks nothing like their profile picture . . . married men using dating apps to commit adultery . . . and then, of course, there are the con artists – out to get their hands on your life savings. That's what Jacqueline's gentleman friend has been trying to do.'

'Do you know this for certain?' Violet said, feeling instant sympathy for Jacqueline.

'It stands to reason, darling. Jacqueline Rheinhart is a very wealthy woman, and she doesn't hide the fact. She drives an expensive car, has a beautiful home, and her clothes are nothing short of exquisite. In short, she's easy prey for a grifter.'

Violet suppressed a smile, surprised her mother knew what a 'grifter' was.

'That's as may be,' Violet said. 'But are you absolutely sure of your facts? Has she really been taken in by this guy, or are you just assuming that's what's happened?'

Rachel drained her teacup before replying. 'At first, I didn't know what was going on. Jacq knew I disapproved, so she was very cagey with me. However, it soon became obvious this chap was out for all he could get. The guy is extremely good-looking and at least ten years younger than Jacqueline.'

'So, what if he is?' Violet said, wondering if her mother was jealous. 'Jacqueline's an attractive woman, and in great shape for her age.'

'I know she is, sweetheart, and I mean no disrespect – but let's face it, she is seventy-four, and no amount of expensive face cream or well-cut clothes can disguise that fact. This boyfriend of hers . . . Duncan . . . is supposed to be sixty-four – although he looks a decade younger – and from the first day they got together, Jacqueline has been showering him with gifts.'

'Maybe she's just being affectionate,' Violet said, trying to put a positive spin on a situation that did, admittedly, sound suspicious.

'If she'd bought him a new shirt, or a book, or even a pair of cufflinks, I might agree with you, but when I say *expensive* gifts, I'm talking about a new iPhone, a MacBook, designer clothes, and – more recently – a brand-new electric car. Dodgy Duncan must have thought all his Christmases had come at once.'

'So what happened to change her mind about him?' Violet said. 'If Jacqueline was besotted with this man, why the sudden change of heart? Or was it the other way around? Did he break it off with her?'

'No, it was definitely Jacqueline who called a halt to things. She finally saw the light when he reneged on his promise to pay for their Christmas cruise. He booked it for them ages ago, on the basis that one of his "insurance policies" was due to mature. He said he wanted to pay for the trip as a thank you for everything Jacqueline had done for him. Then, a few weeks ago, when it was time to pay the balance on the holiday, he said there'd been a hitch. He claimed he wouldn't be able to access his funds until the new year.'

'And I'm guessing he wanted Jacqueline to step in and pay?'

'Of course he did,' Rachel said. 'And that's when Jacq smelled a rat. What's that saying about the scales falling from people's eyes? Finally, for the first time, she began to see Duncan for what he was . . . a sponger. She came to her senses, and immediately gave him his marching orders.'

'So, why is she heartbroken?' Violet said. 'It sounds to me like she's had a lucky escape.'

'I agree, and I'm sure, deep down, Jacqueline knows that too – but what you have to remember is that as well as being relieved, she also feels betrayed and embarrassed. She's upset and pining – not for *Duncan*, but rather the feeling of hope their relationship had given her. Those hopes – however misguided – have been dashed. She feels dejected and despondent.'

'Oh dear,' Violet said. 'We'll just have to try and cheer her up then, won't we? You can make a start tomorrow by bringing her along to the Christmas market. A spot of retail therapy might take her mind off Dodgy Duncan, even if it is only for a couple of hours.'

'That's a jolly good idea, actually,' Rachel said, as she bit into her second mince pie. 'I'll go and pick her up from the hotel in the morning. Now . . . enough about Jacqueline. Tell me what you've been up to. How is life in Merrywell suiting you?'

'Everything's great,' Violet said. 'The business is thriving. Life's good.'

She decided not to spoil her mother's arrival by mentioning Daniel Midship's demise. Hopefully, there would be no need for Rachel (or any of the other visitors to the village) to find out what had taken place in that dark alleyway on Friday evening.

# Chapter 8

The Christmas market had been open for almost three hours when Rachel and Jacqueline made their entrance at the shopping village the next morning. Violet spotted them in the distance, and by the time the pair had wended their way over to *The Memory Box*, it was midday.

'Darling, this is absolutely wonderful,' Rachel said, twirling her arms in the direction of the craft stalls. 'So many fabulous things for sale.'

Jacqueline looked equally enamoured. After adjusting the shopping bag on her arm, she moved in to deliver an air kiss. 'Hello, Violet,' she said. 'Your mother's right. This market is sublime. I've spent a small fortune and I've only been here twenty minutes.'

Violet smiled. 'Hi, Jacqueline, and welcome to Derbyshire. How are you settling in at the hotel? Is everything to your liking?'

'It's perfect. Absolutely perfect. Comfortable, luxurious, and so quaint. I don't know why I haven't visited this area before. It's stunningly beautiful, and I'm looking forward to spending a quiet Christmas here. Apart from this market – which is absolutely buzzing – everything else about the village seems so calm and quiet and peaceful. Merrywell is exactly what I need right now.'

'We're going to the café for a coffee and a bite to eat,' Rachel said. 'Will you join us, darling?'

Violet shook her head. 'Sorry, Mum. We're really busy, and it wouldn't be fair to leave Molly to cope on her own. Go ahead without me, and I'll catch up with you this afternoon.'

The two women reappeared at *The Memory Box* an hour later and, from the sour expression on Rachel's face, it was clear something had upset her.

'What's up, Mum?' Violet said. 'You don't look very happy. Didn't you enjoy your lunch?'

'Lunch was fine. The café was busy, but the food was lovely. I had a brie and cranberry sandwich, and a huge slice of chocolate fudge cake. It was delicious.'

'So, why do you look as if you've been sucking a lemon?' Violet said.

Rachel ran a finger across her left eyebrow and reset her expression. 'If you must know, we've just been accosted by a policeman. He showed us a man's photograph and wanted to know if we'd seen him on Friday.'

Violet cursed inwardly. She hadn't seen either of the police officers herself today – but it was just her luck they would show up precisely where her mother happened to be.

'I told the officer we only arrived in Merrywell yesterday evening,' Rachel said. 'I expect that would have been the end of it – but as he started to walk away, we asked about the man.'

Jacqueline interjected. 'We wondered if he'd gone missing.'

'And do you know what the policeman told us?' Rachel raised her eyebrows. 'He said the guy in the photograph *died* on Friday night, and that he was found here, in the shopping village.'

'I know,' Violet said. 'I was in the bookshop when the body was found.'

Rachel's eyes widened. '*What?* Why didn't you say something? For heaven's sake, Violet! What kind of village *is* this?'

A passing shopper swivelled her head in their direction.

'Keep your voice down, Mum.'

'Why? I'm not saying anything that isn't true,' Rachel said, lowering her voice only a fraction. 'You have to admit there have been an abnormally high number of mysterious deaths since you moved to Merrywell – so much so that I'm beginning to think you've jinxed the place. This village is fast becoming the Derbyshire equivalent of Cabot Cove.'

Violet wasn't thrilled with the comparison, but as a fan of the *Murder, She Wrote* TV series, she couldn't help but smile.

'There's no need to exaggerate,' she said, quick to defend the reputation of her beloved village. 'As far as I'm aware, the man the police are asking about died as the result of an accident.'

'If it was an accident, why are police officers wandering around the market showing his photograph to all and sundry?' Rachel said.

'I expect they're trying to establish what happened, so that they can work out how he died. Whatever their reasons, it's nothing for you to worry about. Just ignore the police presence and go and do some more shopping. Enjoy yourselves.'

'Easier said than done. Jacqueline and I are not as inured to death as you appear to be.'

'I'm not *inured* to anything, Mum. I didn't tell you about this because I didn't want to spoil your visit. I'd like you and Jacqueline to make the most of your time in Merrywell.'

'Well, you *should* have told me,' Rachel said. 'Contrary to popular belief, ignorance is not always bliss. Is there anything else I should know about? Any other horrid secrets you've been keeping to yourself?'

'No, of course not,' Violet said, surprised and a little dismayed by her mother's reaction. 'Can you please stop finding fault and looking for things to fret about? You and Jacqueline are supposed to be relaxing and getting ready for Christmas.'

Jacqueline smiled and squeezed Violet's arm in a show of

solidarity. 'I'm enjoying myself,' she said. 'Even if your mother isn't.'

'I didn't say I wasn't enjoying myself,' said Rachel. 'Although, I admit I was hoping you'd be able to spend more time with us. It hadn't occurred to me you'd be working such long hours.'

'Today is the final day of the "pop-up" booth,' Violet said. 'From tomorrow onwards, I'll be free to take some time off. I thought we could go over to Chatsworth farm shop one afternoon.'

The suggestion seemed to pacify Rachel. 'That would be nice,' she said, sounding much calmer. 'And perhaps we could take a drive if the weather's good . . . give Jacqueline a taste of the Peak District.'

'I'd like that,' Jacqueline said.

'Great,' said Violet. 'I'll be working late again today, but rest assured . . . from tomorrow onwards, the three of us can start to enjoy some quality time together.'

# Chapter 9

The next day was Monday, and Molly's day off. Violet arrived at the office early, intending to stay for only a few hours. She would have preferred not to have gone in at all, but with the 'pop-up' initiative over, she needed to make a start on editing the Christmas memory films, so that she could email them out to the individuals involved. She was expecting it to be an easy but slightly boring process, given the number of video files awaiting her attention. Since Friday, she and Molly had filmed almost fifty people and raised over five hundred pounds for charity.

The Christmas market still had a further six days to run, but Violet was now winding slowly down in anticipation of the holidays. In the run-up to Christmas Eve, she would complete whatever work she needed to do in the mornings, and spend the afternoons with Rachel and Jacqueline.

After two solid hours of staring at her computer screen, she decided it was time for a break. She made herself a much-needed cup of tea, and was carrying it to her desk when the door opened and Charlie Winterton strolled into *The Memory Box*.

'Hello,' Violet said, surprised to see him again so soon. 'This is becoming a habit. People will start to talk.'

He laughed. 'I was in the area, so I thought I'd drop in and give you a quick update, and I wouldn't say "no" to a coffee, if there's one going begging.'

'Sit yourself down,' Violet said. 'The kettle's just boiled.'

'What's the latest then?' she said a couple of minutes later, as she handed a steaming mug of coffee to Charlie.

'The post-mortem has confirmed that Daniel Midship died from the head injury he sustained, and everything points to an accidental death. There's no evidence of a fight, or a struggle. No defence wounds.'

'Has anyone spoken to Zac Wallis?' Violet said. 'PC Turner told me someone matching his description was seen in the rear car park, after the market had closed. *Was* it Zac? Did he see anything?'

Charlie shook his head. 'PC Turner talked to him yesterday, but the lad has denied being anywhere near the shopping village. He could be lying through his teeth, but we have no choice but to take him at his word. Other than one extremely vague eyewitness description, there's no proof that Zac was in the car park. And even if he was, it doesn't necessarily follow he would have seen anything.'

Violet let out a sigh of frustration. 'What about the mark on Daniel Midship's jeans?'

'Interestingly, there was a welt found on Dan's right ankle during the post-mortem . . . a slight reddening of the skin that corresponded with the position of the mark on his jeans. In the opinion of the pathologist, it suggests he tripped over the chain.'

'But how did that happen if the chain was lying on the ground?'

DS Winterton held up his hands. 'I don't know, Violet. I wish I had all the answers – *any* answers – but I don't. Apart from the anomaly with the chain, there's no proof of foul play – which means there's no case to investigate as far as my boss is concerned. I don't agree with her, but she is the senior officer, and in the absence of any compelling evidence, it's out of my hands. I've been told to leave well alone and get on with solving "real" crimes.'

'I see,' Violet said, taking an instant dislike to Charlie's boss. 'I guess you'll have to follow orders, then. Doesn't sound like you have any choice.'

Charlie ran a finger around the rim of his coffee mug. 'There was a time when I might have kicked against the decision, but I'm getting too long in the tooth to be a rebel. I'm not going to risk my career and my police pension by disobeying the boss. Having said that . . .'

Violet leaned towards him, resting her elbows on the desk and her chin in her hands.

'Go on,' she said, eager to hear what Charlie was about to say.

He cleared his throat. 'There's nothing to stop me making a few enquiries in my own time. That way, I'll be able to put my mind at rest without upsetting the DI.'

'Good for you, Charlie.'

She smiled at him, and he grinned back mischievously.

'I've got a lot of hours owing to me,' he said. 'I thought I'd use some of them to make a few phone calls, starting with Dan Midship's old colleagues in Leeds. I'm interested in finding out whether he'd had trouble with anyone in the past – possibly someone he'd arrested who might be holding a grudge.'

'Is there anything I can do to help?' Violet said.

Charlie waved his hands. 'Thanks for the offer, but no. If I do uncover evidence of foul play, we could be dealing with a potentially dangerous individual. This isn't a parlour game, Violet. Police work can be a nasty business – which is why I can't have you putting yourself at risk.'

'I'm no fool, Charlie. I know how to look after myself.'

'I agree, you're the complete opposite of a fool. Even so, I can't have you ending up in a dangerous situation that you're not trained to deal with.'

Violet leaned back in her chair and folded her arms.

'There's no need to look quite so crestfallen,' Charlie said. 'You're not seriously expecting me to let you get involved in a police inquiry?'

'It wouldn't be the first time it's happened – and anyway, you've just told me there isn't going to *be* an investigation. Your boss has expressly forbidden it.'

Charlie frowned. 'That's the situation at the moment, but things will change rapidly if I can discover something of significance related to one of Dan's past cases.'

'So, it's all right for you to make enquiries in your own time, but I'm not allowed to?'

'Correct,' Charlie said. 'I'm a policeman, even when I'm off duty. You're a civilian, and you need to remember that. And why the heck do you want to get involved in this anyway? Why does it matter to you so much? I don't understand you sometimes, Violet. I really don't.'

Violet tilted her head back and sighed. 'I don't always understand me either, but this shopping village is important to me. I care about the people who work here, and I need it to be a place of safety – for me, and for them. Since I saw Daniel Midship in the alleyway, things have started to feel dark, and dangerous. For my own peace of mind, I need to know what happened to him, and understand why he died.'

Charlie nodded. 'I get that, and I sympathise, but some things defy explanation. Finding answers isn't always possible.'

'Don't we owe it to Daniel Midship to at least try?'

'*You* don't owe Dan anything,' Charlie replied. 'I appreciate you want to help, Violet, but the best way you can do that – the *only* way – is to keep your ear to the ground, here in the village.'

Violet sat up, nodding to accept the task allotted to her.

'I can do that,' she said.

'Based on the CCTV footage, I think we can assume Dan Midship saw someone at the shopping village – and the chances are it was someone local. You're acquainted with most of the residents of Merrywell, and your observational skills are second to none, so you have my permission to observe. Nothing more. If you see or hear anything even remotely suspicious, you're to call me straight away. Understood?'

Violet pressed her hands together and smiled. 'Yes, I understand.'

Charlie held up an index finger. 'Remember, eyes and ears only. I don't want to fall out with you, Violet, so please don't be tempted to launch your own investigation.'

# Chapter 10

Violet had arranged to meet her mother and Jacqueline in *Books, Bakes and Cakes* for lunch. At one o'clock she locked up the office and crossed the courtyard. The market was a little quieter today, but the stallholders and shopkeepers were continuing to make plenty of sales, and looked set to do so right up to the final hours of the last day of the Christmas market.

The café was full of customers, but when Violet walked in, she saw that Rachel and Jacqueline had managed to snag a table by the door.

'We've already ordered,' Rachel said, as Violet sat down. 'We've been warned there could be a twenty-minute wait for the food, so I chose for you to save time . . . I've ordered you a BLT on rye and a cappuccino.'

'Excellent. Thanks, Mum. I'm ready for something to eat. I've been editing some of the videos Molly and I filmed over the weekend. What about you two? What have you been up to?'

'We drove into Bakewell this morning,' Jacqueline said. 'It's a lovely town, although trying to find somewhere to park was a nightmare.'

'It's always the same at this time of year,' Violet said, as a waiter appeared, carrying their drinks on a tray. 'Market days can get busy too.'

As Violet sipped her cappuccino, Jill Atherstone wandered past, scanning the room in search of a vacant table.

'Jill!' Violet waved to catch her attention. 'There's a spare seat here, if you'd like to join us.'

Jill came over to their table, pulled out the fourth chair, and flopped onto it gratefully. 'Phew! Thanks, Violet. Am I ready for a sit-down! I've not had a break since nine o'clock this morning and my feet are killing me.'

'This is my mum and her friend Jacqueline,' Violet said, making the introductions. 'They'll be spending Christmas in Merrywell.'

'I'm pleased to meet you both,' Jill said. 'And I appreciate you letting me share your table.'

'Busy day, huh?' said Violet.

'Our busiest so far. Today was supposed to be my day off, but Eric begged me to come in anyway. He's employed two extra people for the whole of December, but neither of them have a clue about bookselling.'

'In my experience, temporary staff can be more of a hindrance than a help,' Rachel said. 'You end up spending all your time training them, instead of doing your own job.'

'You're absolutely right,' Jill said. 'It's been an exhausting and very frustrating morning – which is why I needed to get away from the shop for half an hour.'

'It sounds to me like you're ready for some time off,' Rachel said. 'You must be so looking forward to Christmas.'

Jill see-sawed her head. 'Yes, and no,' she said. 'I have mixed feelings about it. This has been a difficult year for me, so I'm not feeling very festive.'

Rachel's face fell. 'Oh, I'm sorry to hear that. It's not easy getting into the festive spirit when you've had a bad year, is it?'

'No, it's not.' Jill smiled sadly. 'My brother died in the summer,' she said, by way of explanation. 'Steven and I were twins, so we were always close – emotionally, if not geographically. He lived in London for many years, but last April he moved back to Merrywell. I was so happy that he'd returned to the village, but then . . . in June, he died very suddenly. It was an awful shock, one I still haven't quite come to terms with.'

Rachel leaned across the table and squeezed Jill's hand. 'I'm so sorry,' she said. 'You have my sympathy. I know what it's like to lose someone unexpectedly. Violet's dad died almost ten years ago now. He was fine one minute, and gone the next. It's a terrible thing to have to deal with.'

Jill picked up the salt pot from the centre of the table and turned it clockwise between her index finger and thumb.

'I struggled a lot in the weeks after the funeral,' she said. 'Steven and I were a sort of double-act – although he was always far more talented than I was. He left home and pursued a very successful career in the City, whereas I was the boring stay-at-home girl, living with my mum and working for the local council.'

'Is your mum still around?' Jacqueline said.

Jill shook her head. 'She died two years ago. As a matter of fact, it was Mum's death that prompted Steven to rethink his life. At the time, he was earning a huge amount of money, but his job was very stressful, and he was tired of the frenzied lifestyle that went with it. He'd reached the stage where he wanted to ease back a little, which is why he decided to buy a house in Merrywell. He completed on his house purchase in the spring, and was looking forward to doing the renovations over the summer – but sadly, it wasn't meant to be.'

'I can totally understand why you're not looking forward to Christmas,' Rachel said. 'It isn't the same when you've lost someone close to you – and the first Christmas without them is especially tough. The festive season is supposed to be about spending time with those we love, so when someone important is missing from your life, it's hard to drum up any enthusiasm.'

Jill sat back as a waiter placed a cup of coffee in front of her.

'On a more positive note, there has been an upside to all this,' she said, as she tipped sugar into her cup. 'The fact is, if it wasn't for Steven's death, I would never have met Adrian.'

'Adrian?' said Rachel.

'My boyfriend. Well . . . my partner, actually. We moved in together last month. We met at a bereavement group – so you could say that grief brought us together.'

Rachel smiled. 'They do say every cloud has a silver lining.'

'After my brother died, I felt very low,' Jill said, as she stirred her coffee. 'I visited my GP and instead of prescribing medication, she referred me to a bereavement group in Matlock. I wasn't too keen on the idea initially, but it turned out to be a surprisingly comforting experience.'

'I thought about joining something similar when my husband died,' Jacqueline said. 'In the end, I decided it wasn't my kind of thing . . . but if your experience is anything to go by, perhaps I made the wrong decision.'

'That kind of group isn't for everyone, but it certainly helped me,' Jill said. 'By talking to other people who'd lost a partner or close family member, I was able to come to terms with my own feelings about Steven's death. During one of the meetings, I got chatting to Adrian. Like me, he'd lost a sibling. He and his sister weren't twins, but they were close in age and always very supportive of each other.'

'It sounds like you were kindred spirits,' Rachel said.

'Yes, I think we were. Adrian and I just sort of . . . clicked. We started out as friends, but we were both single and – dare I say it – lonely, and so our relationship blossomed.'

'Rachel and I are both widows,' Jacqueline said. 'We know all about loneliness, don't we Rach?'

'We do,' Rachel agreed. 'But we have each other, Jacq. Friends forever, yes?'

Jacqueline gave a wistful smile and raised her coffee cup.

'Here's to friends,' she said.

Rachel lifted her own cup. 'I'm sorry for your loss, Jill, but I'm glad this year has brought some joy as well. Trust me, when happiness comes along, you have to grab it with both hands – that's what I keep telling Violet anyway. I live in hope that she and Matthew will move in together eventually.'

Violet rolled her eyes.

'It's no good pulling a face, darling,' Rachel said. 'Someone needs to stir you into action. It's time you and Matthew stopped shilly-shallying and made a decision.'

'This is neither the time nor the place to have this discussion, Mother,' Violet said. 'Although, for your information, we *have* made a decision. Matthew and I are planning to move in together some time in the new year, once we've found somewhere suitable to live.'

Rachel let out a gasp of delight and clapped her palms together. 'Well, that *is* good news,' she said. 'And about time too . . . but what's all this about finding somewhere suitable to live? You and Matthew both own beautiful homes. Surely you can decide between you which one to live in?'

Violet had planned to have this conversation with her mother in private, but she knew there was no stopping Rachel, once she was in full flow.

'I absolutely love Greengage Cottage – but it's tiny,' she said. 'Matthew's house is bigger, but not big enough. We'd like somewhere with more space. Four bedrooms, ideally.'

Rachel pulled a face. 'What do you need four bedrooms for? There's only the two of you, and that's not likely to change. You're well past your childbearing years. Why on earth do you want to rattle around in a house that's too big for you?'

Violet sighed inwardly. They were obviously going to have this discussion – now – whether she liked it or not.

'There'll be a bedroom for Amelia, and one for Rhys,' she said. 'Matthew and I want our children to know they're welcome to stay whenever they feel like it. We thought a fourth bedroom would be nice for guests – such as yourself – but if you think that's an extravagance, then maybe we should reconsider.'

Rachel spluttered. 'Far be it for me to influence your decision, darling. It's your life. All I'm urging you to do is get on with it.'

Thankfully, the arrival of their food obviated any need to respond. Grateful for small mercies, Violet tucked into her sandwich and changed the subject.

# Chapter 11

The next morning, Violet got to *The Memory Box* at eight-thirty. She had promised to drive her mother and Jacqueline to Hartington later, but there were a few things she needed to do in the office first. On her walk to work, she'd called in at the village shop to buy a carton of milk, and had been pulled up sharp by the front page of the latest edition of the local paper, the *Peak Times*. She picked up a copy, paid for it with her milk, and skim read the article as she walked to the office.

The newspaper was now lying on her desk, the stark headline a reminder of something she'd been trying not to think about. She reread the brief report, feeling frustrated that the only new information it contained was Daniel Midship's age.

**Man dies at local shopping village**

Derbyshire Constabulary has confirmed that a man has died at Merrywell Shopping Village. His body was found at the end of the first day of the retail centre's newly established Christmas market. The discovery was made by a security guard just before 9 p.m. on Friday. Although a formal identification has yet to take place, the deceased is believed to be Daniel Midship (55) from Leeds. His family have been informed.

A spokesperson for Derbyshire Police said: 'There are no suspicious circumstances at this time, but we are appealing for information from anyone who may have seen or spoken to Mr Midship at the shopping village on Friday. Our thoughts are with his family at this difficult time.'

Beneath the headline was a colour photograph of Daniel Midship taken in happier times. He was grinning into the camera, looking carefree and relaxed. There were laughter lines around his eyes, and his cropped grey hair looked newly trimmed. As Violet stared at the photograph, a lump formed in her throat.

She shivered and pushed the newspaper away. She had to stop thinking about this – it was doing her no good. She didn't want to spend another morning puzzling over Daniel Midship's untimely death, so she left the paper at the end of her desk, out of her line of vision. She had work to do: enquiries to deal with, and Christmas films to edit. She needed to crack on.

As she opened one of four unread emails in her inbox, the door opened and Jill Atherstone stepped into the office, bringing with her a blast of cold air. She was wearing a smart, navy-blue coat and a purple beret, and looked nervous but determined.

'Hello, Jill,' Violet said, surprised to see her – especially so early in the morning.

'Hi, Violet. I'm sorry to disturb you. I'm on my way into work, so I won't stay long . . . but there's something I'd like to talk to you about.'

'Sure. Would you like to sit down?' Violet motioned to Molly's empty chair. 'Do you have time for a coffee, or tea?'

Jill sat down, but waved away the offer of a drink. 'No, really. I'm due at the shop in a minute. I'm here because of something you mentioned yesterday. Were you serious when you said you and Matthew are looking for a house to buy in Merrywell?'

'Deadly serious,' Violet replied. 'We want to stay in the village, but we're realistic enough to know it might take a while to find what we're looking for. Properties in this area don't come onto the market very often.'

'Actually, I believe I can help you there,' Jill said, leaning forward conspiratorially. 'I haven't told anyone this yet, but I'm planning to put my house on the market in the new year.'

Violet shifted in her chair, feeling distinctly uncomfortable. She knew Jill lived at Overton Cottage, which she'd inherited when her mother had died. Violet had never been inside the property, but she'd walked past it plenty of times, and from the outside, it looked tiny – even smaller than Greengage Cottage.

'It's very kind of you to think of us, Jill, and I'm sure Overton Cottage is lovely, but Matthew and I are looking for something bigger.'

Jill laughed. 'Sorry, I haven't made myself clear. I don't mean Overton Cottage. I'm talking about Rock House, the property my brother left me. It needs quite a lot of work doing to it, but it's very light and airy and spacious, with four large bedrooms, and three reception rooms. The kitchen's very small – more of a scullery really – and it needs completely refitting, but there's a massive garden, so you could easily knock through at the back and build an extension . . . create one of those amazing live-in kitchens?'

Violet was instantly intrigued, but keeping a firm lid on her excitement. The only thing she knew about Rock House was its location – on a quiet lane that ran behind St Luke's Church, about a quarter of a mile from the centre of the village. She'd driven past it a few times, but the house was set back from the road behind a high hedge, and she had no idea what it looked like.

'Is it a modern property?' she said, wondering if 'light and airy' equated to the spacious but bland architecture of the 1970s. If it did, then she and Matthew wouldn't be interested. They were looking for an older property, something with character.

'I believe it was built in the early twentieth century, just before the First World War,' Jill replied. 'It has an arts and crafts feel about it. It's slightly quirky, but the rooms *are* big, and it's structurally sound too. Steven had had quite a lot of refurbishment work done before he died. The whole house has been rewired, and a new boiler and central heating system have been installed. Steven was aiming to strip everything back and get the basics right, so that he could put his own stamp on it in terms of fitting and decor.'

Jill unclipped her handbag and pulled out a brochure, which she pushed across the desk.

'Those are the estate agent's details from when Steven bought the house. I'm happy to let the property go at the same price, for a quick sale.'

Violet picked up the brochure and noted the asking price. Based on a quick scan of the photographs, floor plan and descriptive blurb, it seemed more than reasonable.

'May I keep this, to show Matthew?'

'Of course,' Jill replied.

'And can I ask you something else?'

'By all means.'

'Why are you willing to sell the house for the same price your brother paid for it? He must have spent several thousand pounds on the new electrics and heating system.'

The last thing Violet wanted to do was bump up the asking price, but it seemed odd that Jill wasn't trying to recover the money her brother had already invested in the property.

'My priority is to get a quick sale,' Jill said, pressing her hands together. 'Plus, if you and Matthew like the house and decide you want to buy it, we can do it as a private sale. What I'll save on estate agent's fees will go a long way towards recouping the money Steven spent on the house.'

Violet scrutinised the sales details more carefully, checking the dimensions and trying to visualise how each of the photographed rooms might look once they'd been renovated. The property *would* need a lot of work – there was no doubt about that – but it looked exactly like the kind of house she and Matthew had been hoping to find.

'I'll understand if it's not what you're looking for,' Jill said. 'But after what you said yesterday, I thought I should mention it to you, because I know properties in Merrywell are hard to come by. I'll let you talk it over with Matthew. See what he thinks, and if you'd like to view the house, just give me a call and I'll take you on a guided tour.'

'Thanks,' said Violet, who was already desperate to see the house, and praying she wouldn't be disappointed. 'I'm sure Matthew will be keen to take a look.'

Jill glanced at her watch. 'There is one more thing I need to add,' she said, holding up an index finger. 'Can I ask that you, me and Matthew keep this between ourselves for now? The truth is, I'm looking for a quick sale because Adrian and I are hoping to buy a business together. We recently put in a bid on a boutique hotel near Ashbourne. Our offer is below the asking price, but the hotel's been on the market for a while, so we're hoping they'll accept. Adrian and I are pooling our resources, and we're obviously keen to get things moving as soon as possible.'

Violet's sense of optimism took a nose dive. 'Matthew and I won't be cash buyers, I'm afraid,' she said, feeling a stab of disappointment. 'Our house purchase will be reliant on us selling at least one of our existing properties, and I'm not sure how long that will take. If we do decide to buy Rock House, there's no guarantee we'll be able to complete the purchase quickly.'

Jill waved away Violet's doubts.

'You and Matthew have beautiful homes. I'm sure both properties will be snapped up the minute they go on the market. Our aim will be to complete on our own purchase within the next three months – and I have every confidence your own property sales will fit in with that timescale.'

'It certainly sounds doable,' Violet said. 'But, like I say, there are no guarantees. We could end up in long property chains, involving lots of buyers. Anything could happen.'

'Let's take it one step at a time and hope for the best,' Jill said. 'If it's meant to be, I'm sure everything will work out in the end.'

'That sounds like a very pragmatic approach, but let's not get ahead of ourselves. Matthew and I haven't even seen the property yet.'

'The thing is . . .' Jill tapped her fingers on the desktop. 'If Adrian and I are lucky enough to get the hotel, it will mean I'll be leaving Merrywell . . . and I haven't broken the news to Eric yet. He knows nothing about any of this. That's why I'd like you and Matthew to keep this to yourselves for now.'

'OK,' Violet said. 'But when are you thinking of telling Eric?'

Jill leaned forward. 'I thought I'd wait until after Christmas. I've worked at the bookshop for a long time now, and Eric isn't just my boss – he's also a friend, and he'll be sorry to see me go. I'll give him as much notice as I can, to allow him plenty of time to recruit my replacement, but I know he'll be upset when he finds out I'm leaving. I don't want to spoil his Christmas, so I've decided to wait, and tell him in the new year. By then, Adrian and I will know for certain whether our offer on the hotel has been accepted.' She gave a lopsided smile. 'I hope you understand, Violet. Will you and Matthew keep my secret, until after Christmas?'

'Of course we will,' Violet replied. 'And you're right – Eric will miss you, but he's also going to be really happy for you, Jill. You and Adrian are embarking on an exciting new adventure . . . making a fresh start together. Eric and Fiona will be nothing but delighted for you.'

'Thanks, Violet. It's kind of you to say so.' Jill stood up and reached for her handbag. 'Let me know what Matthew thinks of the house and, if you do want to view it, you know where I am.'

As she pulled the bag across the desk and onto her shoulder, she dislodged Violet's copy of the *Peak Times*, which fell to the floor. When Jill bent down to pick it up, she stared intently at the front page.

'It's not good, is it?' Violet said. 'Headlines like that aren't the sort of publicity we want for the shopping village.'

But it obviously wasn't the headline Jill was studying. Instead, she was pointing at the photograph of Daniel Midship.

'Is this him?' she said, as she spread the newspaper across the desk. 'This is the man who died?'

'Yes,' Violet replied. 'It's the photo the police were showing around yesterday. Didn't you see it then?'

'No, I was in the storeroom, unpacking a delivery when they came into the bookshop,' Jill said. 'Eric mentioned the photo, but this is the first time I've seen it. The thing is . . . I recognise this guy. He came into the shop, asking about books on classic motorbikes. I sent him upstairs, onto the balcony, to the transport section and, if I remember rightly, he was up there for quite some time – although he didn't buy anything in the end.'

'Did he say anything else to you, other than asking about the books?' Violet said.

'Not really. It was a busy day and there were quite a few people in the shop – and, to be honest, I forgot about him.'

'Do you remember how long he was on the balcony for?'

'Twenty minutes maybe. I can't be sure. I got the impression he'd gone to sit in the book nook to do some reading. People do that sometimes . . . they treat the shop like it's a reference library. They look things up, instead of buying the book.'

Violet gave a wry smile. 'Is there anything else you remember about him?'

'I do recall he left in quite a hurry. He came pounding down the stairs and dashed straight out, through the front door.'

'I take it this was towards the end of the day?' Violet said. 'Early evening-ish?'

Jill shook her head. 'No, it was late morning, around eleven-thirty, I think. Definitely before lunchtime.'

'Eleven-thirty? That's weird. If he was at the market in the morning, why did he come back again later on?'

Jill pushed her hands into her pockets, looking confused. 'I'm not talking about the first day of the market,' she said. 'I saw this guy in the bookshop earlier in the week . . . on Wednesday.'

## Chapter 12

Violet scribbled Charlie Winterton's telephone number onto a piece of paper and handed it to Jill.

'Please call this number and ask to speak to DS Winterton. You need to tell him what you've just told me.'

'Do you think it might be important?' Jill said.

'Potentially. Everyone's been assuming that Daniel Midship's first visit to the shopping village was on the day he died – but if he was here before, the police will want to check the CCTV from earlier in the week. Maybe something happened to him on that first visit . . . something that prompted him to return on Friday.'

Jill looked sceptical. 'He could have just spotted the posters advertising the market and decided to come back to do some Christmas shopping.'

'Our little market is great, but I'm not sure anyone would want to drive all the way from Leeds to shop here,' Violet said. 'And Daniel certainly didn't have any carrier bags with him in the alleyway – although, I suppose he could have bought something small and put it in his pocket.'

'I'll call DS Winterton when I get to the bookshop,' Jill said, as she cast another glance at the photograph of Dan Midship. 'That poor man. It's awful, isn't it? None of us know what fate has in store. It just goes to show . . . you have to make the most of every day.'

Molly got to the office at midday, ready to take over from Violet and cover the afternoon shift.

'Is there anything in particular you want me to do?' she said, as she took off her coat and hung it on the back of her chair.

'It would be useful if you can get all the invoices up to date and chase any that are outstanding. Other than that, there's nothing that needs doing urgently. I know the market's still busy, but now the pop-up booth has finished, I suspect interest in *The Memory Box* will be non-existent between now and the new year.'

The newspaper was still on the desk, and as Molly pulled it towards her, a frown appeared between her eyebrows. As she stared at the photograph, her mouth fell open.

'Oh my God!' Her eyes widened in recognition. 'I saw this guy. I spoke to him on Friday. He visited the pop-up booth.'

'What?!' Violet's head shot up. 'Daniel Midship came into *The Memory Box*? When? I didn't see him. Where was *I*?'

'It was about half past six on Friday,' Molly said, as she settled in behind her desk. 'You'd gone to see Matthew. Things had quietened down, so you took a break, remember? Daniel Midship turned up soon after you left.'

Violet nodded slowly, feeling utterly dumbfounded as she thought through the implications of what Molly was saying.

'I was only gone for about ten minutes, so he couldn't have been here long.'

'He wasn't,' Molly said. 'He was ever so confident in front of the camera, so we got the filming done really quickly. He talked for three or four minutes . . . about his family, and how much he'd loved Christmas when his daughter was young.' Molly's eyes filled with tears. 'Afterwards, he wrote down his email address, and then he wished me a merry Christmas and donated twenty quid to the charity. He was *so* nice. I can't believe he was the man Tim found in the alley.'

Violet pointed to the newspaper. 'The police were showing this photograph around the shopping village yesterday.'

'Well they didn't show it to me,' Molly said, as she wiped away a tear with the heel of her hand. 'I'm sorry, Violet. I'll contact the police and let them know. I had no idea he was the man who'd died, otherwise I would have said something earlier.'

Violet leaned across and patted Molly's fingers. 'You weren't to know. If anyone's at fault, it's the police. They should have been more thorough with their person-to-person inquiries.'

'You realise what this means?' Molly said. 'We have Daniel Midship on camera, talking about how much his family meant to him. It's heartbreaking to think that's one of the last things he did.'

'The video must be one of those I haven't got around to editing yet,' Violet said. 'I'll find the file now and send a copy to DS Winterton. He'll want to see it, but – more importantly – we need to make sure Daniel Midship's family gets a copy. It might just bring them some comfort.'

Molly shivered. 'That man's death was already preying on my mind, but seeing his photo in the paper and realising who he was has totally shaken me up. I don't think I could bring myself to watch the video again. It'd upset me even more than I already am.'

Piped Christmas music was drifting into the office from outside, cheery and irritatingly insistent. Daniel Midship's life was over, but everything else was carrying on as normal.

'If you're getting in touch with DS Winterton, there's something else you should mention to him . . . something Robert told me,' Molly said. 'I wasn't going to say anything because I didn't think it was important but, on reflection, I think the police might want to know.'

'Is it anything to do with Daniel Midship?'

'No, it's about one of the stallholders,' Molly said. 'The guy on the antique stall out there – the bloke with the sheepskin coat? Robert says he's dodgy. His name's Frank Harper and apparently, he's known to most of the antique dealers round here.'

'Known to them in what way?'

'He handles stolen goods,' Molly said. 'Fencing, I think they call it. Robert reckons he pitches up at loads of markets in Derbyshire and South Yorkshire.'

'That's interesting. Daniel Midship was from Yorkshire. Leeds is in West Yorkshire.'

'Do you think they might have known each other?' Molly said.

Violet nodded. 'I wouldn't be surprised.'

'What if . . .' Molly narrowed her eyes as she formulated a theory. 'What if Daniel Midship spotted something he recognised on Frank Harper's stall? Maybe someone had burgled his house and taken a family heirloom, and he saw it for sale at the market?'

'I like your thinking,' Violet said, even though she knew Molly was on the wrong track. 'But what I haven't yet told you is that Daniel Midship was a retired detective. The more likely scenario is that he recognised Frank Harper, rather than one of the items on his stall. If this Harper character is known to the local antique dealers, it's highly likely he's also known to the police.'

'Will you talk to DS Winterton then?' Molly said. 'The police are appealing for information, and you never know . . . it might be relevant.'

Violet gave a thumbs-up. 'Yes, don't worry, I'll let him know.'

'Aye, we know about Frank Harper,' Charlie said, when Violet spoke to him a few minutes later. She'd informed him of Daniel Midship's visit to the pop-up booth, and had sent him a copy of the video footage.

'The word locally is that he sells dodgy antiques,' Violet said.

'Harper does have previous convictions for handling stolen goods,' Charlie said. 'And I'm not breaking the rules by telling you that, because it's information that's already out there in the public domain. However, what the local antique dealers don't know – or maybe they choose not to believe – is that Frank Harper has turned over a new leaf. He claims his days as a petty criminal are behind him and he's now running a legitimate business.'

'Do you think he's telling the truth?' Violet said.

'I do, actually. He's definitely been keeping his nose clean. Having said that, Harper obviously still likes to be economical with the truth in his conversations with the police. He told PC Turner he hadn't seen Dan Midship at the market – but the CCTV cameras tell us otherwise. I got someone to trawl through the footage from earlier in the evening on Friday, and Daniel Midship was caught on camera talking to Frank Harper at 7.10 p.m.

'It was a brief conversation. The West Yorkshire Constabulary have had dealings with Harper in the past, so my best guess is that Dan recognised him, approached the stall, and a short but frosty exchange ensued. After that, Dan walked on, towards the café.

'PC Turner revisited Harper's stall this afternoon after we'd unearthed the CCTV evidence. Harper then admitted, grudgingly, that he and Dan had had a conversation. He said Dan wanted to know if everything on the stall was legit. Harper confirmed that it was, and told him to get lost . . . said he didn't sell stolen goods anymore.'

'Could there have been more to the encounter than he's letting on?' Violet said.

'There's nothing on the CCTV footage to suggest they had an argument. Like I say, it was a frosty exchange, rather than a heated one. I imagine Dan was keeping Harper on his toes by giving the impression the police had their eye on him. When he talked to PC Turner, Harper referred to Dan as "that copper", so he obviously wasn't aware Dan had retired.'

'It sounds like a fairly innocuous encounter,' Violet said.

'Yes, something and nothing, most likely.'

'What did you make of Jill Atherstone's sighting of Daniel

Midship earlier in the week?' Violet said. 'I take it she's spoken to you? I gave her your number.'

'She called about ten minutes ago, and interestingly, what she told me fits in with what I've learned from Dan's old colleagues.'

'You've spoken to them then?' Violet said, wondering how much Charlie would be willing to tell her.

'Only on the phone. Dan met up for a drink with a few of them last week, and he told them he was planning to buy a classic motorbike. Apparently, he'd had a Honda when he was a youth, but he was hoping to get a Harley-Davidson. It seems the lads ribbed him about it – told him he was showing all the symptoms of a midlife crisis – but deep down, they were glad he was finally starting to enjoy his retirement.'

'Had he *not* been enjoying it, then?' Violet said.

'It sounds like he'd been missing work – that's what Dan's old colleagues seem to think, anyway. Bob – the guy I had the longest conversation with – said Dan was having a hard time adjusting. I'll probably be the same when I retire.' Charlie chuckled. 'Like me, Dan had spent over twenty years in the force – and once a copper, always a copper. You can't just switch that off overnight. The job becomes part of who you are, and unless you can find something else to occupy your time, it's notoriously difficult to let it go.

'Anyroad, Dan told his mates he'd seen a motorbike for sale in Derby, and he'd arranged to go and see it. He said he was going to view the bike on Wednesday and then drive home via the Peak District . . . do some sightseeing, have lunch in a country pub et cetera, et cetera.'

'And that was the day Jill saw him in the bookshop?'

'Yep.'

'So, did he buy the bike? Is that why he returned to Derbyshire on the Friday? To collect it?'

'No, that wasn't why he came back,' Charlie said. 'We managed to track down the seller of the Harley-Davidson Dan viewed, and although Dan was impressed with the bike, he didn't offer to buy it. He told the seller he'd think about it, but he didn't contact him again.'

'So, something else must have brought Daniel back to Merrywell?'

'*Someone*,' said Charlie. 'It's like we thought . . . during that initial trip, Dan spotted someone he recognised.'

'Do you know that for certain?'

'Yeah, Bob said that Dan rang him the day after he'd been to see the bike, after a favour. He mentioned he'd seen someone on his trip – a "blast from the past" is how Dan described it – and he asked Bob to run a check on this guy.'

'A background check, you mean?'

'What he was really after was an address, but Bob was annoyed, so he shut the conversation down and refused to get involved. He reminded Dan he was supposed to be retired, and that whoever he thought he'd seen was no longer his responsibility. "Let it go, Dan" – that's what Bob told him to do – "Buy a Harley-Davidson, ride off into the sunset, and thank your lucky stars you don't have to deal with the scumbags and repeat offenders anymore."'

'And did Bob tell you the name of the person Daniel was enquiring about?' Violet said.

'It was someone called Ed, but Bob didn't get a surname. He cut Dan off . . . didn't want to know about it. He feels bad about that now, but he did what he thought was best for Dan – he wanted him to forget about policing and focus on enjoying his life. The job had already cost Dan his marriage, and Bob told him it wasn't healthy to still be worrying about perpetrators five months into his retirement.'

Violet reminded Charlie of what Jill had said about Daniel's sudden departure from the bookshop on his first visit to the shopping village.

'He was up on the balcony, in the book nook,' she said. 'You can see right down into the courtyard from up there, through the big windows at the front of the shop. Do you think Daniel saw someone he recognised and hurried outside to try and catch up with them?'

'That would make sense,' Charlie said. 'And if that person managed to give him the slip, it would explain why Dan returned later in the week.'

'To look for him again? Or to double-check this guy really was who he believed him to be, and find out what he was doing in Merrywell? If his old colleague refused to help, Daniel might have decided to investigate on his own.'

'It's an excellent theory,' Charlie said. 'But unfortunately, it has one major flaw. How would Dan have known that this person he *thought* he'd seen would be at the shopping village again if he went back? There must be hundreds of shoppers passing through every day. Why was Dan so sure this bloke would be there when he returned?'

'There must have been something about him that led Dan to believe he was local.'

Charlie said nothing for several moments – a pause long enough for Violet to check whether her phone had lost its signal. When Charlie finally spoke again, it was with a sense of urgency.

'Do any of the shopping village employees wear uniforms or corporate wear?' he said. 'What about the security guy?'

'If you mean Tim Waldron, he wasn't around on Dan's first visit to the shopping centre. Tim works at the local primary school. He's only covering security for the market on a temporary basis. He was definitely at the shopping village on the first day of the market, and he stood out from the crowd in his high-vis jacket, but he wasn't there earlier in the week.'

'Who normally looks after security for the shopping village?' Charlie asked.

'As the facilities manager, Nick Penfold has overall responsibility – but it's not often he gets hands-on with the actual security side of things. The shopping village has a contract with a security firm. They do regular checks at night, and they're also on call should there be any kind of incident during business hours. Most of the time the traders take care of their own security, and thankfully, we don't have too much of a problem with petty pilfering.'

'Nick Penfold obviously doesn't wear a uniform,' Charlie said. 'When he showed us the CCTV footage, he was wearing dark jeans, and a shirt and jacket.'

'Yes, Nick always dresses smartly,' Violet said. 'He does sometimes wear a baseball cap with the shopping village's logo on it, but never a uniform.'

'What about the other traders?'

Violet thought for a moment, mentally reviewing each of the business units and their staff.

'The guys in the deli wear green polo shirts with a gold *Epicurious* logo embroidered on them, and Fiona Nash and her team wear gingham *Books, Bakes and Cakes* shirts, but the rest of the business owners dress like anyone else would. There's nothing to distinguish them from the shoppers.'

'OK. Thanks, Violet. Now that I know Dan was at the shopping village on Wednesday, I'll get someone to scrutinise the CCTV from that day. If we're lucky, we'll be able to pinpoint who was in the courtyard just before he ran out of the bookshop.'

'Does this mean you're launching a formal investigation?'

'That's yet to be confirmed, but given what I've learned over the last couple of days, I'm going to talk to my DI and recommend we make some further inquiries. It could be a tough sell, though. There are a lot of unanswered questions, but there's still no hard evidence to suggest Dan Midship died in suspicious circumstances.'

'And without evidence, there's technically no case to answer,' Violet said.

'Precisely – but thanks for the information anyway. I'll take a look at the Christmas video file you sent over, and I'll also make sure Dan's family gets a copy.'

'It'll bring a lump to your throat when you watch it,' Violet said. 'He didn't know it at the time, but it was Daniel's last message to his loved ones.'

# Chapter 13

'What do you think?' Violet was studying Matthew's face as he read through the estate agent's particulars for Rock House. His neutral expression was making it hard to gauge his reaction.

Rachel had gone upstairs to run a bath, leaving Violet and Matthew to enjoy an after-dinner glass of Irish single-malt whiskey in front of the fire. With her mother out of earshot, they were free to discuss Rock House in private.

'It's interesting,' Matthew said, as he stared hard at the asking price on the front of the brochure. '*Very* interesting, especially if Jill's brother has had most of the major work done already.'

'She told me he'd "stripped everything back to get the basics right", whatever that means. The whole house has been rewired and it's had a new boiler and central heating system installed, but I've no idea what state the rest of it is in. We can arrange a viewing if you'd like to see it.'

Matthew caught hold of Violet's hand and eased her over onto his side of the sofa. 'Of course I want to see it,' he said, sounding emphatic. 'Don't you?'

Violet grinned. 'Definitely,' she said, pleased by his sudden show of enthusiasm. 'This could be it, Matty. We might just have found our new home.'

There was a sense of anticipation fizzing through her veins. Buying a house with someone was a huge commitment – but one that Violet was ready to make. Despite what her mother might think, she hadn't been dragging her heels about moving in with Matthew. She'd simply been biding her time and waiting until they found the right place in which to start the next chapter of their lives – together.

'Can we afford it?' Matthew said. 'It's a very fair asking price, but we'll have to spend a lot of money to get the house how we want it. We'll need to refit the kitchen, maybe add an extension. That won't come cheap.'

'Once we've sold Greengage Cottage and Tanbeck House, we'll have more than enough money in the kitty to buy the house and do the work.'

Matthew looked into her eyes. 'Are you sure about this, Violet?'

She knew it wasn't her opinion on Rock House he was questioning. What he was really asking was whether she was ready to give up Greengage Cottage and the sense of independence that went with it.

'I'm one hundred per cent sure,' she said. 'About *everything*. I think Rock House could be a great opportunity for us, somewhere we could make our own. Obviously, we'll need to consider the work that needs doing and get some quotes. You're right, an extension won't be cheap, and we'd also need to get planning permission. If our application is turned down, we might have to settle for knocking the existing kitchen through into the third reception room. Is that something you could live with?'

'Probably. I'll know more once we've seen the house. I'll make and fit the kitchen units, so that will help to keep costs down, but we'll need to get the professionals in to do the structural alterations, and an electrician to fit the appliances.'

Violet smiled. 'Before we get too carried away, perhaps we should arrange to view the house. Shall I contact Jill tomorrow, or would you prefer to leave it until after Christmas?'

'What, and risk someone else buying the place?' Matthew said. 'No way. We need to get in there and take a look as soon as we can.'

'And if we like it?'

He put his arm around her and pulled her close. 'Then we'll get the ball rolling. We'll make Jill an offer, appoint a solicitor to sort out the conveyancing, and – most importantly – put our own houses on the market.'

'Let's wait until the new year before we do that,' Violet said. 'Nobody will want to be bothered with house hunting this close to Christmas. Besides, I should probably get my fence repaired before I put Greengage Cottage up for sale. That storm we had the other week made a right mess of the garden. It needs a good tidy-up.'

'Do you want me to fix the fence?' Matthew said.

'No, you're OK. You haven't got time at the moment. I'll get someone in to do it.'

'All right, if you're sure – but it's best you get it sorted ASAP. We'll need to move reasonably fast if Jill wants a quick sale. It sounds like she's got her heart set on becoming a hotelier.'

'I must admit, I was quite surprised when she told me that,' Violet said. 'Do you think she's doing the right thing?'

Matthew wobbled his head. 'It's not my place to say. She's not got any experience of running that kind of business, but Jill's a very capable person. I'm sure she could turn her hand to anything.'

'Adrian's a trained chef, so he'll know about the catering side of things,' Violet said. 'And you're right about Jill. She's very astute, and extremely organised and efficient – in fact, I don't know how Eric's going to cope without her. I love Eric . . . he's great, but he's not the most methodical person in the world. Jill's the one who keeps on top of the paperwork at the bookshop. She might not have run a hotel before, but I get the feeling she could succeed at anything, if she puts her mind to it. I imagine Adrian's worked in plenty of different hotels in his time, albeit in the kitchens. All they need to do is pool their knowledge and skills.'

'It sounds like they'll make a great team,' Matthew said. 'And working together will add to the excitement of their new venture. I like Jill. She's a nice person and she's had a tough time recently. Here's to good times ahead for her and Adrian.'

He reached for his whiskey glass and raised it in front of him.

'And here's to *our* next adventure,' Violet said, clinking her own glass against his. 'Let's hope Rock House turns out to be the home of our dreams.'

'I need to get someone to fix my fence and tidy up my garden,' said Violet, as she was buying a coffee and a croissant in the bakery the following morning. 'Is there anyone you can recommend?'

Fiona fixed Violet with a serious expression. 'It depends how quickly you want it done. A bloke in Bakewell did some work for us earlier in the year, and he was excellent. The trouble is, his services are in high demand, so don't expect him to be available until the spring.'

Violet turned down the corners of her mouth. 'I can't wait that long. I'm planning to put Greengage Cottage on the market in the new year, so I need to get the garden sorted as soon as possible – ideally before Christmas.'

Fiona's eyes widened. 'You're selling your house? Does this mean you and Matthew are finally moving in together?'

Violet laughed. 'You sound just like my mother.'

'I bet Rachel's thrilled for you – as am I, of course. Are you moving into Matthew's place, then?'

'No, we're hoping to buy a house together,' Violet said. 'Matthew's going to put Tanbeck House on the market as well.'

'Ooh, exciting!' said Fiona. 'So, have you found somewhere you want to buy?'

Although Violet was bursting with excitement about Rock

House and desperate to share the news, she couldn't risk Fiona asking questions about Jill's reasons for selling. Eric would be gutted when he found out Jill was leaving Merrywell, and it was important the news of her departure came from Jill herself.

'We've started to look,' Violet said, glad that this, at least, was the truth (if not the whole truth).

'You are staying in the village, I hope?'

'That's the plan, providing we can find somewhere we like – but it's early days. It could take months to find the right house, and even when we do, there's no guarantee we'll be able to sell our own properties in time to seal the deal. I hate moving house. Even the thought of it stresses me out.'

'You won't have any problems selling Greengage Cottage,' Fiona said. 'It's gorgeous. Absolute perfection. The first person who views it will put in an offer – I guarantee it.'

'It won't be perfection unless I can get the fence sorted and the garden tidied up,' Violet said, as she picked up her takeaway coffee.

'If you're desperate, you could always ask Zac Wallis,' Fiona said. 'He's been doing a lot of odd jobs around the village lately, mostly gardening, and he seems to do good work. You'll probably have to get the fence panels delivered, but Zac will fit them for you – no problem. He's cheap too . . . might even do the job before Christmas if you offer him cash in hand.'

Violet furrowed her brow. 'Zac Wallis? Really? I thought he had a reputation as a "bad lad". Someone matching his description was seen in the staff car park the other night, trying car door handles.'

Fiona frowned dismissively. 'I know Zac and his mate are petrol heads, but I don't think he'd stoop so low as to steal a car.'

'Wasn't he convicted for driving without insurance or a proper licence a while ago?'

'Yeah, but the car he was caught driving was his friend's,' Fiona said. 'Zac claimed his mate was over the drink-drive limit, so he put him in the passenger seat and drove them both home himself. That was over a year ago, and Zac's grown up a lot since then, although he definitely still has a thing about cars. It's up to you whether you employ him . . . I suppose it depends how badly you want to get your fence fixed.'

'I'll think about it,' Violet said, deciding to keep an open mind about Zac. 'Perhaps I will have a word with him, see if he's available.'

Fiona laughed. 'He will be. If there's a few quid to be earned, Zac's always available.'

Violet passed Frank Harper's stall as she strolled back to *The Memory Box*. Today he was wearing a beanie hat as well as his sheepskin coat, and he was swinging his arms to keep warm.

'Mornin',' he said, waving as Violet dashed by. 'It's a chilly one today – although, thankfully, the cold weather doesn't seem to be keeping the punters away.'

Violet waved at him and smiled as she hurried towards her office. As she turned the key, she realised the door was already unlocked, and when she stepped inside, she found Molly sitting with her phone in her hand.

'Hi, Molly. What are you doing here? It's supposed to be your day off.'

Molly placed the phone face down on her desk and looked up.

'Yeah, I know,' she said. 'I made Robert a breakfast cob and brought it over for him.' She held up a foil-wrapped roll that was giving off sausage and bacon smells. 'The plan was to drop it off, to surprise him – but he's not here. The shop's closed.'

Molly looked disappointed, and slightly miffed.

'Perhaps he's gone off on a buying trip,' Violet said, as she hung up her coat. 'If you didn't tell him you were coming, it's not Robert's fault you've had a wasted journey. You'll just have to eat the breakfast cob yourself. Shall I make you a cuppa to go with it?'

'No, you're OK. I've already had my breakfast. I'll take this home and warm it up later in the microwave.'

'You could always stick around for a few minutes. Maybe Robert's just running late. He might be here soon.'

'I don't want to end up hanging about all morning,' Molly said, sounding peeved. 'I've got things to do.'

'Give him a call then. Find out where he is and make your decision accordingly.'

Molly picked up her phone again. 'I was about to do that when you arrived,' she said, as she called Robert's number.

Robert answered while Violet was switching on her computer.

'Ey up,' Molly said. 'Where are you?'

To give them some privacy, Violet went into the back room to find a plate for her croissant. To her surprise, when she returned to her desk, the call was already over. Molly was staring at the phone, tears rolling down her cheeks.

'What on earth's the matter?' Violet said. 'What's happened?'

Molly began to blub, dashing away the tears from her crumpled face.

'I . . . I asked him wh . . . where he was,' she said, crying and mumbling at the same time.

'OK,' Violet said, waiting for Molly to catch her breath. 'And what did he say?'

'He said . . . he said he was at the shop.'

'Oh!' Violet's brow settled into a frown. 'Then why is it closed?'

Molly swiped at fresh tears with the heels of her hands.

'I don't know,' she said. 'I didn't ask him.'

'Why not?'

'I'm not sure. I should have said something . . . I know I should, but I was gobsmacked. He's not *at* the shop. I know he's not. He lied to me, Violet. Robert lied. Why would he do that?'

'I don't know,' Violet said. 'That's a question you'll have to ask him.'

'I don't think I can bring myself to.'

'Are you sure you haven't got hold of the wrong end of the stick?' Violet said, as she took a bite of her croissant. 'What exactly did Robert say?'

Molly pulled a paper tissue from the box on her desk and blew her nose.

'I said: "*Where are you?*" And he said: "*I'm in the shop. Where else would I be?*"'

'Perhaps he *is* in the shop. He could be out in the back, in the storeroom.'

'He's *not*,' Molly said. 'I knocked really loudly, and waited for ages. There are no lights on. Everything's closed up. Why? Why would he shut the shop? He's been getting loads of customers since the Christmas market started. Why would he choose to miss out on all that extra trade?'

Violet exhaled. This was one mystery she would prefer not to get involved in – but Molly was clearly upset, and the least she could do was offer a few words of comfort.

'Why don't you ring him back?' she suggested. 'There's bound to be a simple explanation.'

Molly shook her head forcefully. 'No. I don't want to. He's hiding something – I know he is.' She started to weep again. 'I thought Robert was one of the good guys. I trusted him, and now he's lied to me.'

'Robert *is* one of the good guys – I'd put money on it,' Violet said, injecting as much conviction into the words as she could muster. 'I'm sure there's a perfectly innocent explanation for all of this. I know you've been hurt in the past, Molly, and so does Robert. I can't believe he'd do anything to upset you. Not intentionally.'

'Well – intended or not – he *has* upset me. Whatever it is he's up to, why can't he be honest with me? I thought he and I were a team. He should have told me he was closing the shop. It's my day off today . . . I could have looked after things for him.'

'Doesn't Robert's mum usually cover for him in the shop when he has to go out?'

'She does, yes, but obviously she's not available today.'

'Maybe he didn't ask you to step in because he didn't want to put his mum's nose out of joint,' Violet said.

'You might be right about that. His mum doesn't like me very much, so I can't imagine she'd approve of me working in the *Antiques Emporium*.'

'What makes you think she doesn't like you?' Violet said. 'You've never mentioned it before.'

Molly screwed up her nose. 'Evelyn's very . . . aloof, is that the right word? You know what *my* mum's like . . . all warm and huggy? Well, Evelyn's nothing like that – she's the exact opposite, in fact. Prickly, standoffish and . . . cold. Robert's sister was visiting a few months ago, so Evelyn asked me and Jamie round for tea so that we could meet her, but I've never been invited back. I suspect Jamie was too boisterous for Evelyn. You know how excitable he gets sometimes . . . and I admit he can be a handful, especially when he's somewhere new. Tea was served on bone china plates, and I was scared to death Jamie would end up breaking one. I think Evelyn was worried about it too. She seemed to be on edge, like she didn't know how to relax.'

'I think she's just very shy,' Violet said. 'I've tried to engage her in conversation a few times, but she and I have never clicked. I don't think Evelyn's a natural conversationalist. Goodness knows how she copes with some of the pushier customers when she's in the shop.'

'As far as I know, she's fine with the customers. It's me she doesn't like. She doesn't think I'm good enough for Robert. Who knows . . . maybe she's right.'

'Don't be daft,' Violet said. 'You and Robert are perfect together.'

Tears were streaming down Molly's face again. 'Are we? Right now, the only thing I'm certain about is that we're very, very different.'

'That can be a good thing in a relationship,' Violet said.

Molly gave a shrug. 'Sometimes it is, but other times I wonder whether Robert and I have enough in common to go the distance – and maybe he's come to the same conclusion. Why else would he have lied to me?'

Violet threw up her hands. 'There could be any number of reasons why he didn't tell the truth. You need to have more confidence in yourself, Molly, and more faith in Robert. You've never questioned your relationship before, so why start now? There's obviously been a misunderstanding between the two of you. I know you're scared of being hurt, but please don't push Robert away without giving him a chance to explain himself. Give him a call later, and talk to him. The key to any successful relationship is good communication.'

'You might try telling Robert that,' Molly said, sounding thoroughly miserable. 'He's the one who's been lying.'

She blew her nose one more time and then left, taking the now-cold breakfast cob with her.

Violet checked her inbox for new emails, and then pressed on with editing the last of the Christmas films – all the while keeping a close eye on the clock. She had arranged to pick Rachel and Jacqueline up at noon so that she could drive them over to Chatsworth House. They had tickets for the stately home's spectacular Christmas at Chatsworth event, which included decorations in the house, and an interactive light and sound trail in the magnificent gardens. Both Rachel and Jacqueline were looking forward to it immensely.

At eleven o'clock, having caught up with all her jobs, Violet's thoughts turned to Rock House and all of its tantalising possibilities. She did a quick internet search for estate agents, and toyed with the idea of giving one of them a call to get a valuation on Greengage Cottage. The only thing that held her back was the current state of the rear garden. A broken-down fence wouldn't make a good first impression with either the estate agents or prospective buyers.

This might not be the ideal time of year for gardening work, but action was needed. Violet put on her coat, grabbed her car keys and bag, and made a decision she hoped she wouldn't come to regret.

## Chapter 14

Even as she knocked on the front door, she was having second thoughts.

Zac Wallis lived with his mother in a late-twentieth-century semi-detached house on the outskirts of Merrywell. By the looks of the patchy front lawn, it seemed Zac's prowess as a gardener was reserved only for fee-paying customers. His mother's garden was reasonably tidy, but bereft of flowers or any other kind of horticultural adornment.

Violet heard a dog barking inside the house, followed by movement behind the glass panel. A moment later Zac's mother, Marcia, unlocked the door and peered out. She was holding the dog under her left arm, and when it saw Violet, it broke into another frantic bout of barking and tried to wriggle free.

'I'm sorry to bother you,' Violet said, 'but I wondered if I could have a word with Zac.'

'He's not here,' Marcia said, as she shushed the dog.

'Will he be back later?'

'Depends what you want him for.'

'I've got a fence that needs fixing,' Violet said. 'I was told Zac does gardening work. I'm hoping he can fit me in before Christmas.'

The dog had gone quiet, having lost interest in Violet's presence, but it was still struggling to escape from its owner's grasp.

'Hang on,' Marcia said. 'Let me put the dog in the kitchen.'

When she returned, she opened the door a fraction wider, folded her arms and looked Violet up and down before speaking again.

'Our Zac's broken up for Christmas, but he can probably fit you in early in the new year. If you give me your number, I'll ask him to give you a call when he gets home.'

Violet took one of her business cards from her bag and handed it to Marcia.

'That's my mobile number. I've got a couple of fence panels that need replacing, and I'd also like a quick tidy-up in the garden. Weeding, pruning . . . that kind of stuff. The thing is, I'd like it done quickly, if that's possible. I'd be happy to pay cash in hand if Zac could do the work before next week.'

Marcia pushed the business card into the pocket of her jeans and regarded Violet suspiciously.

'You're not from the Inland Revenue, are you? Here to try and catch him out.'

Violet smiled. 'No, I can assure you, I'm not.'

Marcia looked unconvinced. 'As I say, I'll ask him to ring you, but I can't make promises on his behalf. Zac's his own man, and he makes his own decisions. He'll only take on jobs if it suits him – and from what he's told me, he's got a big pay-out coming before Christmas, so I doubt he'll be in a hurry to take on any work at the moment.'

Violet was beginning to regret offering the job to Zac at all. He didn't exactly sound like an enthusiastic worker, or a particularly reliable one.

'If he's not interested, I'll understand,' she said. 'But I'd appreciate him letting me know either way. Could you ask him to call me? Or he can drop in to see me any morning this week in my office. The address is on the business card. I'm based at the shopping village.'

Marcia's face hardened into a scowl.

'I realise who you are now,' she said, looking at Violet through half-closed eyes. 'You're the woman from that video business?'

'*The Memory Box*, yes.'

Marcia sneered. 'You're more of a *Jack*-in-the-box from what I've 'eard . . . always popping up and sticking your nose into things that are none of your business. You're big mates with the police as well, aren't you? Did you know they've been round 'ere giving our Zac grief?'

Violet reeled back, surprised by this sudden vitriolic onslaught.

'You've not come here to get your fence fixed,' Marcia said, stepping forward and using an index finger to poke at Violet's collarbone. 'You were hoping to grill Zac about the night that man died. I'm right, aren't I?'

'No!' Violet said. 'Someone gave me Zac's name . . . said he did odd jobs, and I'm here because I'd like him to work on my garden.'

But even as she refuted Marcia's claim, Violet realised there was an element of truth to it. In coming here, she had (perhaps subconsciously) sought confirmation that Zac Wallis had been in the car park on the night Daniel Midship died.

'You'd better be telling the truth,' Marcia said. 'Because if you're here to cause trouble for my son, you've picked on the wrong family. I won't let anyone . . . and I repeat, *anyone* . . . make trouble for my lad. He may not be perfect, but he's got a good heart, and he's all I've got. So, *lady*, don't even think about accusing him of anything, otherwise you'll have me to deal with.'

'OK,' Violet said, taking another step onto the front path. 'You've made your point.'

'Good. I'm glad we understand each other. Now clear off, before I set my dog on you.'

*I'll take the dog over you any time*, Violet thought, as she made a hasty retreat to her car.

\*

She was still shaking when she pulled up at Greengage Cottage. The encounter with Marcia Wallis had been disturbing on two levels. First and foremost, Marcia had proven to be unexpectedly intimidating. She was a small, slender woman, but her threatening tone of voice suggested she would stop at nothing to protect her offspring.

Secondly, the clash had emphasised Violet's growing (and unwanted) reputation as a busybody. Even Marcia, a relative stranger, had felt justified in accusing her of '*sticking her nose in*'. Violet hadn't set out to garner that kind of attention, but while ever she continued to take an interest in local crimes, she had no chance of changing people's perceptions.

Willing herself to calm down, she got out of the car and went into the house. Her mother was in the living room, applying lipstick and checking her reflection in the mirror above the fireplace.

'Hello,' Violet said. 'I'm not late, am I? I thought we were picking Jacqueline up at twelve.'

'We are,' Rachel said. 'But you'll need to get your skates on if you're going to get changed.'

'I was planning to go like this,' Violet said, holding out her arms.

Rachel looked at Violet's puffer jacket and scrunched up her nose. 'We're going to one of the finest stately homes in the country, darling. If that doesn't warrant wearing your best coat, I don't know what does.'

'Why? I'm not coming into the house with you, Mum. I'm just the driver.'

'Not anymore,' Rachel said, holding up her hands and splaying her fingers. 'I've managed to get hold of an extra ticket so that you can join Jacqueline and me on the tour. So you see, Cinders, you *shall* go to the ball.'

Violet laughed. 'In that case, I'd better look lively and smarten myself up. Thanks, Mum. Give me five minutes to change, and then we'll go and get Jacqueline.'

Violet bounded up the stairs and opened her wardrobe. She took out her smart wool coat, and then put on a green and red holly-print blouse, adding an extra layer in the form of a green V-necked cashmere sweater. As she stood at the bedroom mirror and brushed her hair, her phone rang.

The caller ID showed it was Jill Atherstone.

'Hello, Jill,' Violet said. 'I was going to ring you later . . . about Rock House.'

'Did you talk to Matthew?' Jill said, with a hopeful note in her voice.

'Yes. I showed him the property brochure, and we'd like to arrange a viewing, please.'

'Excellent. When were you thinking?'

'It depends on when you're free. I imagine you're working long days at the bookshop this week.'

'Actually, it's my evening off tomorrow,' Jill said. 'Would six o'clock suit you? I realise it'll be dark, so it's probably not the best time to view a house – but you can always take another look at the weekend, in the daylight. For the first viewing, I'd like to show you around so I can point out the work that's already been done, and talk you through what else needs to be addressed. If you'd like to do a second viewing, I'll let you have the key, and you and Matthew can look around on your own.'

'OK, that sounds great. Shall we meet you at Rock House tomorrow, then? Six o'clock?'

'I'll be there,' Jill said. 'And I was wondering . . . would you and Matthew like to come over to my house afterwards for dinner? I realise it's short notice, but Adrian would love to cook you both a meal.'

'It's kind of you, Jill, but you don't have to do that.'

'I know,' Jill said, 'but we want to. It'll give Adrian a chance to try out some of the new recipes he's been putting together. He's in the process of planning a menu, for when we open the hotel.'

'In that case, thank you. We'd be delighted,' Violet said.

Only a fool would turn down the offer of having someone cook for them, especially when that person was a trained chef.

## Chapter 15

'This is absolutely spectacular,' Jacqueline said, as they entered the Painted Hall at Chatsworth House. A huge, richly decorated tree stood at one end – its delicate blue, green and orange ornaments reflecting the colours in the room's magnificent painted ceiling. The mantelpiece above the fireplace was decked with swags of beautifully decorated greenery. Similar garlands adorned the first-floor balustrades and the banisters of the grand staircase that dominated the other end of the room.

Violet tilted her head and looked up to the top of the twinkling Christmas tree. So far, the stunning decorations were proving to be a delight. She'd heard wonderful things about the Chatsworth Christmas events, but this was the first chance she'd had to experience the magic at first hand. Jacqueline was right – it really was absolutely spectacular.

Together, they climbed the stairs and continued along the Christmas route around the house. The beautiful decorations, the sparkling trees, and attention to detail filled Violet with a sense of festive optimism. For the first time in years, she was overwhelmed by a sense of excitement and anticipation – not just about Christmas, but about the year ahead.

She smiled. Next year, if everything went to plan, she and

Matthew would have their own house to decorate, and would finally have started their new life together. No one could predict what the future held, but it was good to be able to look forward with such positivity.

'You look like the cat that got the cream,' Rachel said, as they entered another bedecked room. 'Is there something I should know about?'

'I was thinking I'll make more of an effort at home next year ... Christmas decoration wise,' Violet said. 'We'll never be able to recreate anything as grand as this, of course, but between us, I think Matthew and I will be able to put together something special.'

'I suppose it will depend on whether you're actually living together by then,' Rachel said.

'I'm pretty sure we will be. I don't want to tempt fate, but we may have found a house we want to buy.'

Rachel's face lit up. 'Well, that *is* exciting!' she said, clasping her hands together. 'Is it in Merrywell? Can I go and see it?'

Violet laughed. 'Hold your horses, Mum. We've not seen it ourselves yet. We've seen photos though, and the estate agent's blurb, and although the property needs work, we're pretty sure it's the one. And yes, it's in Merrywell.'

'Oh, that's wonderful news, darling. I'm thrilled for you. Where's Jacqueline? I can't wait to tell her.'

Rachel searched the room with her eyes, but Jacqueline had moved on to the next display and was admiring a silver-toned Christmas tree.

'Actually, Mum . . .' Violet linked her arm through Rachel's. 'Can we keep this between ourselves for now? The house is being sold privately and, for various reasons, the vendor wants to keep the sale quiet until the new year.'

Rachel regarded her suspiciously. 'What is it with you, Violet?' she said, rolling her eyes. 'Why does everything you get involved with have to be so cloak and dagger? Just for once, why can't things be straightforward?'

'There's nothing cloak and dagger about it. We just want to keep a lid on things until the new year. After that, everything will proceed in the usual way – assuming we do actually decide to buy the house. I'm beginning to wish I'd not said anything. I thought you'd be pleased. You've been banging on about me and Matthew moving in together for ages.'

'Of course I'm pleased – I'm ecstatic. I just want everything to go smoothly for you. I take it you'll be selling Greengage Cottage?'

'Yes, and Matthew will be selling Tanbeck House. We'll be buying the new house together.'

She had almost said *Rock House*, but had managed to stop herself just in time.

'Well, I'm over the moon for you,' Rachel said. 'Really, I am. I'll keep everything crossed that this mysterious house of yours materialises – and if it does, I'll expect to see the biggest, most gloriously decorated tree ever when I visit next Christmas.'

'Why don't we go and have a look on our own in the morning?' Matthew said, when Violet had told him about the arrangements she'd made to view Rock House. 'You know . . . take a sneak peek before the official viewing? We won't be able to see inside, obviously, but we can look through the windows and have a wander around the garden.'

They were sitting in front of the fire at Tanbeck House, enjoying some time on their own. After they'd returned from Chatsworth, Rachel had gone over to the Merrywell Manor Hotel, to attend a jazz evening with Jacqueline.

'It would be nice to get a feel for the place in the daylight, before our first proper viewing tomorrow night,' Violet said. 'We could go before work . . . say eight-thirty? The sun will be up by then.'

Matthew rubbed his hands together. 'Let's do it. Taking a look at the house from the outside will help us view it more objectively – because once we step over the threshold, we'll be swept away by the excitement of it all. An initial visit, on our own, will give us a chance to cast a critical eye over the place. Buying a house is a massive commitment, and we need to be absolutely sure we're doing the right thing. We don't want to have any regrets down the line.'

'It sounds like you're getting cold feet already,' Violet said.

Matthew grinned. 'I'm trying to think with my head, not my heart. Believe me, I want this to work out as much as you do, but we shouldn't allow ourselves to be rushed into making a decision. I know Jill's in a hurry to sell, but we mustn't feel pressured. We should only make an offer if it's the right house for us.'

'I agree,' Violet said. 'And I suspect we'll know the minute we walk into the place. We'll either get "the feels" or we won't – but if either of us are unsure, then so be it. We both have to like the house if we're going to put in an offer.'

## Chapter 16

Daylight was seeping through wispy clouds as Violet pulled up at Rock House the following morning.

'Are you leaving the car on the road?' said Matthew, speaking from the front passenger seat.

'Yes, let's get out and approach the house on foot. We'll get a better impression of it that way.'

They opened the gates and walked onto a short, straight driveway that had tall trees and overgrown shrubs either side of it. As they made their way past the brick-built garage, Violet was struck by how quiet it was here, how peaceful.

When she was ten yards from the house, she stopped and looked up at the imposing, double-fronted façade. In one of the nearby trees, a blackbird was singing, as if in welcome. Cautiously, reverently, she moved forward to join Matthew, who was examining the studded front door, which was wooden and fitted with black ironmongery.

'Nice door,' he said, running his fingertips across its panels. 'It's made of oak, and I'd say it's original to the house.'

'It is a lovely feature,' Violet said. 'And definitely worth keeping.'

'Absolutely,' Matthew said. 'Unlike the windows, which – if the ones at the front are anything to go by – will all need replacing.'

Violet winced. 'That sounds expensive.'

'Yeah, but it'd be a good investment . . . I mean, *look* at this place, Violet. It's bloody brilliant.'

She gave in to the smile of joy that had been tugging at her lips since she walked through the gates. She had been getting seriously good vibes from Rock House, but had been afraid Matthew wasn't 'feeling it'.

'It is impressive, there's no doubt about that,' she said. 'It's so tranquil here, so quiet – and yet we're only a short walk from the centre of the village.'

Matthew squeezed her hand. 'I really like what I've seen so far. So much so, it scares me. Do you think the rest of the house will live up to expectations?'

'There's only one way to find out,' Violet said, tugging his hand and pulling him to the left. 'Come on, let's go and check out the back garden.'

A side gate opened onto a path that led to a semi-circular patio, beyond which lay an enormous sloping lawn that looked out over rolling hills on the other side of the valley. On either side of the lawn were wide flower beds, and another central path that curved down to a summer house in the bottom corner of the garden. Violet had viewed the house on Google Maps, so she knew the ploughed field beyond the stone wall boundary belonged to Merrywell Hill Farm.

Matthew turned to face the house. Shading his eyes from the glare of the winter sun, he looked up at the tiled roof and the two dormer windows that jutted out of it.

'I didn't realise there was an attic,' he said.

'It's not easy to tell from the front because there's only a small Velux window on that side,' Violet said. 'The estate agent's blurb does mention the attic, but it has sloping ceilings and limited headroom, so I don't think they're allowed to officially class them as rooms. It's a good place for storage though. Somewhere to stash our junk.'

They approached the grimy, ground-floor windows and peered through them. The kitchen was exactly as Jill had described it – scullery-like, and in need of total refurbishment – but there was a large, light-filled garden room alongside it, which had a pair of dilapidated French doors that opened onto the patio.

'We'll have to rip the kitchen out,' Matthew said. 'Hopefully, we'll be able to knock through into the room next door, and possibly extend out as well.'

Violet smiled. She liked that Matthew was making plans, talking as if the house was already theirs.

They returned to the front of the house and looked through the bay windows on either side of the wooden door. Beyond the first window was an enormous living room, which had a large fireplace and beams on the ceiling.

Violet wrinkled her nose. 'I'm not sure about the beams.'

'Me neither,' Matthew said. 'But I expect they'll be decorative, rather than structural, so it should be easy enough to get rid of them. Apart from the beams, it's a great room . . . with lots of natural light coming into it.'

The sitting room on the other side of the front door was fitted with dark oak wall panels, a massive, tiled fireplace topped by a large oak mantelshelf, and several lines of built-in bookshelves.

'The fittings make this room look quite dark, but strangely, I quite like them,' Violet said. 'It looks like a cosy place to sit and read. I can picture us lighting a fire and settling down in there in the evenings.'

'I agree,' said Matthew. 'And if the panels are original to the room, it would be sacrilege to get rid of them.'

They linked hands and wandered back and forth a couple more times, appraising the exterior of the house and imagining what it would be like to live there.

'Let's hope it's as good on the inside as it looks from the outside,' Matthew said, as he slung his left arm over Violet's shoulder.

'If it is, do you think we should make an offer?'

He stuck out his bottom lip and nodded sagely. 'I reckon so. The only thing that might scupper things is if the walls are riddled with dry rot or rising damp.'

'I guess we'll have to wait until tonight to find that out.'

Matthew nodded. 'I know Jill wants to give us a guided tour, but I'd much rather look round on our own. It's hard to be critical when the owner of the property is standing right next to you.'

'Once we've completed the initial viewing, I'm sure Jill won't mind if the two of us wander off on our own.'

'Aren't we supposed to be going to her house for dinner afterwards?' Matthew said.

'We are, but there'll be time for us to have another mooch around the house first. It's really kind of Adrian to rustle up something special for us, but I'm not sure how much appetite I'm going to have. Depending on what the house is like inside, I'll either be too excited to eat, or too disappointed.'

Matthew pulled her close and smiled. 'Let's hope for the former, shall we? I have a good feeling about this house, Violet, so let's try and think positively, rather than worrying about what might go wrong.'

They left Rock House reluctantly and drove to the shopping village and their respective places of work. As Matthew let himself into his furniture workshop and Violet opened up *The Memory Box*, Robert Dorman hurried across the courtyard towards the *Antiques Emporium*. He was fumbling for something in his shoulder bag – all the while muttering quietly to himself.

He looked unhappy and distracted, his glum expression suggesting that he and Molly had yet to resolve the previous day's misunderstanding – a state of affairs that left Violet feeling anxious and saddened. Molly had been hurt badly by her previous partner. The thought of her having her heart broken for a second time was something Violet didn't want to contemplate.

'Morning, Robert,' she said, raising a hand to catch the antique dealer's attention. 'How are you today?'

He pulled a set of keys from his bag and then glared up at the grey sky, his blue eyes troubled behind his heavy-framed glasses.

'Cold,' he said.

Violet fixed a smile to her face. 'Cheer up,' she said. 'It may be chilly, but the sun is still shining somewhere behind those clouds.'

Robert hitched his bag onto his shoulder and managed to drop his keys.

'Is everything OK, Robert?' Violet said. 'You don't seem like your usual exuberant self this morning.'

'Everyone has their off days,' he said, as he bent down to snatch up his keys. 'Even me.'

And with that, he gave a half-hearted wave, inserted the key into the door of the antiques shop and went inside.

Molly arrived at *The Memory Box* two hours later, looking equally unhappy. Instead of her usual chirpy greeting, she mumbled a quick 'good morning' and then disappeared into the back room. She re-emerged a few minutes later carrying two mugs of coffee, and it was clear from the puffiness of her eyes that she'd been crying.

'I was going to ask if you're OK, Molly,' Violet said. 'But I can see that you're not.'

'Sorry,' she said, as she put the drinks on the desk and sat down. 'I must look a right mess.'

'There's no need to apologise for being upset,' Violet said, as she warmed her hands on her coffee mug.

Molly's bottom lip quivered for a moment, and then her whole face crumpled as she burst into tears.

Violet pulled a paper tissue from the box on her desk and handed it over.

'I'm here if you want to talk about it,' she said. 'But I'll understand if you prefer not to. And if you want to go home, that's fine too. There's nothing here that needs doing urgently.'

Molly blew her nose noisily.

'I'm OK. I'm just still upset about yesterday.'

'Did you talk to Robert about it?'

'Yes, I did as you suggested, but it didn't do any good.' Molly grabbed another tissue and wiped her eyes. 'He lied . . . again . . . this time to my face.'

Violet frowned. 'That doesn't sound like the Robert *I* know. Don't get me wrong – I'm not trying to defend him, but he's such a fundamentally honest man . . . I wouldn't have thought he was capable of lying.'

Molly snuffled. 'He's not very good at it. In fact, as a liar, I'd say he's completely useless. He was stumbling over his words, and his face was blotchy and red – but even when I told him I didn't believe him, he still wouldn't tell me the truth.'

'What did you say to him exactly?' Violet said. 'How did you broach the subject?'

'I didn't pussyfoot around. I told him the truth: that I'd gone to the *Antiques Emporium* yesterday morning, and that it was closed.'

'And how did he respond?'

'He blustered for a second, and then he said he must have been in the storeroom. When I asked why the door was locked and the "closed" sign was showing he went bright red. At that point, he suddenly and very conveniently remembered he *had* locked up for a few minutes while he checked on a new piece he'd acquired. I didn't believe him, and I told him so. He has new stock delivered every week, and I've never known him close the shop before.'

'How did he react when you told him you didn't believe him?'

'In fairness to him, he looked mortified. In fact, I began to feel quite sorry for him – but then he stood in front of me as bold as brass and repeated the same pathetic lie. He said the shop was closed because he was sorting out an important new acquisition. Honestly, he made it sound like he was taking delivery of the crown bloody jewels.'

'You didn't manage to resolve things, then?' Violet said. 'I'm guessing not, because I saw Robert earlier, and he looked like he'd got the weight of the world on his shoulders.'

'Serves him right,' Molly said.

'So, how did you leave things with him? You haven't broken up with him, have you?'

Molly pressed a fresh tissue to her eyes. 'No. I thought about it, but I couldn't bring myself to. He looked so contrite and worried when I said I didn't believe him. He told me he loved me, and that if I loved *him*, then I needed to trust him. So, in the end, I caved. He ordered a takeaway and we had a glass of wine, and I acted as if everything was fine. But it isn't fine, Violet. I should have challenged him, instead of backing off – but the truth is, I don't want to lose him. I know Robert's not everyone's idea of a great catch, but I love him. *Really* love him. At least I thought I did. Now, I'm not sure that's a good idea. I can't risk getting my heart broken again. And I have Jamie to think about too. He never sees his dad, and Robert's becoming a father figure to him.'

'So, what are you going to do? Do you have a plan?'

Molly raised her shoulders and held up her hands. 'Not really, although I have told him I don't want to see him tonight. I need time to think . . . to decide whether I can trust him.'

'Don't give up on him just yet,' Violet said. 'There has to be a rational explanation. I can't believe Robert would be deliberately deceitful. If he's being evasive, he must have his reasons.'

Molly pulled in a shuddering breath. 'Do you really think so?'

'I do,' Violet said. 'Although, if I'm wrong and Robert is messing you about, I'll have his guts for garters.'

## Chapter 17

By the time Violet left the office at eleven-forty-five, Molly was looking slightly more cheerful, although she was still far from being her normal, chirpy self. Violet knew she would have to wait and see what happened, all the while hoping that the situation with Robert would resolve itself.

Outside in the courtyard, the market was filled with the background hubbub of conversations between stallholders and customers. Before heading home, she needed to buy a few things from *The Epicurious*, and as she skirted around the first row of stalls she bumped into Nick Penfold, who was coming from the opposite direction with a takeaway coffee in his hand.

'Hi, Nick,' Violet said. 'How's things?'

'Not so bad, thanks, Violet – although I'll be glad when this bloomin' market is over and I've broken up for Christmas.' He thumbed over his shoulder towards the busy stalls.

Violet smiled. 'I know what you mean, but we mustn't complain. I'm just pleased the whole thing has been a success.'

'Yep, it's all gone really well,' Nick said. 'Apart from that man dying on the first day, of course.'

'Talking of which, have the police been in touch to ask for the CCTV footage from last Wednesday?'

Nick stared at his feet and swung the toe of his right shoe in an arc across the cobbles.

'They've asked,' he said, looking uncomfortable. 'But unfortunately, I haven't able to provide it. The system is supposed to back up automatically, but some of the files from last week weren't saved.'

'Why not?' Violet said, feeling instantly distrustful.

Nick swigged his coffee and did his best to look unruffled, despite the red flush of shame that was creeping up his neck. 'I honestly don't know. Something similar happened before, during a power outage, but we only lost a couple of hours of footage on that occasion. This time, we're missing two whole days' worth, including that from last Wednesday.'

'Are you saying it was never recorded?' Violet said. 'Or has it been deleted?'

Nick shrugged. 'There's no way of knowing – and believe me, I've done my best to find out what went wrong. I've been getting a lot of grief from that detective over it. He is not a happy man.'

'I'll bet he's not,' Violet said. 'DS Winterton was banking on that footage. He was hoping to identify someone who was around during Daniel Midship's first known visit to the shopping village.'

'Yeah, he told me,' Nick said. 'What I don't understand is why it's so important. I thought Daniel Midship's death was an accident.'

'Maybe it was, maybe it wasn't. That's what DS Winterton is trying to establish.'

Nick grimaced. 'I see. Now I understand why he was so annoyed.'

'How easy would it be for someone to delete the files?' Violet said. 'Accidentally or otherwise.'

Nick wobbled his head. 'Once you were logged into the system, it'd be a piece of cake, providing you knew which files you were looking for. However, this is the shopping village's security system we're talking about. It's password-protected, and only three people have access: me, Matthew, and Eric Nash.'

'What about Tim Waldron? You must have given him access if he's working as a security guard?'

'Oh, yeah. I forgot about him. I've given him a temporary login, but I doubt whether he's used it. I don't think he's the most tech-savvy of people.'

'Is there any way of finding out when each of those users last logged in?' Violet said.

'There is, but I don't need to,' Nick said. 'I've spoken personally to Matthew and Eric and they both said they haven't accessed the system in months. I trust them, so I don't need to check up on them.'

'I trust them too,' Violet said. 'But I think DS Winterton would want you to check anyway. And if you find out that someone has logged in recently, you'd better let him know.'

'I'm surprised your mum didn't want to come along,' Matthew said, as they drove to Rock House for their six o'clock rendezvous with Jill.

'She did, but I told her this was something you and I needed to do together. On our own. She was disappointed, but I told her she'll have to curtail her curiosity for now.'

Matthew smiled. 'I've not said anything to my parents yet. They'd want to know all about it – and until we have some actual news, I'm better off saying nothing. The last thing we want is for Eric to hear about Jill's departure before she's had time to tell him herself.'

They passed the White Hart and were approaching St Luke's Church when Violet recalled her earlier conversation with Nick Penfold.

'When were you going to tell me about the missing security footage?' she said.

It was clear from Matthew's puzzled expression that he didn't have a clue what she was talking about.

'What missing footage?'

Violet filled him in on her earlier conversation with Nick, and how it impacted on Charlie Winterton's inquiries.

'Nick did ring me this morning to ask when I'd last logged into the security system, but he didn't say anything about any footage going missing.'

'When did you last log in?'

'Ages ago,' Matthew said. 'I'd say getting on for a year. To be honest, I've hardly used the system. I'm not sure I'd know how to go in and delete files, if that is what's happened.'

'Why were you granted access to the system in the first place?'

'The traders' association decided to appoint a couple of back-up users, in case Nick wasn't around for some reason. Eric and I were chosen, but as far as I'm aware, neither of us have been called upon to access the system.'

'Well, someone must have used it,' Violet said. 'There's no way those files went missing accidentally.'

'You don't know that, love. In fact, you know even less about the shopping village's security system than I do. You shouldn't leap to conclusions.'

Violet would have liked to argue the point, but they had arrived at Rock House. The gates were wide open, and Jill had already arrived. Every light in the property had been switched on. It made the house look warm, intriguing and inviting, and Violet couldn't wait to go inside.

She was experiencing the same positive vibes from this second visit that she had felt the first time she'd seen the property. She sensed that Rock House was the kind of place that would be good for her soul. Whenever she felt stressed or overworked, or distracted by the world, she would only have to stand at the front door, listening to the birds in the trees, to feel at peace.

They parked in front of the house this time, behind Jill's ruby red Fiesta. As they got out of the car, the front door opened.

'Welcome to Rock House,' Jill said, waving at them from the front step. 'Come in and have a look round.'

Compared to the cold nip of the winter evening, the hallway was comfortably toasty.

'I've been keeping the heating on a low setting, to keep the chill off,' Jill said. 'I got here an hour ago and whacked up the thermostat, so I hope you'll be warm enough as you go from room to room.'

Violet touched the radiator in the hall. The new central heating system was working like a charm, blasting out heat.

'Adrian sends his apologies,' Jill said. 'He wanted to be here, but he's busy preparing dinner. He said he'll catch up with you both later.'

They entered the living room on the right – the one with the beamed ceiling. Violet stood for a moment, absorbing the ambience. She was intrigued by empty houses. To her, it always felt as if the air inside them was holding on to the echoes of previous owners.

'This is the main reception room,' Jill said. 'It's as good a place to start as any – but rather than following you around the house and pointing out the obvious, I've decided I'll wait here and let the two of you look around on your own. Adrian won't be serving dinner until seven-thirty, so there's plenty of time. Take as long as you want, and let me know if you have any questions.'

Violet and Matthew took in the generous proportions of the room, imagining it fitted out with their own furniture and decorated to their taste. After examining the fireplace and checking that the ceiling beams were indeed decorative, they went through into the dining room, which had an old-fashioned serving hatch into the kitchen next door.

Matthew opened the connecting door and tapped his knuckles on the wall near the hatch.

'It's hollow, so it's not a supporting wall,' he said. 'Knocking it down shouldn't be a problem.'

Violet tried to visualise what the kitchen and dining room would look like opened up as a single room. There was certainly plenty of space, so maybe they wouldn't need to build an extension after all.

A door from the dining room led into the second reception room. Its wood-panelled walls were old-fashioned, but cosily cocooning. A nylon rose-pink carpet covered the floor, but when Violet peeled a corner of it back, she discovered a parquet floor hidden beneath.

Matthew's eyes lit up when he saw it. 'Depending on its condition, we might be able to restore this to its former glory,' he said, as he bent down to take a closer look.

Violet nodded enthusiastically. 'We should try and save as many of the original features as we can. I've been thinking . . . we could talk to Robert Dorman, get him to source some early-twentieth-century furniture for us. I wouldn't want it everywhere, but I'd love to furnish this room in keeping with when the house was built.'

They spent the next thirty minutes exploring the house, checking for signs of damp and assessing the level of work that would be required to bring the property up to modern standards. They admired the stained-glass window halfway up the stairs, and debated whether the fireplaces in the bedrooms were worth keeping as a decorative feature. There was only one bathroom, which would need refitting, but a small dressing room next to the master bedroom was perfect for converting into an en-suite.

Jill joined them after a while, eager to point out a couple of areas where the plaster work needed attention. She then unlocked a door on the first-floor landing and took them up to the top floor, which consisted of two attic rooms and a small bathroom. The larger of the rooms was fitted with a tiny kitchenette in one corner.

'Someone told me the family that lived here in the Sixties had a nanny,' Jill said. 'I assume these rooms must have been hers.'

There was an old chaise longue in the centre of the room,

and off to one side was a small Formica table with two chairs tucked beneath it.

'The reason I brought you in here was to show you this,' Jill said, pointing up to a worryingly bowed ceiling. 'I don't know if the problem is with the roof, or the ceiling joists, but it will definitely need looking at.'

'It's the sort of thing that will be assessed during the survey, but thanks for drawing it to our attention,' Matthew said. 'Regardless of their condition, these attic rooms are an unexpected bonus. They hardly get a mention in the estate agent's brochure.'

'I don't think my brother came up here very much,' Jill said. 'He was six four, so he found the lack of headroom quite restrictive. It is a great space for storage though. Somewhere to put all of the clutter one accumulates over the years.'

Violet laughed. 'Matthew and I definitely have our fair share of that, although we've vowed to get rid of as much of it as possible before we move.'

Once their inspection of the attic was over, they returned to the ground floor and went into a boot room at the rear of the house, where the new boiler was located. When Jill had shown them how it worked, she unlocked the door and they went out into the garden – but even with torches, it was difficult to see anything in the dark.

'If you'd like to come back at the weekend, you can collect the keys from me on Saturday morning, at the bookshop,' Jill said. 'I want you to be absolutely sure about the house before you decide whether to make an offer. Buying a property is a massive financial commitment.'

'It is,' Violet said. 'And yet, I read somewhere that the average time spent viewing a house is between thirty minutes and an hour.'

Jill laughed. 'It's ridiculous, isn't it. I spent more time shopping for my last winter coat than I did looking at the hotel we're planning to buy. I'm keen to go there again next week for another look around, but Adrian thinks we should wait until our offer's been accepted. He says we shouldn't set our hearts on the place until we've got a buyer for Rock House. He's worried about me getting my hopes up – and quite rightly. I'll be devastated if someone else buys the hotel.'

'I know exactly what you mean,' said Violet, who was already feeling the same way about Rock House. 'The place you're hoping to buy is near Ashbourne, you said? It's a lovely town, and quite touristy in the summer – so it's an ideal location.'

'The Brighouse Hotel is about four miles from the town, on the main road between Ashbourne and Hartington,' Jill said. 'It's surrounded by hills and beautiful countryside, so the setting is very picturesque.'

She pulled out her phone and swiped through the photographs in the camera roll.

'Here.' She turned the screen towards Violet and Matthew. 'That's the dining room. At the moment, it's only used by hotel guests, but Adrian's going to turn it into a proper restaurant . . . open to the general public.'

She scrolled through a couple more photos, one showing the arched front door of the hotel, and another taken in the garden. Adrian was standing with his back to the camera, next to a red-haired woman who was staring into a large pond.

'That's Tammy, the current owner,' Jill explained. 'She told us there are koi carp in the pond, but we couldn't see any.'

'It looks like an amazing place,' Violet said. 'And the garden is fabulous. I'm very impressed.'

'The photos don't do it justice,' Jill said. 'We were asked not to take pictures, so I had to be a little bit sneaky and take a few on the sly. Trust me though, the Brighouse Hotel is picture-perfect. Owning a place like that would be a dream come true.'

Violet and Matthew completed one more circuit of the house on their own, walking from room to room, and making copious notes on the work that needed doing. At ten to seven when they were satisfied they'd seen all there was to see, Jill switched off the lights, turned down the heating, and locked up the house.

'Are you sure you don't want to stay longer?' she said, as the three of them stepped onto the driveway.

'We've seen enough for tonight,' Matthew replied. 'But we'd definitely like to come back at the weekend and take a proper look in the daylight.'

'No problem,' Jill said, as she fished her car keys from her pocket. 'Does that mean you like what you've seen so far?'

Violet and Matthew exchanged a smile.

'We do,' Violet said. 'We'll need to work out some costs . . . but we are very, *very* interested.'

Jill gazed up at the front of the house. 'It is lovely, isn't it? Adrian and I toyed with the idea of moving here ourselves, but I'm not sure what we'd do with all that space.'

Matthew chortled. 'I'm not sure what Violet and I will do with it either.'

'You have family,' Jill said. 'I know your kids don't live with you anymore, but it's nice for them to have their own rooms waiting for them when they do visit. This was built to be a family home, and at forty-one, I think we can safely say I've left it too late to start a family.'

'Not necessarily,' Violet said. 'If that's what you want, there's still time.'

Jill shook her head and smiled sadly. 'Ten years ago, there's nothing I would have liked more – but I hadn't met the right person back then. Adrian is wonderful, and I know he'd make a great dad, but he and I are going to be far too busy running our business to look after a child.'

They got into their cars and drove to Overton Cottage, which was on the western side of the village. Jill put her Fiesta in the garage at the side of the house, and Matthew parked on the road. In the time it took them to reach the front of the house, Adrian had opened the door, ready to greet them and take their coats.

'Let me get you a drink,' he said, as he ushered them into the living room, which was warm and snug compared to the temperatures outside. 'What would you like?'

Violet plumped for a small glass of red wine. As the designated driver for the evening, Matthew opted for a tonic water.

'So?' Adrian said, as he handed over their drinks. 'What did you think of the house?'

'We were impressed,' Matthew said. 'Very impressed.'

'Does that mean you're going to buy it?' Adrian said.

Matthew gave a wry smile. 'There are a few things we need to discuss before we make a final decision.'

'Right.' Adrian looked slightly crestfallen. 'Of course.'

'We're going to view the house again at the weekend,' Violet explained. 'We want to see it properly . . . in the daylight.'

Jill slipped a hand into the crook of Adrian's elbow and squeezed his arm. 'Don't put them under pressure, love. Violet and Matthew are our dinner guests . . . let them relax. If they have any questions about the house, I'm sure they'll ask – but for now, let's talk about something else. You can start by telling us what's on the menu this evening.'

As a starter, Adrian served mozzarella, tomato and basil arancini on a bed of wild winter cress. They were deliciously crispy and cheesy, and served with a smoky tomato dip. The main course was succulently cooked chicken breasts with a wild oyster mushroom and Stilton sauce, accompanied by dauphinoise potatoes, buttered carrots, tender stems of broccoli, and braised red cabbage. The food was delicious, perfectly prepared, and beautifully presented.

'If this is the sort of meal you're planning to serve in your restaurant, you'll be inundated with customers,' Violet said, as she savoured every last mouthful of the flavoursome meal.

'I'm glad you've enjoyed it,' Adrian said, accepting the compliment with a modest smile.

'When did you train to be a chef, Adrian?' Matthew asked.

'I started at catering college when I was nineteen, and went on to work in some of the best restaurants in the north of England,' he said, as he rested his knife and fork on top of his plate. 'Working in a kitchen can be stressful, but in my opinion, there's nothing quite like it. I loved being a chef. The dream was always to run my own restaurant, specialising in dishes that include wild and foraged food.'

'Are you into all that then?' Matthew said. 'Foraging for food?'

'I am.' Adrian smiled self-consciously. 'Unfortunately, there's not much of it to be found at this time of year, but the wild cress and oyster mushrooms in the meal you've just eaten were foraged. I enjoy incorporating wild ingredients into my dishes, and hopefully it's something different that will set us apart from our competitors. Our USP, if you like.'

'You must be thrilled to be opening your own restaurant at last,' Violet said.

'Yes. It's all very exciting. To be honest, I'd pretty much given up on the idea. I attempted to open a small bistro six years ago, but I couldn't get the money together. I gave up cheffing at that point and went to work for a friend – still in the hospitality trade, but in sales rather than cooking.'

'What kind of things were you selling?' Matthew said.

'Catering equipment mainly, and industrial kitchen supplies. It was a complete change to what I was used to, and I can't say I enjoyed it – but I was good at it. Whenever I got a bonus or some extra commission, I squirrelled it away, into my restaurant fund – because even though I'd given up cheffing, I never gave up on my dream of becoming a restaurateur. As it turns out, those years of scrimping and saving and working in a job I hated weren't necessary. Ironically, I'm funding my half of the hotel from the inheritance I received from my sister.'

His eyes were swimming with tears. 'I was her next of kin, so when she died, I got everything. Her house. Her savings. It was more than enough to buy my own restaurant . . . but you know what? I didn't want it . . . any of it. I loved my sister. It was *her* I needed, not her money.'

As he spoke, his voice cracked, and Violet began to understand how he and Jill had developed such a close bond so quickly. Each of them had lost a cherished sibling. They were in mourning, and in sharing their grief, they were easing each other's pain and finding new ways to move on with their lives.

'I'm sure your sister would have been happy to know you're making good use of your inheritance,' Violet said.

Adrian dabbed his napkin against his mouth, taking a moment to rein in his emotions. 'She'd be delighted,' he said, giving a lopsided smile. 'Finally, I'll be realising my dream. More importantly, Jill and I are going into business together. We're buying a hotel! Can you believe that?'

Violet smiled. 'I'm thrilled for you both, truly I am. The pair of you will do a great job of running a business. You're a dream team – and if the meal you've prepared tonight is anything to go by, people will be queuing up to eat in your restaurant.'

'I'll second that,' Matthew said. 'Everything you've served tonight has been exceptional, and packed with flavour. You're onto a winner with these dishes. No doubt about it.'

'And the meal isn't over yet,' Adrian said, as he got to his feet. 'Pudding is banana curd tarte with dark chocolate shavings, served with homemade honeycomb and toffee ice cream.'

Violet licked her lips and closed her eyes. 'I think I've died and gone to heaven.'

They stayed at Overton Cottage until well after nine. Over pudding, they talked about Rock House; the Christmas market; the Merrywell Manor Hotel, where Adrian was working on a temporary basis during the busy Christmas lunchtime period;

and Jill also talked about how much she would miss working at the bookshop.

Much to Violet's relief, Daniel Midship didn't get a mention. She and Matthew, and Jill and Adrian were in a buoyant, optimistic mood, looking forward to starting new chapters in their lives. By unspoken agreement, they avoided downbeat subjects and dwelt instead on positive outcomes and the fulfilment of dreams.

# Chapter 18

After two glasses of excellent red wine and with her appetite sated by a top-notch meal, Violet was feeling decidedly 'chilled'. As Matthew drove them to Greengage Cottage, she leaned into the headrest and closed her eyes. Despite it being a short journey, she felt herself drifting off . . . sinking gradually towards sleep . . . lulled by the sound of the car engine.

And then suddenly, her sense of calm was shattered by the heart-stopping wail of a siren. Startled back to full consciousness, she opened her eyes in time to see flashing blue lights appear behind them. Matthew pulled over in front of the village shop to let the approaching ambulance overtake.

'That's not good,' Violet said, as the sound of the siren faded into the distance. 'Do you think it's someone from Merrywell?'

'At this time of night, I'd say it's a racing certainty,' Matthew replied, sounding more than a little worried. 'I'm just glad the ambulance wasn't coming from Mum and Dad's end of the village.'

'I wonder if there's been a road accident,' Violet said. 'The forecast did warn about the possibility of black ice.'

'Well, whoever it is in that ambulance, let's hope they'll be OK. If it's someone local, we'll find out about it soon enough.'

There were downstairs lights on in Greengage Cottage when they pulled up outside.

'Looks like your mum's back from her dinner with Jacqueline,' Matthew said. 'I won't come in. I'll let the two of you have some time on your own.'

'She'll think you're avoiding her. You're not, are you?'

He laughed. 'No, I just want to be on my own for a while so I can think about Rock House, and maybe sketch out a few plans for the kitchen. Give your mother my best wishes and tell her I'll see her tomorrow.'

Violet's phone rang at seven-fifteen the next morning, jolting her out of a deep slumber. She pushed an arm out from under the duvet and answered it without checking the caller ID.

'Hello,' she said, her voice muffled with sleep.

'Have you heard the news?'

It was Fiona. As a baker, she was up with the lark every day, except Sundays. Seven-fifteen was early for Violet, but for Fiona it was virtually the middle of the day.

Violet sat up in bed, instantly alert.

'What news? I've no idea what you're talking about. I've just this second woken up.'

'Sorry,' Fiona said, sounding contrite. 'I shouldn't have called you so early. I forget that not everyone gets up at the crack of dawn like me – but I thought you'd want to know. There was a hit-and-run up at the cross last night.'

The 'cross' was the local name for the crossroads on the north-eastern edge of the village. It marked the meeting point of four country lanes and lay quite some distance from the nearest houses, and well away from the main roads. Consequently, it wasn't a busy crossroads, but a public footpath cut through it that was popular with dog walkers during the daytime.

Violet ran a hand through her bed-ruffled hair, remembering the ambulance that had sped through the village the previous night. Presumably, it had been carrying the victim of the hit-and-run.

'Do you know who was involved?' Violet said. 'Were they badly hurt?'

'No, and yes,' said Fiona. 'I only know what I heard on the radio this morning. The victim is in intensive care, but they haven't been named. The police have put out an appeal for witnesses or dashcam footage from anyone driving in the area between eight-thirty and nine o'clock last night.'

'That's an odd time for someone to be walking around in the dark up at the cross. Not to mention dangerous. There are no street lights up there.'

'Whoever it was, I bet they were up to no good,' Fiona said. 'Some sort of illicit meet-up, no doubt. I'm sure we'll get to hear more before long.'

'Let's hope whoever it is makes a full recovery. Matthew and I saw an ambulance last night. It zoomed past us at about twenty past nine with its lights flashing and siren on – so I'm assuming it must have been taking the victim to hospital.'

'You didn't see anything suspicious, did you?'

'No,' Violet said. 'We were on our way back from—'

She stopped herself just in time. If she revealed they'd been at Jill's house, Fiona would want to know why – and that would lead to questions that Violet wasn't in a position to answer. It felt sneaky, keeping Fiona in the dark about Rock House and the meal with Jill and Adrian, but until Jill had informed Eric of her plans, Violet had no choice but to hold her tongue.

'I spent the evening with Matthew,' she said, because this was, fundamentally, true. 'He drove me home, and that's when we saw the ambulance. I hope the victim's not someone we know. You will keep me posted if you hear anything else?'

'Course I will,' Fiona said. 'I guarantee that sooner or later, someone will come into the bakery who knows what's happened. I'll speak to you later. I've gotta go, there's another batch of gingerbread people I need to take out of the oven. They're selling really well, but – quite honestly – I'm sick of the sight of them. It's got to the point where I'm icing silly expressions onto their faces, just to keep myself from screaming.'

After the call had ended, Violet was tempted to lie down and go back to sleep, but she could hear sounds of movement coming from the bedroom next door. Rachel was up already. Another one of life's early risers.

Half an hour later, the two of them were eating breakfast at the kitchen table. Violet was consuming a bowl of porridge and blueberries, and Rachel was rasping butter across a piece of wholemeal toast.

As Violet scooped the last spoonful of porridge into her mouth, her phone rang again. This time, Charlie Winterton's name flashed onto the screen.

She got up, put her empty bowl on the draining board, and moved into the living room so that her mother wouldn't be able to overhear the conversation she was about to have.

'Morning, Charlie,' she said, as she accepted the call. 'Are you ringing about the hit-and-run?'

'You've heard then?' Charlie said.

'Fiona Nash heard it on the radio. She rang earlier to tell me about it – although she didn't know who the victim was. Is it someone from the village?'

There was a pause before Charlie spoke again.

'It's Zac Wallis,' he said. 'He's still alive, but he's in a coma. In a bad way, so they say.'

'Zac?' Violet dropped onto the settee. 'Oh my God!'

'That's exactly what I said when I heard the news – or words to that effect. What do you make of it? Do you think it's a coincidence?'

'I'm always wary of coincidences,' Violet said, her mind racing with possibilities and unanswered questions. 'I prefer to listen to my instincts, which right now are veering towards there being some kind of link between Zac's accident and Daniel's accident.'

Charlie gave a long sigh. He sounded exhausted.

'I agree, but finding that link is going to require a lot of conjecture. First off, it requires an assumption that despite his denial, Zac Wallis *was* in the car park when Dan Midship died, and he saw what happened.'

'Which would make him an important witness,' Violet said. 'And a potential target for someone who wants to guarantee his silence.'

'Precisely. The trouble is, it's a theory based purely on guesswork . . . a castle built on sand. There's no proof that Zac was at the shopping village, and no evidence of any third-party involvement in Dan's death. You and I can hypothesise until the cows come home, Violet – we can even make a case to connect our separate, unproven theories – but the truth is, we may never know the full story of what happened to Dan and Zac.'

Violet moved the phone to her other ear. 'It's not all theoretical now though, is it?' she said. 'A crime *has* been committed. Someone ran into Zac Wallis at the cross and drove away – so there is a case to investigate.'

'That's true, and we're doing everything we can to track down the person responsible.'

'Are you allowed to tell me who found Zac, and rang for the ambulance?' Violet said.

'It was his mother, Marcia Wallis. She and Zac were at home together earlier in the evening, but at ten to eight, Zac announced he was going to the cross to meet someone. Marcia was annoyed, because she'd just ordered in a pizza. Zac told her to chill . . . said he wouldn't be long, and promised to be home before the pizza was delivered.

'At half past eight, when the food arrived and Zac still wasn't back, Marcia realised something must be wrong. She told me that pizza is Zac's favourite food, and there was no way he'd have wanted to miss out. She asked a neighbour to drive her up to the cross, and they found him lying unconscious in the middle of the road. It's a good job they found him when they did, otherwise sooner or later, another car would have come along and there's no way the driver would have seen him lying there in the dark. Zac's badly injured as it is. He certainly wouldn't have survived being hit twice.'

'Did he say anything at all to Marcia about *why* he was going to the cross?' Violet said. 'It seems a strange place to walk to in the dark. He must have had a compelling reason to be there.'

'All he said before he left was that he was going to meet someone, and he wouldn't be long. His mum assumed it was some kind of drop-off or pick-up. She thought he might have been buying drugs.'

'Is that something he does regularly?' Violet said.

'Occasionally, according to Marcia – although she doesn't recall him meeting up with anyone at the cross before.'

'Maybe he was there transacting some other kind of business,' Violet said, thinking aloud. 'If Zac was at the shopping village when Daniel Midship died, there's every chance he saw something, or someone. He might even have witnessed the so-called accident. What we have to ask ourselves is: why wasn't he willing to tell the police what he saw?'

'Perhaps he thought he could use that information to his advantage,' Charlie said. 'Someone like Zac might see it as an opportunity to make some dosh. If he saw someone with Dan – someone he recognised – then maybe he got in touch with them afterwards and demanded money in exchange for his silence.'

'Blackmail?'

'Why not?' Charlie said. 'If I'm right, it backfired in the worst possible way, but Zac wasn't to know that would happen.'

Violet recalled the antagonistic exchange with Marcia Wallis. 'Actually, it does tally with something Marcia said on Wednesday. I went round there to find out if Zac could do some gardening work for me.'

She heard Charlie tutting on the other end of the line.

'There are any number of decent gardeners out there, Violet. Why the hell would you want to employ Zac Wallis?'

'I need the work doing quickly, and I thought he might be available. He wasn't in when I called round, but his mum said he wouldn't be interested in doing any work before Christmas. I'm trying to recall what she said . . . something along the lines of Zac not being in a hurry to take on new jobs because he was expecting a big pay-out.'

'And you think by "pay-out", she meant "pay-off"?' Charlie said. 'Zac demanding money from someone, in exchange for keeping quiet about what he'd seen?'

'It's possible, although he obviously hadn't told Marcia what he was up to.'

'So, what's the theory? That the person Zac was blackmailing arranged to meet him at the cross, but instead of handing over money, decided to run him over?'

'Yes, either to warn him off, or silence him altogether,' Violet said. 'Is there any way of checking Zac's phone records and messages to find out if he'd arranged to meet anyone?'

'Unfortunately, his phone is missing,' Charlie said. 'It wasn't in his possession when they got him to the hospital, and we've done a search of the immediate area around the cross. There's no sign of it. We do know that the phone's switched off, so we're working on the assumption that whoever ran Zac down got out of their car, found his phone, switched it off and drove away with it. That in itself is a red flag. In most hit-and-run cases, the driver flees the scene as fast as they can. It's rare for anyone to hang around, let alone long enough to steal the victim's phone.'

'It sounds like they didn't want anyone reading Zac's messages.'

'We're working with the phone provider to access the data, but that could take a while. And if this was a planned attack on Zac, whoever's behind it will have been savvy enough to use a burner phone – so we won't be able to trace them anyway.'

'What's your boss's take on all of this?' Violet said. 'Does she think there could be a connection between Daniel Midship's death and the incident with Zac?'

'She accepts that the two things could be linked. As a matter of fact, she's told me to look into Dan's death. Officially.'

'Is that why you called me?' Violet said. 'To warn me off what is now an official investigation?'

'Do I need to?' said Charlie. 'I thought we'd agreed your only involvement would be as a pair of "eyes and ears" in the village.'

'The question is, do you still want me to do that?'

'I don't think you'd stop, even if I asked you to,' Charlie said, laughing quietly to himself. 'I'm more than happy for you to keep an ear to the ground, Violet, providing you get in touch the minute you see or hear anything of interest. You've already provided me with some useful information, especially in relation to Dan's earlier visit to Merrywell Shopping Village.'

'I hear that piece of info has been a bit of a damp squib,' she said. 'Nick Penfold told me he hasn't been able to let you have the CCTV footage from Wednesday, because it's gone missing.'

Charlie huffed. 'Yeah. Missing, or never recorded in the first place. Either way, it's very convenient for someone, don't you think?'

'Highly suspicious,' Violet said. 'Has Nick been able to confirm who's logged into the system recently?'

'Yes, I got the information from him yesterday. Nick has logged in several times himself, of course, and Eric Nash logged in on Saturday morning.'

'Eric?' Violet said. 'He must have been trying to download the footage that PC Turner requested on Friday evening. He certainly wouldn't have been logging in to delete the data.'

'I spoke to him on the phone about it. Eric Nash denies having logged in at all. Either he's lying, or someone else accessed the system using his ID.'

'How?' Violet said. 'They'd need his login name and password.'

'Eric told me he has it written down in a notebook, which he keeps in an unlocked drawer under the bookshop counter. Keeping a book of passwords is a classic error – but it's only really a problem if someone knows about it.'

Violet thought back to Friday evening in the bookshop, when Eric had been under pressure to retrieve the CCTV footage.

'When PC Turner asked about the security cameras on Friday, Eric said something about needing to log in to access the system,' she said. 'As he was talking, he pulled out a notebook from under the counter. He didn't say as much, but based on what you've just told me, I assume it was his book of passwords. Anyone who was there at the time could have noticed it.'

'Who *was* there? Can you give me their names?'

Violet thought for a moment. 'There were quite a few of us. Me and Matthew Collis, Eric and Fiona Nash, Jill Atherstone and Adrian Billings, Judith and Andrew Talbot, Molly Gee and Robert Dorman, and Tim Waldron. And PC Turner of course, who told Eric not to worry about the CCTV . . . that it could wait until the morning.'

'So in theory, any one of those people could have clocked the notebook?'

'Yes,' Violet said. 'But to get the login details, they'd have had to get their hands on it without anyone seeing them – and it was very busy in the shop the next day.'

'Which would have made it difficult, but not impossible.'

'I suppose not,' Violet said. 'Matthew and Tim have their own access to the security system, so if either of them had wanted to delete the footage – and obviously I'm not saying they did – they would have used their own logins.'

'Not if they wanted to point the finger of blame elsewhere.'

'That's not something Matthew would do, I can promise you that,' Violet said, realising that in giving this latest information to Charlie, she had inadvertently thrown suspicion on Matthew and her friends.

'I'd better go,' she said, eager to bring the call to an end. 'Thanks for the update and for putting me in the picture regarding Zac Wallis.'

'We'll be holding a press conference at lunchtime, so I'm not telling you anything that won't be public knowledge within a few hours.'

'What will happen next?' Violet said.

'We'll make an appeal for information during the press conference, and we'll also be following up some other lines of inquiry – but that's for me to worry about. The main reason for this call, apart from updating you, is to wish you a happy Christmas and all the very best for the new year.'

'Aw, thanks, Charlie,' Violet said, feeling an unexpected rush of warmth for the curmudgeonly detective. 'Have a good one yourself. And if our paths do cross again next year, let's hope it's not in connection with another crime in Merrywell.'

## Chapter 19

And that should have been the end of it. Except, of course, it wasn't. Shadows were already gathering in the nebulous gloom of the grey and drizzly day ahead.

Fearing for her carefully straightened hair, Violet made the short journey to work in her car. Her plan for the morning was to spend half an hour in the office, buy a few last-minute gifts from the Christmas market, and then meet her mother for coffee.

When she got to the shopping village, there were only four vehicles in the staff car park; Fiona's car was there, as was Nick Penfold's, and the *Antiques Emporium* van stood next to a silver Vauxhall Astra. Violet parked alongside Fiona's grey Nissan, got out, and made her way towards the alleyway. As she reached the edge of the car park her footsteps slowed and her stomach flipped.

A young woman was standing by the bollard, holding a bunch of flowers – baby pink roses surrounded by yellow chrysanthemums and purple irises. Violet stopped, watching as the woman bent down and laid the bouquet on the ground between the chain barrier and the bollard. This must surely be a relative of Daniel Midship's, come to pay her respects.

Silently, Violet veered to the right, intending to walk around and enter the shopping village via the main entrance. Whoever this person was deserved privacy and some time alone to grieve their loss.

Violet stole away as discreetly as possible, but she'd only gone a few yards when she heard the woman calling to her.

'Excuse me?' she shouted. 'Do you work here?'

Violet stopped. Turned around.

'Yes, I do,' she replied. 'Can I help you with something?'

'Do you know anything about the man who died here the other night?'

Violet retraced her steps, closing the distance between herself and the young woman.

'I was on site when the security guard found him,' she said.

Tears pooled in the woman's eyes and she pressed her hands against her cheeks.

'Are you a friend of Mr Midship's, or a relative?' Violet asked.

'I'm Lucy, his daughter.'

Violet moved closer and gently placed a hand on the young woman's forearm.

'I'm sorry for your loss, Lucy. It must have been a terrible shock.'

Lucy nodded, and a tear dripped from her eye.

'I can't explain it, but I felt I needed to come here?' she said, applying an upward inflection that seemed to question her own decision. 'I wanted to see where Dad died. The police told me that this is where he was found.'

Violet wondered whether to say anything about waiting with the body, but on reflection decided it would only cause further upset.

'Nobody seems to know what happened,' Lucy said. 'All the police have told me is that Dad ran into the alley, and must have fallen over. They say he banged his head on this.' She pointed to the bollard.

Did Lucy know a full investigation into her father's death was now officially underway? It didn't sound as if she did, but it wasn't Violet's place to tell her.

'I run a videography business in the shopping village,' she said, changing the subject in order to check on something. 'We recently organised a pop-up booth to raise money for charity, and your dad visited it on Friday. My colleague filmed him talking about his favourite memories of Christmas. I sent the file to the police and asked them to forward a copy on to you. I hope you've received it.'

Lucy shook her head. 'Not yet, but they did tell me about it. They said they're going to email it to me.'

Violet pulled a business card from her bag and handed it over.

'I'm sure they will, but if for some reason you don't get the video, here's my number. All you have to do is send me a message with your email address, and I'll make sure you get a copy.'

Lucy smiled weakly. 'Thanks. I'm desperate to see it, but I know it'll make me cry.'

'Did you know your dad had visited Merrywell once before, a few days before he died?'

'He told me he'd gone to Derby earlier in the week to look at a motorbike, but I didn't know he'd called in here until the police told me. He must have stopped off on his way to see the bike, or on the way back.'

'Have you any idea why he came back here on Friday?'

'The police asked me the same thing,' Lucy said. 'They think he may have seen or met someone he recognised – but if he did, he didn't say anything to me about it when I rang him on Thursday evening. He didn't mention that he was planning to come back either.

'I had no clue about why he might have returned, but then – last night – I spoke to my Aunty Helen, Dad's sister. She told me he called her on Wednesday evening, asking about someone she'd dated three or four years ago in Leeds. Dad said he thought he'd seen him. He didn't say where, but I'm guessing it must have been here, and that's why he came back on Friday.'

A sudden gust of wind blew a fine spray of horizontal rain into their faces.

'My office is in the shopping village if you'd like to talk somewhere warmer,' Violet said. 'I can offer you a cup of tea or coffee, or we could go to the café, if you prefer. It'll be opening in a minute.'

Lucy glanced at her watch. 'Thanks, but I left my partner looking after the kids. He's supposed to be working from home, so I should probably get back. I wouldn't mind using the loo though, before I set off.'

'It's this way.' Violet nodded towards the alleyway. 'Have you had to travel far to get here?'

'I live in Durham, so it's been quite a journey,' Lucy replied, as they walked into the courtyard together. 'I set off early to avoid the worst of the rush hour, but the traffic was pretty heavy by the time I got onto the M1.'

They stood outside *The Memory Box* and Violet pointed to where the public toilets were located.

'Can I ask you something before you go?' Violet said. 'Have you told the police about this guy your aunty knew? The one your dad thought he'd seen?'

'Not yet, but I will do. Aunty Helen only told me about it last night, so I haven't had chance. The guy . . . the one she used to go out with, was called Ed Hampton.'

Violet remembered what Charlie had said about Daniel asking his old colleague to run a check on someone called 'Ed'.

'It was a whirlwind romance – which, with hindsight, should have rung alarm bells,' Lucy added. 'My aunty was absolutely besotted with Ed, until he took off with ten grand of her savings.'

'Oh, no!' said Violet. 'That sounds like a horrible experience. Did she manage to track him down and get her money back?'

Lucy shook her head. 'She chose not to pursue it, which

infuriated Dad, who was a serving police officer at the time. He told Aunty Helen to call Action Fraud and report him, but I think she was reluctant to step forward and report the crime because she felt embarrassed.'

'When something like that happens, it's only natural for people to feel a sense of shame or embarrassment,' Violet said, thinking about Jacqueline Rheinhart's unwillingness to talk about her recent brush with 'Dodgy Duncan'. 'It's how these fraudsters get away with it. They prey on people, often those made vulnerable by loneliness, and then rely on them being too embarrassed to tell anyone what's happened to them. My mum's friend had a lucky escape recently. She ditched a guy – a total sponger by the sound of things – but not before she'd bestowed several expensive gifts on him.'

'These things happen more frequently than you might think,' Lucy said. 'My aunt's an intelligent woman, but she was so totally smitten with Ed that she completely failed to see him for what he was. His stealing from her was the worst kind of betrayal. Helen was angry and hurt – and yet still, she refused to report him.

'She told Dad she wanted to put it down to experience and move on. He was livid – furious with Ed for ripping off his sister, and exasperated by Helen's refusal to report the crime. I'm pretty sure Dad would have gone ahead and arrested Ed anyway, but he'd scarpered by the time Dad found out what had happened.'

'Couldn't he have tracked him down? As a policeman, he was in an ideal position to find him.'

Lucy shook her head. 'He did try to trace Ed, but he couldn't locate him. Dad told me that fraudsters are experts at concealing their identities and reinventing themselves, and they know all about finding new ways to trick and deceive people. Having said that, he never completely gave up on finding him. Dad had a memory like an elephant, and he never forgot a face.'

'Do you really think it could have been Ed Hampton that your dad saw at the shopping village?'

Lucy glanced at her watch again. 'I don't know for certain, but it seems likely. Dad didn't say anything to me about it, but his conversation with Aunty Helen has to be significant. He told her about seeing Ed on the very day he first visited Derbyshire. That can't be a coincidence.'

'It's really important you tell the police about this,' Violet said. 'Give them a call as soon as you can, and ask to speak to DS Winterton.'

'I'll make the call when I get home,' Lucy said. 'I'm not sure what good it'll do though.'

'It might help them work out what caused your dad's accident.'

'Yeah,' said Lucy. 'But it's not going to bring him back, is it?'

After Lucy had gone, and not wishing to leave anything to chance, Violet messaged Charlie Winterton. He'd asked her to let him know if she saw or heard anything important, and the conversation with Lucy was definitely something worth reporting.

FYI, Daniel Midship's daughter (Lucy) was here this morning, laying flowers in the alleyway where her dad died. She told me the person Daniel recognised could have been her aunt's old boyfriend – a guy called Ed Hampton. It sounds like he was a con man and fraudster, which would account for why Daniel was so eager to speak to him. Lucy's going to call you later to give you more info, and you might also want to speak to Daniel's sister, Helen.

Lucy also said she hasn't received a copy of the video file I gave you . . . Can you chase it up? Daniel's favourite memories of Christmas were those spent with his daughter, so it's important she gets a chance to see the video.

Charlie replied to the message five minutes later.

> Thanks for that. Very useful. It fits with Dan asking his colleague to run a check on someone called 'Ed'. He must have been talking about Ed Hampton. Now that I've got a surname, I'll do some digging – see what I can find out. I take it there's no Ed Hampton living in or around Merrywell?

Violet waited a few minutes before replying (she didn't want Charlie to think she had nothing better to do with her time than send messages to the police).

> The name isn't familiar to me. As far as I'm aware, there's no Ed (or Edward or Edmund) Hampton in Merrywell, but I'm sure that's something you can easily check on the PNC. A thought occurred to me about the CCTV footage from Friday though . . . Remember we thought Daniel might have been shouting *hey* or *oi* as he ran into the alley? Knowing what we know now, do you think he could have been shouting *Ed*?

Charlie's reply pinged onto her phone as she was locking up the office.

> That would make sense. I'll take another look at the footage. Leave it with me, and enjoy your time off at Christmas.

The arts and crafts supplier in the shopping village also stocked a wide range of jigsaw puzzles. At ten o'clock, Violet went inside the shop and bought a thousand-piece book-themed puzzle for Joyce Collis, Matthew's mum, who loved nothing better than completing a jigsaw by the fire on dark winter evenings. Next, Violet joined the crowds milling around the craft stalls in the market. She made several purchases, including two bars of rose-petal-scented soap, a pair of heavy marble bookends, and a couple of felt animal Christmas tree decorations (one in the form of a cat that looked a lot like Rusty, and the other a white and tan dog that resembled Molly's dog, Alfie).

She concluded her spending spree with a visit to *The Epicurious*, where she bought vast quantities of local cheeses, two large boxes of savoury biscuits, a jar of piccalilli, and some caramelised onion chutney.

Finally, she waited in line in the bakery to replenish her stock of mince pies and buy bread for the freezer (back-up supplies that would keep her family going over Christmas when the bakery would be closed for a few days).

When she reached the head of the queue, she was greeted by Fiona, who looked tired and slightly harassed.

'I've found out who the hit-and-run victim is,' she said, leaning forward and lowering her voice. 'It was Zac Wallis. I can't chat now, but I'll call you later to fill you in on the details.'

Violet feigned surprise, being careful not to let on that she'd already been given the same information by Charlie Winterton.

'He's still alive, but apparently it's touch and go,' Fiona said, as she filled a paper carrier bag with Violet's purchases. 'Terrible, isn't it? Poor Marcia. I don't particularly like the woman, but there are some things you wouldn't wish on your worst enemy.'

'Let's hope he pulls through,' Violet said. 'And that they catch whoever left him for dead.'

'It could have been a drunk driver – someone who'd had one too many snifters at the office Christmas party and should have called for a taxi instead of driving themselves home.'

'I guess that would explain why the person didn't stop, or report the accident,' Violet said.

What it didn't explain was why Zac's phone had been taken, but that was information she wasn't at liberty to share.

'The other possibility is that it was one of the local boy racers,' Fiona said. 'They're regularly seen driving up and down the lanes, going far too fast – and I'm sorry to have to say it, but Zac's usually one of those behind the wheel.'

# Chapter 20

That evening, Violet and Matthew took Rachel and Jacqueline to the White Hart, the pub run by Molly's parents, Cathy and Billy Gee, who were holding a special quiz night with Christmas-related questions. The music round was to focus on popular Christmas hits, and Billy had also promised rounds on festive food, traditions, and the nativity story.

Knowing they would need all the help they could get, Violet enlisted Rachel and Jacqueline as the fifth and sixth members of their team – which also included Brian and Joyce Collis, as well as herself and Matthew. On the next table was Team Nash, which this evening was made up of Eric and Fiona, their son Tom and his partner Darren, and – in the absence of Sophie Nash – Eric had recruited help from Jill and Adrian.

During the music round, Jacqueline emerged as Team Collis's secret weapon. Her musical knowledge was extremely impressive, and she was confidently familiar with almost every Christmas number-one song since the 1960s.

There was a short break at the halfway point in the quiz. As Matthew and Brian went to the bar to replenish the drinks and Joyce went to powder her nose, Jill and Adrian got up and came over for a chat.

'Had any more thoughts about the house?' Jill whispered, as she sat down next to Violet.

'We'll make a decision at the weekend, after we've had our second viewing,' Violet replied, aware that her mother was only a few feet away. Despite making a great show of sipping her drink and casually minding her own business, Rachel's ears were pinned back and listening in.

'I'll bring the keys with me to work tomorrow,' Jill said, speaking quietly. 'If you call into the bookshop, I'll hand them over when Eric isn't looking.'

Violet nodded. 'You've still not told him then?'

Jill shook her head. 'No, although I did think about it, now that things appear to be moving forward with the hotel.'

'When you say "things are moving forward", what do you mean?'

'Our offer's been accepted,' Adrian said, grinning at Jill and giving her hand an affectionate squeeze. 'We're thrilled, aren't we, love?'

'Yes,' Jill said, smiling from ear to ear. 'It's the best early Christmas present ever.'

The conversation was curtailed by a brief squeal of feedback from the microphone. Billy Gee stood at the bar, ready to make an announcement.

'Listen up, ladies and gentlemen,' he said, waving his hand to get everyone's attention. 'In a few minutes we'll be making the annual draw for this year's Christmas hamper, so please have your tickets ready.'

'If I win it, I think I'll donate it to Marcia Wallis,' Jill said. 'I take it you've heard about what happened to Zac?'

'I have,' Violet said. 'It's awful news. It must have happened while Matthew and I were at your house. The ambulance hurtled past us as we drove home.'

'Any news on how he's doing?' Adrian said.

'The last I heard, he's still unconscious,' Violet said. 'Let's hope he's able to make a full recovery, but it doesn't sound good.'

Billy tapped the microphone and began his preamble to the draw, thanking the local businesses who had contributed to the Christmas hamper, and letting everyone know that the £485 raised from the ticket sales would be going towards repairs to the village hall.

'Come on,' Adrian said, as he gently tugged Jill's hand. 'It's time to head back to our table for part two of the quiz.'

Rachel smiled as she watched them go and then leaned in to whisper into Violet's ear. 'I take it they're the people you're hoping to buy a house from?'

'Yes, Mum, they are,' Violet said, as Matthew returned with a tray of drinks, including a tonic water with ice and lemon for her. 'But let's not talk about it here. I'll tell you more when we get home.'

'OK, and while you're at it, you'd better fill me in on what's happened to this Zac character I heard you talking about. Please tell me there's not been another calamity in the village.'

Brian Collis won the hamper (much to his delight) and Team Nash won the quiz. After one final round of drinks, the members of Team Collis put on their coats and left the pub. Outside, the sky had cleared and the stars were twinkling high above them.

'It looks like we're in for an overnight frost,' Matthew said, as he waved to his parents, who were making the short journey home on foot. 'If the temperature keeps dropping, we might have a white Christmas.'

'Snow scenes are the preserve of Christmas cards and made-for-TV movies,' Violet said, as she unlocked the car and got into the driver's seat. 'In all of my forty-seven years, I don't ever remember it snowing on Christmas Day.'

'We used to get white Christmases when I was a child,' Rachel said. 'I remember Jack Frost on the inside of the windows . . . snow drifts . . . dripping icicles.'

'The good old days, eh, Mum?' Violet said, laughing as she

switched on the car's heated seats. 'Whereas the twenty-first century is the era of central heating and global warming.'

They set off in the direction of the Merrywell Manor Hotel, to drop off Jacqueline.

'The tall man with the intense blue eyes?' Jacqueline said, speaking from the back seat. 'I take it that was Jill's partner?'

'Trust you to notice the colour of his eyes,' Rachel muttered, as she stared out at the darkness through the car window.

In the front seats, Violet and Matthew exchanged a smile.

'Yes, that's Adrian,' Violet said. 'Sorry, I should have introduced you.'

'It's OK,' Jacqueline said. 'I wondered who he was, that's all. I've seen him at the hotel a couple of times.'

'He's a chef,' Matthew said. 'He works in the kitchen at lunchtimes, helping out temporarily in the run-up to Christmas.'

Rachel sighed. 'You know, these short-term contracts are no good to anyone. Whatever happened to job security? You watch. Come the new year, Adrian will be given his marching orders. Chefs are surplus to requirements once the Christmas and new year celebrations are out of the way. In January, people have a tendency to stay in and eat at home.'

'I go out for at least one meal every January,' Violet said.

'Of course you do, darling – for your birthday – but trust me, most people prefer to stay in. They're either short on money after the expense of Christmas, or they've made a new year's resolution to lose weight. Whichever way you look at it, January is all about belt-tightening. It's the direst month of the year for restaurant owners.'

'I don't think Adrian's too concerned about his job at the Merrywell Manor Hotel,' Matthew said. 'He's got other irons in the fire.'

'And are they in any way connected to the house that he's selling you?'

Matthew shot a questioning look in Violet's direction.

'Mum overheard my conversation with Jill,' she said, giving an eye-roll that only Matthew could see.

'You did say you'd tell me more when we got out of the pub,' Rachel said. 'Come on, Violet. Spill the beans. I'm good at keeping secrets, and so is Jacqueline.'

'It's not Adrian who's selling us the house,' Violet said, surrendering to the inevitable. 'It's Jill.'

'It's the property she inherited from her brother,' Matthew added.

'OK,' Rachel said. 'But what's with all the secrecy?'

They were halfway along the tree-lined driveway that led to the Merrywell Manor Hotel, which looked extremely grand and welcoming with its floodlit frontage and strings of outdoor lighting.

'Jill wants to keep things quiet because she and Adrian are planning to leave the village,' Violet said. 'She doesn't want anyone to know that yet – especially Eric and Fiona. Obviously, it means she's going to have to resign from her job, but she wants to wait, and tell Eric in the new year to avoid spoiling his Christmas.'

'I see,' Rachel said. 'I guess it's a shame for Eric, but it's jolly good news for Jill. It all sounds wonderfully romantic, and she and Adrian do seem like a lovely couple.'

'I agree,' said Jacqueline, as Violet pulled up in front of the hotel. 'And who wouldn't want to ride off into the sunset with a man whose eyes are bluer than Paul Newman's?'

She opened the car door, placed her feet on the gravelled driveway and turned back to deliver her parting shot.

'However, my own recent experience with Duncan has left me feeling rather pessimistic and cynical about romantic love. Let's hope for Jill's sake that everything is as it seems. Goodnight, everyone.'

# Chapter 21

'Well, she certainly knows how to put a dampener on things,' Violet said, as they watched Jacqueline mount the steps to the hotel's front entrance. 'What do you suppose she meant by that?'

'Probably nothing at all,' said Rachel. 'Ignore her. She's feeling emotionally wounded and, I suspect, a tad jealous. Seeing Jill and Adrian this evening, happy and loved up, must have been a stark reminder of her own less fortunate experience. The good news is, she's finally spoken openly about Duncan. That's progress, I suppose. Prior to this evening, she refused to even mention his name, let alone talk about what happened. I've tried broaching the subject on several occasions, but she completely clams up and refuses to discuss it. We should view Jacqueline's parting words this evening as the first positive step on a long road to recovery – although it's going to be quite some time before her faith in men is fully restored.'

'We're not all cads and bounders, you know,' Matthew said, as they pulled away from the hotel and turned onto the road that led into the village. 'Most of us are quite nice.'

Violet took her left hand off the steering wheel and squeezed Matthew's knee.

'You're more than nice,' she said. 'And I'm very lucky to have you in my life.'

'Let's have a nightcap, shall we?' Rachel said, when they got back to Greengage Cottage. 'Come on, Violet. Pour us all a brandy and then you can tell me what happened to this Zac chappie I heard you talking to Jill about.'

After she'd poured the drinks and added a couple of fresh logs to the burner, Violet sat down and explained about the hit-and-run, and how – potentially – the incident might be linked to Daniel Midship's death.

Rachel looked thoroughly disgruntled. 'This whole thing began with what you described as a straightforward accident. Now the situation appears to be turning into one of your ghastly mysteries. What is going on?'

'Initially, the police did think that Daniel Midship's death was an accident,' Violet said. 'Now they're not so sure.'

Rachel took a sip of brandy and stared at Violet over the rim of the glass. 'I do hope you're not getting involved in another criminal investigation.'

'I'm not *involved*. I've just been helping DS Winterton by sharing information . . . things I've overheard or found out about.'

A wry smile passed between Rachel and Matthew.

'And exactly *how* have you learned those things?' Rachel said, pausing only briefly before answering her own rhetorical question. 'By being far too curious for your own good – that's how. Honestly, Violet, you do have a propensity for getting drawn into potentially dangerous situations. Why put yourself in harm's way? Just because you were there when this man was found in the alleyway, doesn't make him your responsibility.'

'I'm not in any danger, Mum.'

'I sincerely hope not. I've driven all this way to spend Christmas with you, and I'd like us to have a lovely time together. Goodness knows I see far too little of you as it is. I'd rather this visit didn't coincide with your latest preoccupation with yet another local incident.'

'Violet's been looking forward to your visit for weeks,' Matthew said. 'I'm sure she intends to make the most of it.'

'I most certainly do,' Violet said, grateful that Matthew had spoken up in her defence. 'I'm sorry if you think I've been neglecting you, Mum. The truth is, when something happens, I'm instantly curious – you know that better than anyone.'

'Instantly curious?' Rachel said. 'That's one way of putting it. Inquisitive is another. Nosy would be an even better description.'

Violet folded her arms. 'I can't help it. It's the way I am. My brain is wired in such a way that when I'm presented with a puzzle or a mystery, I can't bear to put it aside until I know the solution.'

'So, how are you going to find the answer to this latest conundrum?' Rachel said.

'I'm not sure. Now that it's officially in DS Winterton's hands, I'm hoping *he'll* solve the case.'

'Does that mean you're giving up?' Rachel took another sip of brandy. 'Washing your hands of the whole thing?'

Violet shrugged. 'Isn't that what you want me to do?'

'At the risk of sounding contradictory, I want you to do whatever makes you happy. I have absolutely no problem with you puzzling something over, providing you don't take an active role in hunting down criminals.'

'That's my take on this sleuthing malarkey as well, Rachel,' said Matthew. 'I've come to accept that curiosity is part of Violet's personality – it's one of the things I love about her. There are times when I find it irritating, but it's a deeply ingrained part of her nature and I wouldn't want to change that.'

'Good, because I don't think you'd be able to, even if you tried,' Rachel said, knocking back what was left of her drink and signalling for Matthew to pour her another one. 'So, tell me

Violet, darling, how does this normally work? When faced with a mystery, how do you approach it?'

Violet looked into her glass and swirled the contents around in a clockwise direction.

'As with every good puzzle, it's a case of following the clues, and examining things from several different angles. I tend to start with the facts . . . the things I'm sure about, as well as those I believe are true, and I try to build a case from there.'

Rachel held up an index finger. 'There's your problem. Based on what you've told me so far, there aren't any certainties in this case.'

'The one thing Charlie Winterton and I are fairly sure about is that Daniel Midship saw someone he recognised on his first visit to the shopping village,' Violet said. 'We believe that person was a man called Ed Hampton.'

'Right . . . so who is this guy, and where is he now?' Rachel said. 'Have you tried googling him?'

Violet laughed. 'Of course I have. That's one of the first things I did when Lucy told me his name. Unfortunately, there are scores of Ed Hamptons online, and there's no way of confirming whether any of them are the man Daniel recognised.'

'Ed Hampton,' Rachel said, leaning back and letting the name roll around on her tongue. 'It sounds like a town in the Home Counties. It doesn't give you a lot to go on, does it? And who's to say it's not an alias? If this man is a fly-by-night fraudster, there's every chance he'll have changed his name at least once.'

'I've thought about that,' Violet said. 'And if Ed Hampton is now living or working in Merrywell under a different name, it stands to reason he must be a relative newcomer to the village.'

'How did you reach that conclusion?' Rachel said.

'Three or four years ago Ed Hampton was in Leeds, dating Daniel Midship's sister, so it seems obvious to me that he must have moved to Merrywell since then.'

'Who do we know who would fit the profile?' said Matthew. 'By which I mean men of about the right age who've joined our community in the last four years.'

'There must be loads of people,' Violet said.

Matthew shook his head. 'Not necessarily. Most of the locals have lived in Merrywell all their lives, or for a very long time. Newcomers are relatively thin on the ground.'

Violet got up, opened a drawer and pulled out a notepad and pen.

'It sounds like it's time for me to compile one of my famous lists,' she said. 'Although, as a newcomer myself, I'm probably not the best person for the job.' She nodded in Matthew's direction. 'You know the local population better than anyone. Give me a name.'

Matthew took a swig of brandy.

'Tim Waldron,' he said, wriggling slightly as if uncomfortable with the idea of drawing up a written list. 'He moved to Merrywell a few months before you did, right after he got the caretaker's job at the school.'

'He's only just in the right age bracket,' Violet said, sounding dubious. 'And Tim was the one who found the body.'

'That's what he told everyone,' Matthew said. 'The question is, do we believe him? Who's to say he wasn't in the alley when Daniel Midship died? In fact, I'm sure I read somewhere that there's a fifty per cent chance that the person who finds the body is the killer.'

'If you did, it was probably in a crime novel,' Violet said. 'I don't think we can rely too heavily on that kind of fictional statistic.'

'Maybe not, but you can't deny that when Tim told us he'd found a body, we all took him at his word. The truth is, we have no idea what really happened out there. He was wearing a high-vis security jacket as well. Didn't you say you were looking for someone wearing a uniform?'

'In Tim's defence, he only started working as a security guard on the first day of the market. He wouldn't have been around the first time Daniel visited the shopping village.'

'He might have been,' Matthew said. 'I've often seen him in the courtyard in his school caretaker uniform. He regularly comes over to buy lunch from the bakery.'

'Fair enough,' Violet said. 'I'll put his name on the list. Is there anyone else you want to put forward?'

'There's Nick Penfold,' Matthew said. 'He doesn't wear a uniform, and he doesn't live in Merrywell – but he's only worked as our facilities manager for a couple of years. As I recall, he worked in Wakefield prior to that. How far is Wakefield from Leeds? Ten miles? Twelve maybe?'

Violet shuffled forward. 'Nick doesn't wear a uniform, but he does sometimes come to work in a baseball cap that has the shopping village logo on it. I saw him wearing it the other day. He also knows about the positioning of the CCTV cameras. Plus, he has full access to the security system, which means he could easily have deleted the footage from Wednesday of last week. He maintains he couldn't send it to DS Winterton because the back-up system failed, but maybe he was saying that to cover up his own actions.'

'Why is the footage from last Wednesday so important anyway?' Rachel asked.

'That's the day of Daniel's first visit,' Violet said. 'He saw someone he recognised, and DS Winterton was hoping the CCTV cameras might have picked up who it was.'

'Actually, there's something else you should know about Nick,' Matthew said.

'What?' Violet said, her ears pricking up.

'He resigned today. Handed in his notice.'

'You're kidding?' said Violet. 'That's highly suspect, don't you think? Why? Is he jumping before he's pushed?'

'I'm not sure I follow you.'

'Come off it, Matty. The last few days have been an unmitigated disaster for Nick Penfold. He's responsible for the shopping village's maintenance, and someone has just died in an unlit alleyway. Even if it turns out to be an accident, the broken sensor light may well have been a contributory factor. Add in the missing CCTV footage, and things don't look good for Nick. I'd say the traders' association would be well within their rights to discipline him, or even dismiss him.'

'That's not going to happen,' Matthew said. 'He's not leaving because he's worried he's going to get the sack. He's moving on because he's set up his own security firm. He's going to run his new business from home, in Chesterfield. Apparently, he's been planning the whole thing for months.'

'Even if that's true, I'm still going to put him on my list.'

Violet wrote down Nick's name, but with a diminishing sense of conviction. Privately, she thought this whole discussion was turning into an exercise in futility.

'Then, of course, there's Adrian,' Matthew said. 'He only appeared on the scene in the summer, so he's the newest newcomer of them all. He's a lovely bloke, but what do any of us really know about him?'

'He is very charming and likeable,' Violet said. 'And kind. Gentle. A great cook. But . . . what was it Jacqueline said as she got out of the car?'

'She said: "*let's hope for Jill's sake that everything is as it seems*,"' Rachel said. 'Maybe Jacq's right. Appearances can be deceptive. No one knows that better than her.'

'What are you saying? That Adrian is too good to be true?' Matthew said. 'Is that fair? Can we really label him as a suspect based purely on what Jacqueline thinks?'

'Probably not,' Violet said. 'Quite honestly, I've never heard anyone say a bad word about him, and I think we all agree he's extremely likeable – but maybe it's time we viewed him from a more objective standpoint.'

'We can view him as objectively as you like,' said Matthew. 'But the one thing we do know for certain is that Adrian Billings wasn't responsible for the hit-and-run. You and I were with him when Zac was run over.'

'You're right. We were,' Violet said. 'OK. I'll add him to the list, but only in the "maybe" category.'

Matthew finished off his brandy and cleared his throat.

'I've got another name for you to consider, but you're not going to like it.'

Violet narrowed her eyes. 'Go on.'

'Do you promise not to jump down my throat?'

'Just tell me, Matthew. Hit me with it.'

'Robert Dorman.' He held up his hands. 'I know . . . I can't believe I'm saying it either, but like it or not, Robert is one of the male newcomers. He opened *The Antiques Emporium* about three years ago. Prior to that, he'd worked in an auction house in Sheffield, and he was also a freelance antiques dealer – so he probably travelled all over the place.'

'Please don't ask me to put Robert's name on the list,' Violet said, as she tapped her pen against the notebook. 'He doesn't fit the profile. He's too young, and too nice. I'm sorry, but you'll have a hard time convincing me that Robert Dorman could run someone over and leave them for dead.'

'I agree,' Matthew said. 'Robert's one of the most honest people I know. I'm only throwing his name into the mix because you asked about Merrywell's male newcomers.'

Violet groaned. 'All right, then. For the purposes of completeness, I will put his name on the list, but I can't believe Robert is capable of any kind of wrongdoing.'

For a brief moment, she allowed a thread of doubt to weave its way into her thoughts and linger there. Robert hadn't been with the rest of the gang in the bookshop when Daniel Midship's body was found, and he hadn't been with Molly on the night of the hit-and-run because she'd told him she didn't want to see him. More worryingly, Robert had been acting out of character recently, lying to Molly. Could it be there was something going on with him that she didn't know about?

# Chapter 22

'Have you given any more consideration to your list of suspects?' Rachel said the following morning, as she placed a mug of coffee on the kitchen table and sat down. 'Now that you've had a night to sleep on it, have you managed to home in on a prime suspect?'

'It's not like there's a big pool of names to mull over,' Violet replied. 'There are only four people on the list: Robert, Tim, Adrian and Nick and, in the cold light of day, they all seem like perfectly normal, harmless people. What about you? Have you formed any kind of opinion overnight?'

Rachel dunked a piece of shortbread into her coffee. 'Gosh, that's way beyond my remit, darling. You're the amateur detective around here, not me.'

'You listened very attentively to everything I told you, so you must have formed an opinion. And actually, as an outsider, you're in a far better position than I am to view this objectively. If you had to pick a prime suspect from one of the four names we discussed, who would it be?'

Rachel stared up towards the ceiling as she pondered the question. 'I believe we can rule out the security guard. I've seen him at the shopping village and without wishing to sound mean, I can't picture him in the role of a smooth-talking manipulator.

He's a nice enough chap, and very friendly, but otherwise unexceptional. Definitely not the sort of man women would fall head over heels for.

'Nick is a possibility. I haven't spoken to him personally, but I have seen him swanning around the market. He seems very sure of himself, and he is good-looking, in a rough-and-tumble kind of way. And although Matthew might not agree, I do think we should question his sudden resignation.

'As for Robert . . . I'd liken him to the antique furniture he sells: solid and dependable, but slightly dull and old-fashioned. He *is* very sweet though, and men like him often worm their way into women's affections by bringing out their protective instincts.

'And then, of course, there's Adrian. I think we all agree he's extremely likeable. Charm personified, in fact – but that doesn't mean we should rule him out. Just because he's affable doesn't necessarily mean we should trust him.'

Violet grimaced. 'I hope we can, because Jill is buying a hotel with him, and that is one hell of a huge commitment.'

'It is a big step,' Rachel agreed. 'But Jill is a woman of a certain age, and there are times in life when one feels compelled to make changes . . . do something different . . . go in a completely new direction. Goodness knows there have been plenty of occasions when I've felt that way.'

Violet stared at her mother, taking in her wistful expression. 'You never said.'

'You never asked,' Rachel said, as she brushed shortbread crumbs from her sweater. 'Anyway, I'm talking about years ago. There was a time – when your dad had his career, and you were off studying – that I felt rather lost. I wish *I'd* been brave enough to embark on a new business venture back then. Not a hotel, like Jill – that would never have suited me – but for a while I did yearn for something . . . something *more*. The trouble was, I could never work out what it was I was looking for.'

'That's a shame,' said Violet.

'Not really,' Rachel said, dismissing the subject with a flick of her fingers. 'The feeling soon passed, and I got a part-time job instead. On reflection, I was always better suited to being an employee than running my own business. The point I'm trying to make is that I totally get why Jill is doing what she's doing. She's committed herself to a major change – a decision that may turn out to be a rash one – but even if it doesn't work out, she's at least had the gumption to try.

'You took a similar leap of faith when you set up *The Memory Box*, Violet. Not all new businesses succeed, but you've established yourself successfully and you're doing well. I'm proud of you.'

Violet smiled, basking briefly in her mother's praise.

'I understand what you're saying. *The Memory Box* was a risk – but I went ahead anyway because it was something I felt I *had* to do. If I hadn't tried, I would always have wondered if I could have made a go of it.'

'And it's for exactly that reason that I believe Jill is making the right decision,' Rachel said. 'Only time will tell whether she's chosen the right business, or the right investment partner – but she has my admiration, no matter how things turn out. I wish her every success.'

'The place they're buying is called the Brighouse Hotel,' Violet said. 'It's near Ashbourne. It's a lovely town, with a lot of tourists, so it's as good a location as any to run that kind of place.'

She picked up her phone, searched for 'Brighouse Hotel' + 'Ashbourne', and opened up the business's website, which included a gallery of beautiful photographs.

'Here you go, Mum. Have a look,' she said, as she handed the phone to Rachel.

'Wow! It looks fabulous,' Rachel said, as she scrolled through the images. 'What a super place. Hotels like that don't come cheap. I wonder how much it's on the market for?'

She passed the phone back to Violet, who immediately typed in a new search term: 'Brighouse Hotel' + 'for sale'.

'That's odd,' she said, as she scanned the search results. 'Nothing's come up.'

'Maybe it's a private sale. Perhaps the vendor is doing it on the QT because they don't want anyone to know they're moving on. When you think about it, Jill is selling her house in exactly the same way.'

'Well, yes . . . but Jill's not selling a business, is she?' Violet said. 'To get the best price for the hotel, you'd expect it to be advertised online. I wonder how Jill and Adrian even found out about it?'

'I expect they'll have approached some kind of agent – one with exclusive rights to sell. I bet Jill and Adrian were carefully vetted before they were allowed to view the property.'

Violet revisited the Brighouse Hotel's website and took another look at the photographs. The restaurant was small but chic, with a menu that offered contemporary cuisine. Artfully composed photographs showed colourful dishes that were beautifully presented.

The website's 'About' page explained that the hotel had been built as a private residence in the 1840s, and then converted into a hotel in the early 1920s. Violet clicked on a link to a subpage called 'Our Team'. A group photograph showed half a dozen people, including Tammy – the owner of the hotel, who Jill had pointed out when she'd shown them the pictures on her phone. The striking redhead was easy to pick out. She was sitting off to the side of the photograph, on the back row.

'That's the owner,' Violet said, holding up her phone to show the photo to her mother. 'The one with the curly red hair. Jill said her name's Tammy.'

'As the owner of the hotel, wouldn't you expect her to be sitting front centre?' Rachel said.

Violet checked the photo caption, which provided a list of staff names, all of which were hyperlinked to further subpages. Tammy's surname was Buckland. When Violet clicked on the name, she was taken to a page that included a flattering portrait shot of Tammy. She was staring into the camera with impenetrable brown eyes, and smiling with a carefully glossed mouth. Below the photo was a brief résumé of Tammy's role at the hotel.

Tammy is the newest member of our team. She runs the reception and manages front-of-house services, and has extensive customer service experience. With Tammy in charge, guests can rest assured their booking is in good hands.

Violet's mouth dropped open. 'You're not going to believe this,' she said.

# Chapter 23

'Tammy Buckland isn't the hotel's owner,' Violet said. 'According to this, she's the customer service manager.'

Rachel reached for the phone and squinted long and hard at the name, title and job description on the screen.

'That can't be right,' she said.

'You can say that again. Jill specifically told me that Tammy was the hotel's owner. She was *definitely* under that impression.'

'So, why is she listed as the customer service manager? Do you think Jill and Adrian are being taken for a ride?'

'Goodness knows,' Violet said. 'Hang on, I'm going to get a second opinion on this. I'll FaceTime Matthew and see what he makes of it.'

Matthew was in his workshop when he answered.

'I agree it's odd,' he said, after Violet had explained what they had discovered on the hotel's website, 'but let's not leap to the wrong conclusion. We should think this through for a minute . . . see if we can come up with a logical explanation.'

The three of them fell silent, mentally running through the possibilities and clarifying their thoughts.

'Perhaps Tammy Buckland showed Jill and Adrian around precisely because she *is* the customer service manager,' Rachel said. 'There's no online sales listing for the hotel – not one we can find at any rate – so it's safe to assume the owner wants to keep the sale of the hotel under wraps. Maybe Tammy is in on the secret and has been asked to conduct the viewings on the owner's behalf.'

'So why not be upfront about that?' Violet said. 'Why did she tell Jill and Adrian she was the owner?'

Matthew rubbed his chin pensively. 'Actually, we don't know that she did. They might just have assumed that she was. Think about it, if Tammy really *was* trying to pull the wool over Jill and Adrian's eyes, wouldn't she have doctored her page on the hotel's website, so that it matched her story?'

*Matthew's right*, Violet thought. *Am I looking for trouble where it doesn't exist? There has to be a logical explanation to this.*

'It's Rock House you and I are hoping to buy,' Matthew said. 'Let's not lose sight of that. I realise you have Jill's best interests at heart, but her purchase of the Brighouse Hotel is nothing to do with us.'

'And she won't be happy if she finds out you're sticking your nose into her business,' Rachel added.

'That's not what I'm doing,' Violet said, making a perfunctory effort to defend herself. 'But I have every right to be concerned, given everything that's been happening in the village recently. Daniel Midship died shortly after seeing someone he recognised, and Zac was knocked over at the cross – possibly because he witnessed what had happened to Daniel.'

'We don't know that for certain,' Matthew said.

'And even if we did, I don't see how it ties in with Jill and Adrian buying a hotel?' said Rachel.

Violet hesitated before replying, but only for a moment.

'It would make sense if the person Daniel and Zac saw at the shopping village was Adrian Billings.'

Matthew let out a sound that was a cross between a gasp and a scoff. 'Whatever you do, Violet, please do *not* say that to anyone else. There is such a thing as slander, you know. You can speculate all you like when we're discussing these things between ourselves, but you have absolutely no proof that Adrian is anything other than an upright citizen.'

'You don't really think Adrian could be this man, Ed Hampton?' Rachel said, sounding shocked.

'I don't know,' Violet said. 'There's no conclusive proof pointing to *any* of my suspects. All I have is an accumulation of information gathered over the last few days . . . bits and pieces and snippets that I'm doing my best to make sense of. Right now, I'm simply putting Adrian Billings under the spotlight and weighing up the possibilities. Where's the harm in that? We know that Daniel Midship's sister was in a troubling relationship with someone who disappeared with her savings, and now Adrian Billings has asked Jill to invest in a hotel that we have no proof is even for sale. Is it possible there's a correlation between those two scenarios?'

'No,' Matthew said, shaking his head. 'I might think differently if we knew for sure that Ed Hampton and Adrian Billings are one and the same, but we don't. You're playing guessing games, Violet.'

'Sometimes guessing games are the quickest way to get to the truth,' she said. 'Occasionally it's good to speculate – wildly if necessary. By testing theories, we might eventually work out who our prime suspect is.'

'I think you're right to be suspicious,' Rachel said. 'These kind of rackets happen more often than you might imagine. I mean, look at Jacqueline . . . the reason she's here in Merrywell is because she's been in a difficult relationship – one that, fortunately, she had the good sense to get out of.'

Matthew was beginning to look exasperated. 'What point are you trying to make, Rachel?'

'My *point* is that con artists can be very convincing, and it's easy to be taken in by them. Not everyone is as straightforward and trustworthy as you are, Matthew.'

He smiled. 'Thank you – I'll take that as a compliment – but let me play devil's advocate for a second. How do you know *I'm* not a con man? Who's to say I won't run off with your daughter's money when she sells Greengage Cottage?'

'I know instinctively that you would never betray her in that way. Violet trusts you with her life, and that's good enough for me.'

Matthew smiled. 'And I'm guessing that's precisely how Jill feels about Adrian. If *she* trusts him, that should be good enough for us. Do you really think it's fair to accuse him of being a fraudster?'

Violet sighed. Without conclusive proof of any wrongdoing, she knew Matthew would continue to defend the innocence of each and every suspect on her list.

'Forget about Adrian for a minute,' she said. 'Let's talk about why Tammy – the woman Jill believes is the owner of the hotel – is listed as the customer service manager on the website. How do you explain that?'

'I think it's like your mum said,' Matthew replied. 'For whatever reason, the real owner wants to keep the sale of the hotel hush-hush. Perhaps they don't want to be identified or involved, or maybe they're the owner in name only. It's possible they bought the hotel as an investment and now they're cashing it in. Tammy Buckland must be acting on behalf of the owner.'

'So why hasn't she told Jill and Adrian that?'

'I don't know,' Matthew said. 'But let's not get into a tizz about it. Don't forget, when someone buys a property, there are a whole series of legal channels and processes to go through. Money changes hands through a solicitor to make sure everything's above board.'

'I hope you're right, because I'd be devastated if the money we hand over to buy Rock House ends up disappearing without a trace.'

'That's not going to happen. We'll make sure we appoint a

decent solicitor – one who'll go through all the due processes rigorously. There's absolutely nothing for us to worry about.'

'But can you say the same for Jill?' Violet said. 'I truly hope Adrian Billings is genuine, but what if he *is* Ed Hampton, and he's about to pull off his latest swindle?'

Matthew let out an exasperated sigh. 'If you feel strongly about this, then perhaps you should talk to Charlie Winterton. If you really think that's the right thing to do, then go ahead – but I for one am not comfortable accusing someone based purely on a gut feeling, so please don't involve me in any of this.'

'OK,' Violet said, trying to think on her feet. 'But if it's proof you're after, then how about this . . . DS Winterton thinks the person Daniel Midship saw was wearing a uniform, correct? Or at least something distinctive that connects them to the local area.'

'Yes, I believe we've already established that.'

'Right, so, Adrian works in the kitchen at the Merrywell Manor Hotel. What if he was in the courtyard on the day of Daniel's first visit to the shopping village . . . cutting through on his way to work or something?'

Matthew grinned. 'You call that proof? What are you suggesting – that he was wearing a chef's hat? I'll admit he'd definitely stand out from the crowd in one of those, but I think it's unlikely, don't you?'

'Obviously I don't mean a chef's hat, but he could have been wearing chef's whites.'

'He could, but it's winter, which means it's cold. If Adrian was out and about in his chef's whites, wouldn't he have worn a warm coat over the top of them?'

'They'd still be visible, if the coat was open at the front.'

Matthew ran a hand through his hair – a sure sign that he was irritated.

'You seem to be giving a lot of credence to this,' he said. 'You know DS Winterton better than anyone. If you think he'll take you seriously, then go ahead and share your suspicions with him.'

'I'll think about it,' Violet said, still not sure whether she was barking up the wrong tree. 'I'm not going into work today, so I might give him a call later.'

'You are still planning to go to the bookshop?' Matthew asked. 'To collect the keys to Rock House from Jill? Or do you want me to do that?'

Violet smiled. 'It's all right, I've got to go to the bakery anyway, so I'll pick them up then. Actually, if you're free at lunchtime, I was thinking we could go to Rock House today, rather than wait until tomorrow. What do you reckon?'

Matthew smiled. 'I like the sound of that. I'm dying to see it again. I can close the workshop for an hour or two this afternoon. Would you be able to pick me up at two o'clock? That'll give us a couple of hours of daylight to have a proper look at the house and take some photos.'

'Sure,' Violet said. 'I'll see you at two.'

## Chapter 24

Violet drove over to the shopping village half an hour later and parked in the staff car park. As she strolled past Robert Dorman's van on her way to the alley, she cast a critical eye over the vehicle. It was a classic white Ford Transit with decals of the *Antiques Emporium* logo and phone number on either side. As usual, its bodywork was dusty and in need of some TLC. In many ways, the van was a lot like its owner: messy and slightly unkempt. Part of the front registration plate was missing, and Violet made a mental note to let Robert know about it. She was pretty sure that driving with a broken number plate was illegal, and an automatic MOT failure.

As she moved on, another thought occurred to her. She retraced her steps and bent down to examine the damage more closely. As well as the broken number plate, there was a scuff on the bumper.

A vision of the hit-and-run at the cross flashed through her mind.

No. Impossible. Robert would never do anything like that.

Would he?

Admittedly, his name *was* on her list of suspects, but she refused to accept that he would get involved in any kind of criminal activity.

Even so, discovering the broken number plate had unsettled her. She would go and see Robert and ask him about it, in the hope there would be an innocent explanation.

He was rearranging a display of ceramics when Violet entered the antique shop, presumably making room for a new acquisition. He spun around and smiled, leaning forward slightly as if questioning her presence.

'It's not often I see you in here, Violet. Is there something I can help you with? Are you Christmas shopping?'

'No, sorry, Robert. I dropped by to let you know that part of the number plate on the front of your van is missing. I noticed it just now as I walked through the car park.'

He frowned. 'That's a pain. I'd better get it sorted, otherwise I'll have the police pulling me over. Thanks for the heads-up. I appreciate it.'

She waited, hoping he might say more, but Robert carried on with his rearranging. She watched as he reached into a box and pulled out a ceramic floral-patterned charger.

'Beautiful, isn't it?' he said, holding up the large plate so that Violet could see it properly. 'It's a Charlotte Rhead. Absolutely gorgeous.'

'Yes, it's very nice,' she said, refusing to be sidetracked. 'But to go back to your number plate for a minute, can I ask how it got broken?'

Robert gave her an odd look as he placed the charger in the newly created display space. 'It got damaged the other day. Someone reversed into me in a car park. Why do you ask?'

'No particular reason,' she said. 'Just curious. I noticed your front bumper was scuffed too. I hope you got the person's details.'

He gave a casual shrug. 'I didn't bother. The driver did stop and wait while I checked for damage, but the only thing I could spot was a crack in the number plate. I'm not precious about my van, so I didn't make a fuss. The crack was obviously worse than

I thought, and I must have lost part of the plate on my journey home. I've not been out in the van since then.'

'So it didn't happen in the car park here?' Violet said.

Robert looked flustered. 'No . . . no. Somewhere else. On one of my buying trips.'

'When? When did it happen?'

'Erm . . . last Wednesday,' Robert said, as he pushed his glasses onto the bridge of his nose and stared through them with penetrating blue eyes. 'What's with all the questions, Violet? Why do I get the feeling I'm being cross-examined? Has Molly put you up to this?'

'Molly? No, of course not. Why would she? I'm just curious. You know what I'm like.'

'I do,' Robert said. 'And I'm also aware that your curiosity tends to kick in when you're trying to catch someone out.'

Violet blustered. 'That wasn't . . . I'm not . . .' She stopped talking and held up her hands in submission. 'I'm just here to make you aware of the number plate problem. Sorry, Robert. I'll let you get on with your work.'

As she left the *Antiques Emporium* it dawned on her that instead of clearing things up, her conversation with Robert had muddied the waters even further. The hit-and-run had happened on Thursday evening. If Robert had last used the van on Wednesday, then there was nothing to worry about. But was he telling the truth?

As Violet entered *Books, Bakes and Cakes* and approached the bookshop counter, she toyed with the idea of asking Jill about the hotel. Should she come straight out with it and tell her what she'd found out about Tammy Buckland, or adopt a more softly-softly approach? Or was it best to say nothing at all?

Jill and Eric were both dealing with customers, so she stood aside, waiting to catch Jill's eye. As Eric engaged someone in conversation, Jill spotted Violet and took the opportunity to slip away from the counter into a quiet corner of the bookshop, where the two of them could talk privately.

'I'm here for the key,' Violet said, keeping her voice low. 'If you've no objections, Matthew and I would like to do the second viewing this afternoon.'

'That's fine,' Jill said. 'I've been carrying them around in my pocket, waiting for you to come in.'

She smiled furtively as she dug around in her jacket and pulled out a pair of keys. 'These are the spares, so there's no rush to get them back to me. Keep them over the weekend. That way you can have a third or even a fourth viewing, if you want to.'

'Thanks, Jill. That's really kind of you. I'll return them to you – discreetly – on Monday morning.'

'Do you think you'll have come to a decision by then?'

'I imagine so. To be honest, we've pretty much made up our minds to buy the house, but there are a few things we want to check before we make a final decision.'

'Take as long as you need,' Jill said. 'There's a lot less urgency now.'

'Oh dear.' Violet knitted her brow. 'I hope your offer on the hotel hasn't fallen through?'

'No, quite the opposite. It's all systems go. Subject to us paying a small exclusivity fee and a ten per cent holding deposit by the end of play today, the owner has agreed to take the hotel off the market. She's happy for us to complete on the sale once our funds are available.'

'I see,' Violet said, trying to sound pleased but feeling instantly nervous on Jill's behalf. 'It sounds as if the seller is being unusually flexible and cooperative. You are sure it's going to be a legally binding agreement? You're not going to lose your deposit if you can't complete within a set timescale, are you?'

'No, we've been assured we'll get a refund if we're unable to exchange contracts for some reason. It's been agreed that the existing staff will continue to run the hotel until such time as we can take over. We'll probably keep several members of the team on anyway. Adrian and I won't be able to run the place on our own.'

'Right, that's . . . good news,' Violet said. 'Just so long as you know what you're doing. Buying the hotel is a huge financial undertaking, so I'm sure you must have considered it long and hard before committing yourself.'

'Yes, Adrian and I have talked about nothing else for weeks. He has an excellent solicitor – which is good, because the conveyancing process is all very new to me. I inherited Overton Cottage from Mum, so I've never actually bought a property before.'

Violet took a deep breath. 'Jill, are you absolutely sure about all of this? About the hotel, and most of all about Adrian?'

Jill took a step back. 'Of course I am. Why would you say that? Are you trying to hurt me, Violet?'

'No, hurting you is the last thing I'd want to do. I'm just checking that you're a hundred per cent certain about everything.'

'Why wouldn't I be?' Jill sounded stroppy now, although she was doing her best to keep her voice at low volume. 'I'll have you know, this is the chance of a lifetime for me. I've waited years to meet someone like Adrian, and he and I are in this together. We're buying the hotel on a fifty-fifty basis, equally committed – both financially and emotionally. I'm sure your heart's in the right place, Violet, but you really do need to learn to think before you speak. Sometimes you are much too forthright for your own good.'

Violet had been going to say something about Tammy Buckland's role at the hotel, but it was clear from Jill's reaction to her previous question that any further meddling would not be welcome.

'I'm sorry if I've offended you,' she said, opting to say nothing further for now. 'That wasn't my intention.'

'Perhaps not,' Jill said, her face red with anger. 'But even so, you *have* offended me. Now . . . please have a good look around

Rock House – and if you and Matthew would like to buy it, I'd be very happy to sell it to you. On the other hand, if you're not interested, that's not a problem either. I'll soon find another buyer for the house if you don't want it. Goodbye, Violet. Please return the keys when you're ready.'

And with that, Jill marched over to the shop counter to serve a waiting customer. She was upset and furious; that much was obvious. Hanging her head in shame, Violet left the bookshop – admonishing herself for once again saying the wrong thing.

# Chapter 25

Violet didn't like the feeling of uncertainty that came with not knowing who to trust. Overall, she liked to think of herself as dependable – someone who looked for the best in everyone, rather than the worst, and for that reason she was deeply troubled by the niggling doubts she'd been harbouring over the last few days. The raw truth was, she hadn't completely eliminated any of the names on her list of suspects – although Tim Waldron did seem to be the least likely culprit, so she had pretty much ruled him out. That left Nick, Robert and Adrian – and currently the focus of her attention was fixed firmly on the latter. She needed to establish once and for all whether he was on the level, and the fastest way to do that would be to run her half-formed notions past DS Winterton.

When she got home from *Books, Bakes and Cakes*, she unloaded her shopping and put her phone on charge ready to make the call to Charlie. As she plugged it in, she noticed an unread text from Eric Nash, sent ten minutes earlier.

Is there something happening with Jill that I should know about?

Violet cringed. She was tempted to ignore the message – answering it would only lead to more questions. On the other hand, she knew from past experience that Eric was as persistent and stubborn as she was. He wouldn't give up asking, even if she chose to ignore him.

What do you mean?

Hopefully, her four-word reply would elicit more information from Eric to help her judge how much he suspected.

I saw the two of you talking a little while ago. I don't know what you said to her, but she's been in a foul mood ever since.

To avoid a series of messages bouncing back and forth, Violet decided to bite the bullet and call him.

'Hi Eric,' she said when he answered. 'I thought I'd ring, rather than text. I'm sorry if I've upset Jill.'

'What on earth did you say to her?' Eric said. 'She's been storming around the shop like she's about to explode.'

'I think she took offence at something I said about Adrian.'

'What? What did you say about him?'

'Nothing much, just a throwaway remark,' she said, being deliberately vague. 'I asked whether she was sure about him. It was wrong of me, and I apologised – but I could see she'd taken the huff.'

There was a moment of silence on the other end of the phone.

'What made you ask that?' Eric said. 'Is there something about Adrian that concerns you?'

Violet had no way of explaining herself without giving him the full story, which she wasn't willing to do.

'I really can't say.'

'Can't, or won't?'

'Look,' Violet replied, trying to avoid being drawn any further into the conversation and ending up saying something she'd regret. 'I hardly know Adrian – so I'm in no position to have an opinion on him.'

When Eric spoke again, she noticed that he had lowered his voice.

'I don't know him very well either, but that doesn't stop me wondering about him. On the face of it, Adrian's great – a top bloke – and since she met him, Jill's been the happiest I've ever known her.'

'But?' said Violet, wondering where this was heading.

Eric sighed. 'I'm slightly concerned about the speed at which things are moving. They'd only known each other for a few months when they moved in together. Or, more precisely, when he moved in with her.'

Violet wondered what Eric would think if he knew about the couple's plans to buy the hotel.

'Have you talked to Jill about this?' she said.

'I don't feel it's my place to. She and I have to work together. If I wade in with my opinion and upset her, it might create an atmosphere in the shop.'

'But you have doubts about Adrian?' Violet said, desperate to hear Eric's thoughts, but being careful not to influence him either way.

'Not doubts as such,' he said. 'It's more a lack of certainty. I feel awful saying this, because Adrian's been nothing but kind to me... but I can't help thinking we know very little about the man.'

*I'm learning more and more by the minute*, thought Violet. *At least I think I am.*

'We know he and Jill met at a bereavement group, and they've both lost siblings this year,' she said. 'And we know that Adrian works at the Merrywell Manor Hotel.'

'He does for now,' Eric said. 'But that's only a temporary job. I've got a friend who works there, and he says that Adrian will be laid off once Christmas is over.'

'What does your friend do at the hotel?'

'He works in the office. Looks after the accounts.'

'Including the payroll?'

'Probably,' Eric said. 'Why?'

'Do you think you could ask him for Adrian's date of birth?'

She heard the ever-so-virtuous Eric suck in his breath. 'That would be a serious breach of confidentiality. It would break all the rules on data protection. My mate could be sacked if he was caught giving me that kind of information.'

'OK, OK,' Violet said. 'It was just a thought.'

'What do you want to know his date of birth for anyway?'

'Like you, I have a few doubts about Adrian,' Violet said, doing her best to defend the indefensible. 'If I were to do a little digging, it might put both our minds at rest. If I knew Adrian's birth date I could look him up online. I don't need the year – I can estimate that. Just the day and month will do.'

'I can't just ring up out of the blue and ask for someone's date of birth. Nor can I expect someone to risk their job in order to satisfy my curiosity.'

'Your friend isn't going to lose his job, Eric. Why don't you say you want to surprise Adrian on his birthday, but you don't know when it is.'

'The first thing my mate will want to know is why I haven't asked Jill for that information.'

'In which case, you can say you're planning a joint surprise for them both, and that you don't want Jill to know.'

Eric whistled through his teeth. 'Gee whizz, Violet. You have a devious mind.'

'I know its slightly underhand, but if I can find out when Adrian's birthday is, I can check whether he's all he purports to be.'

Eric sighed. 'I want it on record that I'm not happy about this. It's not the sort of thing I'd usually have anything to do with – but I am concerned about Jill, so leave it with me. I'll have a think . . . see what I can do. I'm not making any promises, mind. When it comes to ducking and diving and subterfuge, I'm hopeless.'

'Try your best, Eric. That's all I can ask.'

'I've upset Jill,' Violet said, as she drove Matthew to Rock House later that afternoon.

'Why?' He turned to look at her. 'What have you said to her? I thought you were going to keep your suspicions to yourself for now.'

'I didn't air any suspicions. I just asked whether she was sure about everything.'

'When you say *everything*, do you mean buying the hotel, or Adrian?'

'Both,' Violet said, looking at him out of the corner of her eye.

'Seriously?' Matthew shook his head. 'How would you feel if someone questioned *our* relationship, or the wisdom of us buying a house together? Actually . . . you don't need to answer that, because I know exactly how you'd react. You'd be livid.'

'Yes, I would,' Violet said, as she drove past the church and turned off toward Rock House. 'I'd be absolutely furious. But you know what? No one in Merrywell would ever ask that question – because they know you. They've known you all your life. Unfortunately, the same can't be said of Adrian.'

'Being new to Merrywell isn't a crime. You're a relative newcomer yourself, remember?'

'I can't find Adrian on any of the top five social media platforms,' Violet said, ignoring Matthew's barbed comment. 'In fact, as far as I can tell, he has no online presence whatsoever.'

'So what?' Matthew said. 'You can't blame him for that, not with the way social media has been going lately. I'll admit we don't know much about Adrian's background, but we don't need to. *We're* not in a relationship with him. If Jill wants to check whether or not he's genuine, that's up to her. She's a grown woman, and more than capable of making her own decisions. It's not your place to advise her.'

Violet pulled onto the driveway at Rock House and parked in front of the garage. 'That's me told then. You obviously think I'm on the wrong track with Adrian, so there's no point me saying any more, is there?'

'I'm not saying you're on the wrong track, but I do think you should focus on your own life and stop worrying about other people. I've known Jill for years, and I'm sorry to say she's always carried a lingering sadness around with her – as if life hadn't quite turned out as she'd expected it to. Things have changed for the better since she's met Adrian. She's more confident, and she has a far more positive outlook. You can think and say what you like about him, but you have to give Adrian *some* of the credit for that. For the first time in her adult life, Jill seems happy. Let her savour it while she can.'

Violet chewed her bottom lip. 'You're angry with me.'

'A little bit,' Matthew replied. 'Don't get me wrong; I love that you care about people, but there are times – like now – when you overstep the mark.'

'I try not to,' Violet said, feeling too emotionally drained to justify her actions. 'But I know I go too far sometimes. Do you think Jill will forgive me?'

Matthew smiled. 'She will when you tell her we want to buy Rock House. Assuming we still do when we've had another look around. Come on, Brewster. Cheer up. Let's go inside and see what the place looks like in the daylight.'

## Chapter 26

Their exploration of Rock House went well. They scrutinised the house carefully, measuring and assessing the condition of each and every room, ending their inspection in the wood-panelled sitting room downstairs, where they hunkered down on the rose-pink carpet. After discussing their findings, they came to the conclusion that the house was a gem of a find, and they'd be fools not to offer Jill the full asking price immediately.

As they'd both skipped lunch, they decided to head to the *Books, Bakes and Cakes* café for a cup of tea and a sandwich – but their first port of call would be the bookshop. They would find Jill and, providing Eric wasn't within earshot, make their offer on the house and agree to get the ball rolling as soon as possible.

'Let's just hope she's not changed her mind about selling to us,' Matthew said, as – arms linked – they entered the shopping village.

'She wouldn't do that, would she?' Violet said, panicking slightly at the thought of losing the house.

'She might do, after what you said about Adrian.'

'Jill won't let *that* get in the way of a sale,' Violet said, her confidence restored. 'And for your information, I don't regret saying what I did. I agree I should have been more subtle in my approach, but Jill's situation does worry me – so I'm glad I've raised my concerns, even if they do prove to be unfounded.'

'All right, but please don't mention them again today. You've aired your views – now it's time to keep your thoughts to yourself. We're here to make a successful bid on Rock House. That's our priority. Agreed?'

'Roger that,' Violet said. 'Let's do it.'

They entered *Books, Bakes and Cakes* through the bookshop portion of the premises. Eric was behind the counter, looking slightly harassed. His son, Tom, was over in the contemporary fiction area, shelving new stock. Of Jill, there was no sign.

'It doesn't look like she's here,' Violet said, stating the obvious. 'Shall we go to the café and get something to eat and hope she's here when we come back?'

'Why don't we just ask Eric where she is?'

She pulled a reluctant face. 'He'll want to know why we're looking for her, and I don't want to have to lie to him.'

'Then leave it to me,' Matthew said. 'I'll do the talking.'

They approached the till, where Eric was ringing up a sale. Despite looking tired, he was smiling contentedly. Business was booming, and the last few days of the Christmas market were bringing in even more customers than usual for the time of year.

'Hi, Eric,' Matthew said. 'Is Jill around?'

Eric's smile disappeared. 'No, she's not. Is it her you need to speak to, or can I help you with something?'

'She's been trying to locate a book for me . . . *Frank Lloyd Wright: Writings and Buildings*. It was published in 1960, so it's out-of-print, but Jill was going to track down a second-hand copy.'

'She hasn't mentioned it, but if you give me a couple of minutes, I'll see if she's got it on order.'

'It's OK,' Matthew said. 'There's no rush for it. I can see that you're busy. I'll call another time when Jill's back at work.'

'I'm not sure when that's going to be,' Eric said, sounding disconcerted.

'Is everything all right, Eric?' Violet said. 'Jill was here earlier . . . I thought she was supposed to be working all day.'

'She was, but about an hour after you and she had words, she announced she wasn't feeling well and said she was going home.'

Violet's stomach churned. 'I hope she's not unwell because of something *I* said.'

'I doubt it,' Eric replied. 'In fact, I don't think she was ill at all. She looked fine to me. In my opinion, there was nothing wrong with her.'

'I wouldn't have thought Jill was the sort to throw a sickie,' said Matthew.

'She's not,' Eric said. 'I suspect there's something going on that she hasn't told me about, although I'm sure she'll put me in the picture when the time's right. We're really busy, so when she went home, I had to call in the cavalry. I've recruited Tom to help for the rest of the afternoon, although I don't think he's too thrilled about it . . .'

'I'm not,' said Tom, who had returned to the counter with an empty cardboard box, having finished his shelf-stacking duties. 'I can stay until six o'clock at the latest, Dad. After that, you'll have to cope without me.'

'I hope Jill's all right,' said Violet.

'So do I,' Eric said. 'I rang her a few minutes ago, to check on her and find out whether she'll be in tomorrow, but her phone's switched off. I am slightly worried about her, to be honest. She's been out of sorts for a few days. It's late night opening tonight, otherwise I'd have called in at Overton Cottage, to see how she is.'

'Matthew and I are going for a sarnie in the café now, but we can drop by Jill's house on our way home. Make sure she's OK.'

Matthew shot Violet a look, which she ignored.

'Only if it's not out of your way,' Eric said. 'I'm sure she'll be OK. She's probably just having a kip.'

'I'll text you later to let you know how she is.'

'Thanks,' said Eric. 'And Violet?'

'Yes?'

'I did as you asked . . .' he said, dropping his voice. 'I rang my mate at the hotel. He wasn't able to tell me when you-know-who's birthday is – but not because he was worried about data protection. He couldn't tell me, because Adrian isn't an employee and therefore, he's not on the payroll.'

'But he does work there?' Violet said.

'Yes, but on a freelance basis. Adrian gets paid by the hour, and submits a weekly invoice under the name of his business, Tamed Forager.'

'Thanks,' Violet said. 'That's really useful. If he has his own company, I'll be able to check it, and him, out. Hopefully, whatever I learn will provide the reassurance we've both been looking for. Cheers, Eric.'

He nodded. 'The only thing I need to be reassured about right now is that Jill is OK and that she'll be here in the morning, bright and early.'

As they left the bookshop, Violet heard someone calling her name.

'Violet! Wait up,' Robert Dorman was pushing through the crowds towards her. 'I'm glad I spotted you. I know we talked earlier, but I wonder . . . might I have another word?'

'We're about to go into the café,' she said. 'Do you fancy joining us?'

Robert frowned. 'It's very noisy in there. I'd prefer it if we talked in the *Antiques Emporium*? I won't keep you long, I promise.'

'You go and have a chat with Robert, and I'll order the food,' Matthew said.

So, for the second time that day, Violet found herself in the antiques shop. As usual, it was crammed with an eclectic and quirky mix of items. Traditional pieces of brown furniture stood alongside retro G-Plan tables and teak sideboards. Inside the door a display of kitchenalia was dominated by a huge pair of vintage shop scales. There were piles of exquisite antique quilts and Welsh blankets, and row upon row of glass cabinets filled with silver, glass, ceramics and other intriguing curios. Robert definitely had an eye for quality.

'So, what's up?' Violet said, feeling unexpectedly apprehensive about what Robert was going to say. 'What is it you want to talk to me about?'

'I should have said something when you were here earlier,' he said, leaning on the front counter, which was half-covered with boxes. 'I know Molly thinks the world of you, Violet, and I know she confides in you . . .'

Violet stuffed her hands in her pockets, waiting for him to continue. If Robert wanted to initiate a conversation about Molly, it was up to him to do the talking.

'I . . . I wonder if she's said anything to you?'

He put his head on one side and looked at her expectantly.

She smiled noncommittally. 'Molly and I work together, so we talk all the time, about lots of things. If you're asking about something in particular, you'll need to be more specific.'

Robert cleared his throat and adjusted the position of one of the boxes on his desk, lining it up neatly against the others.

'I'm worried,' he said. 'She's not been herself the last few days. I think . . . maybe . . . she's gone off me.'

Violet pulled her hands from her pockets and placed them on the edge of the counter.

'It's Molly you should be talking to about this, not me,' she said. 'And if something has gone wrong between the two of you, perhaps you should ask yourself why that is.'

'Oh God,' Robert said, pulling off his glasses and running a hand up and down his face. 'This is all my fault – I know it is. She came here the other day, when I wasn't here. She rang me and asked where I was, and I told the tiniest of white lies.'

He gave Violet a sideways look and grimaced guiltily.

'I thought I'd got away with it,' he said, 'but Molly's been off with me ever since . . . withdrawn and distant.'

Violet felt a twinge of frustration. If Molly had been standing alongside Robert right now, she might have been tempted to bang their heads together – although that would be difficult, because Robert was very tall and Molly was only five foot two.

'Don't ever underestimate Molly,' she said. 'She's very astute, and she's been lied to in the past, which means she has a built-in fib detector. If you want things to go back to how they were between you, you'll need to come clean and admit to Molly that you lied.'

'I can't!' Robert said, clouting the counter in exasperation. 'If I do, she'll want to know why – and I can't tell her the truth, not about this. That's why I need to ask a favour of you, Violet.'

'What kind of favour?'

'Will you talk to her . . . persuade her that she can trust me?'

Violet raised an eyebrow. 'I'm sorry, Robert, but you've been behaving erratically over the last few days. If you want me to put in a good word for you, you're going to have to convince me that Molly *can* trust you. If you aren't able to do that, then I'm afraid you're on your own.'

He tilted his head and sighed. 'You know what . . . forget it. Forget I said anything. Molly can trust me – I promise you that. She means the world to me.'

'Then you need to tell her that. Talk to her. Put her mind at rest.'

'Believe me, I will,' he snapped. 'Just not now. There are things I need to sort out first.'

'OK.' Violet took a step back. 'I'm sure you know what you're doing. Just don't leave it too late.'

# Chapter 27

When she got to the café, Matthew announced that he'd ordered a pot of tea for two, and club sandwiches – but by the time the food arrived, Violet had lost her appetite. She ended up sliding one half of her sandwich onto Matthew's plate, watching as he wolfed it down.

'What did Robert want?' he said, as he poured himself a second cup of tea.

'He asked me to put in a good word for him, with Molly.'

Matthew pulled a face. 'Why would you need to do that? I thought the two of them were besotted with each other. They are, aren't they?'

'They appear to have hit a rough patch, and neither of them seems willing to talk it through. I'm trying to keep out of it, hoping the situation will resolve itself.'

Matthew laughed. 'Young love, eh? All the angst and misunderstandings. I'm glad we're not like that.'

'You and me both.'

Violet smiled, but deep down she was worried. Why was Robert being so uncommunicative? What was it that he was so keen to hide?

After leaving the café, they had a quick browse around the market stalls before heading for the exit.

'Are we really going over to Jill's house?' Matthew said, as they left the shopping village and turned onto the main street. 'We don't have to make an offer on Rock House today. There's no rush. If Jill's not feeling well, it can wait another day or two.'

'I'd like her to know that we want the house,' Violet said. 'And besides, I promised Eric we'd go over there to check she's OK.'

Matthew gave a resigned nod, and they set off in a westerly direction, towards Overton Cottage. There was a lot of traffic in the village. Most of the cars were heading to the Christmas market, which was good news for the traders, but Violet couldn't help but look forward to January, when Merrywell would once again become the sleepy village she was used to.

There was no sign of life at Overton Cottage – no plume of smoke drifting from the chimney, and no lights on inside, despite the gloomy winter half-light. There was no sign of Jill's car either – although it was possible it was parked in the garage.

Violet rattled the door-knocker and waited. After a minute, when the door remained firmly closed, she knocked again.

'If she's not feeling well, she could be in bed,' Matthew said. 'Don't bother knocking again. She obviously doesn't want to be disturbed.'

Violet looked up at the first-floor windows.

'The curtains are open,' she said. 'I don't think she's in. Let's go and see whether the car's in the garage.'

She marched over to the small window at the side of the brick-built structure, and Matthew followed behind at a less urgent pace.

'It's empty,' Violet said, as she pressed her face against the windowpane. 'No car.'

'Mystery solved then. She's obviously gone out.'

Violet scrunched up her nose. 'So why did she tell Eric she was feeling unwell?'

'Maybe she and Adrian have had to go and sign some documents at the solicitors,' Matthew said.

'On a Saturday?'

'All right, maybe there's been some other kind of emergency that she didn't want Eric to know about.'

Violet pulled out her phone and called Jill's number. It went straight to voicemail.

'It must be switched off,' she said.

'Or it could be she's not in a position to answer.'

A vertical worry line appeared between Violet's eyebrows. 'You don't think she's had an accident, do you?'

Matthew gave an exasperated smile. 'I was thinking of something a lot less calamitous. More along the lines of her phone running out of charge, or perhaps she's in the car . . . driving.'

Violet bit her bottom lip, unable to shake off a feeling of impending doom.

'You'd better send a quick text to Eric to let him know she's not here,' Matthew said. 'If it'll make you feel any better, we can call again later and see if she's back. For now, let's go home, have another cup of tea and wrap some Christmas presents.'

Later, as they sat on the sofa watching a Christmas movie on TV, Violet received a WhatsApp message from Lucy Midship.

> I wanted to let you know that I've received the video from the police and I watched it today. As predicted, it made me cry – but it's also something I will treasure always. Dad and I hadn't seen much of each other recently, so it's good to know he was thinking of me and cherishing the memories of the Christmases we spent together when I was a kid. He wasn't to know it, but making the video was one of the last things he did, and it's good that I was in his thoughts. Thanks for making sure I got a copy.

Violet felt a warm glow of satisfaction as she showed Matthew the message.

'It must have been a hard watch for her,' he said. 'A poignant reminder that she'll never get another message from her dad.'

'At least she'll have the video as a memento. I'm glad the police have sent it at last.'

They paused the movie so that Matthew could make a fresh pot of tea. While he was in the kitchen, Violet used her phone to check Jill Atherstone's social media accounts – half hoping there would be a post of her having a meal somewhere or enjoying an afternoon out with Adrian – but there were no new updates on her Facebook or Instagram accounts. Violet scrolled through some of the more recent photos, noting once again that Adrian was noticeable only by his absence. She knew that some people preferred not to post pictures of themselves online. Everyone had the right to protect their privacy, including Adrian Billings, but it was a pity there were no images of him at all. If there had been a photo, Violet could have sent it to Lucy Midship to ascertain once and for all whether he was the man she knew as Ed Hampton.

Out in the kitchen, she heard the rattling of cutlery and the kettle coming to the boil. Before Matthew returned with the tea, and before she had time to talk herself out of it, she sent a reply to Lucy.

> I'm so glad you received the video and got some comfort from seeing it. It brought tears to my eyes when I saw it, so I can only begin to imagine how you must have felt when you watched it.

> When we met the other day, you mentioned someone called Ed Hampton. Can you tell me what he looked like?

Lucy's reply pinged back as Matthew brought in a loaded tea tray, including a plate of chocolate chip cookies.

Violet smirked. 'Those biscuits are supposed to be for Mum,' she said, as he placed the tray on the coffee table. 'They're her favourite.'

'What the eye doesn't see, the heart doesn't grieve over,' Matthew said. 'Besides, your Mum's eating at the Merrywell Manor Hotel again this evening, courtesy of Jacqueline. She'll be having something a lot posher than shop-bought chocolate chip cookies.'

As he poured the tea, Violet glanced at the latest WhatsApp message from Lucy.

It's a few years ago, and I didn't know Ed very well, but I do recall he was quite tall, with blue eyes and glasses. His hair was short, and a sort of mousy colour. Why? Do you think you might have seen him?

Violet tapped out a quick reply.

Possibly. I'm not sure.

The response had obviously piqued Lucy's interest, because she messaged again immediately.

I can ask Aunty Helen whether she still has any photos of him, if that helps?

Violet felt a surge of anticipation as she sent her reply.

That would be really useful. ☺ Thank you.

Matthew picked up the remote control. 'Are you ready for the second half of the film?'

'Yeah, sure,' Violet replied, as she dunked one of the biscuits into her tea cup. 'Let it roll.'

When the film had finished, Violet cooked some pasta, and then they got some fresh air and after-dinner exercise by taking a walk around the village. At Violet's insistence, they swung by Overton Cottage again, but their knock at the door went unanswered once more.

'They could have gone away for the weekend,' Matthew said.

'Maybe,' Violet said. 'If they've paid the deposit today, perhaps they've gone somewhere to celebrate. They might even have gone to Ashbourne to stay at the Brighouse Hotel.'

'Tell me again how they've ended up exchanging contracts already? I thought their purchase of the hotel was subject to Jill selling Rock House.'

'They've paid a holding fee and a ten per cent deposit, but I don't think they've actually exchanged contracts yet,' Violet said, as she outlined the arrangements that had been agreed with the hotel.

Matthew looked dubious. 'That sounds very unorthodox. I'm surprised the solicitors let them go ahead. If Jill and Adrian can't raise the rest of the money in time to complete on their purchase, they'll lose the deposit.'

'Not according to Jill. She said the owners were happy to wait as long as it took.'

Matthew gave a brief shrug. 'Maybe there are different rules when you're purchasing a business premises,' he said, sounding unconvinced. 'But I don't think our solicitor would be happy if we tried to get a similar arrangement for the purchase of Rock House.'

They swung past the White Hart, calling in for a swift drink before wending their way home to Greengage Cottage. Rachel was in the living room watching television when they arrived, having returned from her dinner with Jacqueline.

As Violet pottered around in the kitchen making a mug of hot chocolate for her mum, she heard the distinctive ping of another WhatsApp message.

Unfortunately, Aunty Helen says she tore up her photos of Ed (a decision she has never regretted!). Like me, she described him as tall with pale blue eyes and said he was 'sweet' (although how she can still think that after what he did to her, I've no idea). I described Ed's hair as mousy, but Helen says it was quite dark, but starting to go grey at the sides. He had a sister, but we only ever met her a couple of times (Aunty Helen took an instant dislike to her).

That was interesting. Ed had a sister . . . the same as Adrian. Violet rattled off a reply.

The guy I'm talking about had a sister too, but she died.

Violet carried the hot chocolate into the living room and gave it to her mother, along with what was left of the biscuits. As they chatted about their plans for the following day, Lucy's reply popped onto the screen of Violet's phone.

She sat bolt upright as she read the message. Adrenaline was rushing through her body, her ears were roaring, and even the sound of her own breathing seemed unnaturally loud.

'What's the matter, sweetheart?' said Rachel. 'You look like someone's poked you with a cattle prod.'

Matthew placed a hand on Violet's shoulder. 'Are you OK, love?'

Violet's mind was whirring, and her hand shook as she passed her phone to Matthew so that he could read the latest message from Lucy.

That's a shame. Helen never liked Tamsin, but none of us would have wished her dead.

'Ed Hampton's sister was called Tamsin,' Violet said. 'Tamsin. Tammy. Very similar names, don't you think?'

## Chapter 28

'Are you saying Tammy Buckland is Ed Hampton's sister?' Matthew said.

'She could be,' Violet said.

'OK,' said Rachel, drawing out the last syllable as she absorbed this latest revelation. 'But even if you're right, we still don't know who Ed Hampton is.'

'No, but I think we can assume he's somewhere in the village. He must be living or working in Merrywell under a different name.'

Matthew rubbed his chin. 'We can eliminate Adrian, then. His sister's dead, isn't she?'

'That's what he told us,' Violet said.

She revisited the website of the Brighouse Hotel, navigated to the page featuring Tammy, and saved the photo. Then she WhatsApped it to Lucy with the caption: 'Is this her?'

Lucy's reply pinged back almost immediately.

Yes, that's definitely Tamsin. Why, have you seen her? Do you think she was there when Dad died?

Violet thought carefully about her reply, not wanting to alarm Lucy unnecessarily.

> I've not seen her myself, so I don't know. I'll talk to the police. They can speak to Tamsin to determine where she was on the day your dad died. I'll ask them to keep you updated.

Giving a loud yawn, Rachel picked up her mug of hot chocolate and got to her feet. 'Much as I'd love to stick around to find out what's going on, it's been a long day and I'm tired. I think I'll go up . . . have an early night.'

Violet stood up and gave her mother a hug. 'Night, night,' she said. 'I promise I'll give you a full update in the morning.'

As Rachel exited the room, Violet's phone began to ring. She looked at the screen and frowned.

'That's odd. It's Robert Dorman.'

'Why is he calling at this time of night?' Matthew said.

'I don't know, and I'm not sure I want to.'

Violet's stomach was churning as she answered the call. 'Hello, Robert. Is everything OK?'

'Yes . . . yes, everything's fine. I'm sorry for ringing so late, but I wanted to apologise for the way I snapped at you earlier. I've been feeling guilty about it all evening.'

Violet hoped that a snappy tone of voice was the only thing Robert had to feel guilty about.

'I also want you to know how much I care about Molly,' Robert continued. 'I love her – which is why I was hoping you'd talk to her. To reassure her.'

'If you don't mind, I'd prefer to keep out of it,' she replied. 'If something's gone wrong between the two of you, you need to work things out between yourselves.'

Robert sighed. 'You don't trust me, do you?'

'I didn't say that.'

'You didn't need to. I can hear it in your voice. You think I'm hiding something.'

'Well, you are, aren't you?'

'I . . .' He hesitated briefly before continuing. 'Yes. You're right. I am, but it's nothing bad. Honestly it isn't. If I let you into a secret, do you promise not to say anything?'

Violet winced, wondering what this 'secret' was that Robert wanted to share. Was she better off not knowing?

When he spoke again, there was a pleading note to his voice. 'Please, Violet. Hear me out. I had to lie. I had no choice.'

Pressing the phone to her ear, Violet sat back and listened as Robert told her everything.

# Chapter 29

'What was that all about?' Matthew said, when the call was over.

'I'm sworn to secrecy,' Violet said, pulling an imaginary zip across her lips. 'All I can say is, the conversation has affirmed my faith in Robert.'

'I didn't realise any affirmation was required. Have you been having doubts about him then?'

'I did have concerns, but only briefly,' Violet said, feeling a rush of shame and regret over her misgivings about Robert. She would make it up to him by complying with his request: she would keep his secret, and do everything in her power to convince Molly of Robert's trustworthiness.

Now, having eliminated her inchoate suspicions about the young antiques dealer, it was time to focus her attention elsewhere.

'I think it's time I rang Charlie Winterton,' she announced.

Matthew went to stand with his back to the log burner. 'Before you do, tell me what you're thinking.'

Violet tapped her chin. 'We now have confirmation that Tammy Buckland is Ed Hampton's sister – which means, in all probability, Ed Hampton is here in Merrywell, operating under an assumed name.'

'OK.' Matthew frowned. 'But what name? Who do you suspect? Adrian?'

Violet thought carefully before setting out her hypothesis.

'Yes. We've established that Tammy Buckland is Tamsin, so it's reasonable to assume that Adrian must be Ed, and that the two of them are working their scams together.'

Matthew let out a long breath. 'How certain are you about this?'

'I'd say . . . eighty per cent.'

Violet held up her left hand and began counting things off on her fingers. 'First of all, we know Adrian Billings is working at the Merrywell Manor Hotel on a self-employed basis. He submits an invoice to them every week in the name of his business – Tamed Foragers. When I heard what his company was called, I assumed he'd named it after his interest in cooking with wild and foraged foods – but what if it has a different meaning altogether? Tamed Forager. Tamed. Tam-Ed.'

Matthew's jaw dropped as he absorbed the significance of the word.

'And "foragers" could have a hidden meaning too,' he said, as he typed out a search on his phone. 'Here's the definition . . . foragers are "people or animals that go from place to place searching for things they can eat or use".'

'I'd say that describes Ed and Tammy to a tee,' Violet said. 'They're "people who go from place to place" in search of vulnerable people they can take advantage of. They swindled Daniel Midship's sister out of ten grand a few years ago, and who's to say how many other victims they've targeted since then. Jill could be the latest of many.'

'If we're right . . . if *you're* right . . . Adrian and Tammy have had to invest a lot of time and effort into this latest scheme with Jill. Adrian's had to foster a serious and relatively long-term relationship with her, and Tammy has had to get a job at the Brighouse Hotel. It's an audacious plan, I'll give you that, but also one that is fraught with difficulty.'

'They've obviously been playing the long game, hoping nothing goes wrong,' Violet said. 'They were probably aiming to rip Jill off to the tune of five hundred thousand pounds or so – in other words, half the cost of a hotel that's not actually for sale. However, because of Zac Wallis, I suspect they've had to scale down and bring forward their plan.'

'There's one glaring problem with that theory,' Matthew said. 'You and I were with Adrian when the hit-and-run occurred.'

'True. We were with *Adrian* – conveniently on hand to confirm his alibi, in fact. But where was Tammy Buckland that evening?'

'Driving the car that mowed down Zac Wallis?' Matthew said.

'Got it in one.'

Violet picked up her phone, searched for the Companies House website, and clicked on 'Find company information'. In the 'Search the register' box, she typed *Tamed Forager*. On the company information page she clicked on the 'People' tab. One name was listed twice – once as a 'director' and again as the company 'secretary'. That name was Tamsin Buckland.

Violet slapped her hands together. 'That's it,' she said. 'Finally, we have hard evidence of a connection between Adrian and Tammy Buckland. Tamed Forager – the company name Adrian has been using on his invoices – is owned by Tamsin Buckland.'

'Bloody hell!' Matthew ran his hands through his hair. 'Charlie Winterton definitely needs to hear about this. You'd better make that call.'

'He also needs to find Jill,' Violet said. 'Where is she, and where is Adrian? And what about Tammy Buckland? If she's capable of hurting Zac Wallis, she'll have no qualms about doing whatever it takes to silence Jill.'

# Chapter 30

Violet called DS Winterton and told him everything she'd learned about the mysterious Tamsin. Charlie listened without interrupting, making no comment, even though she sensed he was desperate to ask questions.

'Jill told me they were due to pay a ten per cent deposit on the hotel today, along with some kind of holding fee,' she said. 'As far as I can tell, the Brighouse Hotel isn't on the market – but if it were, a property like that would fetch in excess of a million pounds. Even if Adrian claims to be paying half of the so-called deposit, Jill will have had to cough up a minimum of £50,000.'

'And presumably any documents will have been faked in order to perpetrate the scam,' Charlie said.

'Exactly,' Violet said. 'It may not be possible to recover the money – it's probably long gone by now – but we do need to find Jill. It's her whereabouts that most concerns me. If the deposit has been paid, Jill will have served her purpose. Adrian and his sister will have no further use for her, which means she's expendable. If Tammy Buckland was responsible for Zac Wallis's injuries, she won't think twice about hurting Jill.'

'I'll give this top priority,' Charlie said. 'We'll do everything we can to trace them, and we'll run background checks so that we know who we're dealing with. If Tammy Buckland and Adrian Billings – or Ed Hampton, whatever the hell his real name is – have done this before, they will have left a trail, no matter how careful they've been.'

'You will call me if you find Jill? Please, Charlie . . . even if it's the middle of the night. I won't be able to sleep anyway, not until I know she's all right.'

Overnight the temperature plummeted, and by the following morning Merrywell was covered in a layer of frost so thick it looked (at first glance) like a light sprinkling of snow. Violet got up at seven-thirty, having had a restless night, and Rachel joined her twenty minutes later. Over a breakfast of muesli, yoghurt and slices of kiwi fruit, Violet updated her mother on the conversation she'd had with Charlie Winterton.

'Please don't tell Jacqueline about any of this, Mum. And if you're going over to the shopping village today, remember that Eric and Fiona know nothing about it either.'

'Don't you think you should say something to them?' Rachel said. 'It sounds like Eric's already very worried. If he rings Jill again today and she's still not answering her phone, he's likely to call the police himself.'

'I'm not in a position to do anything until I hear from DS Winterton. Once Jill's been found, she'll be able to explain everything to Eric herself.'

'*If* she's found.'

'Don't.' Violet held one hand aloft and pressed the other against her churning stomach. 'I feel guilty enough as it is.'

'What have you got to feel guilty about?' Rachel said. 'None of this is your fault.'

'Isn't it? If I hadn't insisted on asking questions about Daniel Midship's death, things might not have turned out the way they have. I feel as though I've made a bad situation worse.'

'Nonsense,' said Rachel. 'The person responsible for all this is

Adrian or Ed, or whatever his name is. If your assumptions are right, he's spent months spinning a web of lies and worming his way into Jill's life with the sole intention of relieving her of as much money as possible. Talk about callous.'

'His plan would have started to fall apart the minute his cover was blown,' Violet said. 'He obviously hadn't anticipated running into Daniel Midship, nor could he have predicted that Zac Wallis would be around to witness whatever took place in the alleyway. If Zac regains consciousness and tells the police what he saw, it'll be game over for Adrian and his sister. The clock's ticking for them, and they'll know that. I'll bet they were hoping to con Jill out of a lot more than a ten per cent deposit – but they'll have had to step things up in case Zac wakes up and talks to the police – hence the sudden "arrangement" with the hotel.'

By nine o'clock Violet had received no further update from DS Winterton. Eric had texted to say he'd been ringing Jill and Adrian since eight o'clock, but hadn't been able to get hold of either of them. He ended his message by saying he was growing increasingly concerned that something might have happened to them.

> Me too. I've alerted Charlie Winterton. The police are looking for them. Try not to worry.

Violet sent the reply knowing it would do little to reassure Eric. He *would* worry. How could he not?

At half past nine, unable to wait any longer, Violet called DS Winterton's number, half expecting to get his voicemail message.

'We haven't found her yet, if that's why you're ringing,' Charlie said, surprising her by answering the call.

'That's not the news I wanted to hear. What's happening, Charlie? What are you doing to find her?'

'Everything we can,' he replied. 'Tammy Buckland's car has been picked up on the ANPR system. She's fled from the hotel and is currently just outside Wigan, heading north on the M6. There are two patrol cars in pursuit.'

'And what about Jill and Adrian?'

'We've set up an ANPR alert on Jill Atherstone's car, but nothing's been triggered as yet. There's no car registered to Adrian Billings or Edward Hampton – who, you'll be interested to know, we have now established are the same person. He could have taken Jill Atherstone's car and be driving it using false plates.'

'Of course he'll have taken it,' Violet said. 'He's taken her money, hasn't he? He's been living in her house. Clearly, the man has no shame. He's a snake.'

'If you're going to liken him to a reptile, you'd be better off opting for a chameleon . . . because it would appear he's very good at blending in with his surroundings. It's early days, but we believe he's used several different aliases over the last few years. He and his sister work as a team, running elaborate scams, and constantly changing their M.O. in order to keep one step ahead of us. From what we can tell, the sister sets up what appear to be legitimate businesses, always short-lived. He changes his name and, occasionally, his appearance in order to pull off whatever scheme they're perpetrating. Once the latest scam is complete and money has been paid into their business bank account, it's quickly transferred and the business is closed down.

'The bank has confirmed that yesterday, Jill Atherstone transferred £50,000 into Tamed Forager's account via the Faster Payment system.'

'And is it still there?' Violet said.

'No, it was moved on almost immediately to another account, but thankfully we've managed to put a freeze on that. For now, the money isn't going anywhere, and I'm hopeful that Jill Atherstone will, eventually, get it back.'

'Well, that's a relief,' Violet said. 'I just hope she's still alive and well enough to spend it.'

'If it's of any comfort, there's no history of violence connected to any of their previous frauds,' Charlie said. 'If I had to guess, I'd say Ed Hampton, aka Adrian Billings is miles away by now, driving on false numberplates. He'll have arranged to meet up somewhere with his sister so they can start to scout out their next victim.'

'So where the hell is Jill?'

'I don't know, but I'll do everything in my power to find her.'

'Adrian and Tammy need to be caught and punished,' Violet said, feeling furious on Jill's behalf. 'And not just for the scams they've pulled on unsuspecting, innocent people. If they were responsible for Daniel Midship's death and the hit-and-run that injured Zac Wallis, they need to go to prison for a long, long time.'

'There is some good news about Zac,' Charlie said. 'He's regained consciousness, although he still isn't well enough to talk. The doctors are hopeful of a full recovery eventually, but it's likely to require a long period of rehabilitation.'

'So, what happens now?' Violet said. 'How are you going to find Jill?'

'We'll be bringing Tamsin Buckland in for questioning shortly. Hopefully, she'll realise the game is up and tell us where Jill is. If not, we'll call a press conference to alert the public and make an appeal. Adrian Billings can't hide out forever. He's managed to stay under the radar for a long time, but everyone's luck runs out sooner or later.'

'The sooner that swine gets his comeuppance the better,' Violet said. 'The longer this goes on, the more likely it is that something's happened to Jill. They could have left her for dead somewhere, in which case time is of the essence.'

'Yes, I'm aware of that,' Charlie said. 'I promise you we've got maximum resources on this. She'll turn up soon. Bound to.'

Violet ended the call feeling a lot less optimistic than Charlie appeared to be.

'Was that your detective chum on the phone?' Rachel said,

as she came into the kitchen wearing her best coat. 'Have there been any further developments?'

'The police are in pursuit of Tammy Buckland as we speak. She's currently driving north on the M6. Unfortunately, there have been no sightings of Jill or Adrian.'

'Gosh, that doesn't sound good,' Rachel said. 'It must be getting on for eighteen hours since she left Eric high and dry in the bookshop. If she's not at home, where the heck is she?'

'I wish I knew,' Violet said, as she stood up and switched on the kettle. 'I'm making myself a brew . . . I'd offer to make one for you, but as you've got your coat on, I assume you're going out?'

'I promised I'd meet Jacqueline at the shopping village,' Rachel said. 'It's the last day of the Christmas market and there are a couple of things I've been umming and ahhing about that I've finally decided to buy. But don't worry . . . if I run into Eric or Fiona, I promise not to say anything about Jill.'

'If things carry on as they are, they'll hear soon enough. If there's no sign of Jill within the next hour or so, the police will hold a press conference and make a public appeal, and they'll want to talk to whoever saw her last – which was probably Eric.'

Rachel gave her a brief hug before heading for the back door. 'Try not to worry, darling. If you carry on as you are, you'll have ulcers by the time you're fifty.'

After waving her mother goodbye, Violet carried her mug of tea to the table. Closing her eyes, she took a series of deep breaths and tried to calm her mind. As she drifted into a semi-meditative state, the door flew open again and Rachel burst into the kitchen.

Violet opened her eyes. 'Mum! What are you doing back so soon?'

'You'll never guess who I've just seen,' Rachel said, pausing only briefly before continuing. 'Jill and Adrian. Together.'

'What? Where?'

Violet told herself this was good news. Jill was safe – at least for the time being.

'They drove past me as I set off for the shopping village,' Rachel said.

'In a ruby red Fiesta?'

'Yes. Adrian was driving, and Jill was in the passenger seat.'

'Which way were they going?' Violet said, as she picked up her phone and found DS Winterton's number.

'They were heading in the direction of the church. As they went past, I could see them laughing together. Everything looked perfectly normal to me.'

'Really? What the devil is going on with those two?' Violet said, her face etched with worry. 'I'd better ring Charlie.'

'And I need to get going,' Rachel said. 'Otherwise, Jacqueline will wonder where I am. Call me though, if you find out anything.'

As Rachel exited the kitchen for the second time, Violet waited for DS Winterton to answer his phone.

'Any idea where they might be heading?' Charlie said, when Violet had filled him in on what her mother had seen.

'They were driving away from Jill's house, not towards it. They might be going to Rock House, although I'm not sure why they'd want to.'

'Where's Rock House?'

'On the lane that runs behind the church, behind a pair of double gates. It's the house Jill inherited from her brother.'

'We'll go and check it out,' Charlie said. 'Don't worry. If they've been spotted in the area, it's only a matter of time before we find them.'

'Rock House is the property that Matthew and I are hoping to buy,' Violet said, wondering if that was nothing more than a pipe dream now.

'That could be where they're heading. We'll go over there, and if they are at the house and refuse to open the door, we'll use the big red key to gain entry. We don't need a warrant if we believe someone's life is in danger.'

Violet had a vision of the police using a battering ram on Rock House's beautiful wooden door.

'You won't need your big red key,' she said. 'I have a set of keys to the house in my handbag.'

# Chapter 31

'I'll get a team together,' Charlie said. 'Meet us there in twenty minutes. Wait for us on the road, and you can hand over the keys when we get there. You should probably take Matthew with you. I know what you're like. If you go on your own, you'll be tempted to go into the house.'

'Well, I do have a set of keys,' Violet said. 'It's not as if I'd be breaking and entering.'

'Just because you're in possession of a key doesn't mean you have permission to enter the property,' Charlie said.

'Actually, I do. Jill told Matthew and I that we could go back as often as we liked over the weekend.'

'Please don't argue with me, Violet. And do *not* let yourself into Rock House.'

'OK,' she said, realising that their bickering was wasting time. 'Message received and understood. You've made your point. I'll do as you suggested and take Matthew with me. He'll make sure I don't do anything I shouldn't.'

'Why didn't you ask the police to pick the keys up from your house?' Matthew said, after Violet had collected him from the shopping village and they were driving past the church.

'It'll save time if we meet them there,' Violet said.

He frowned. 'A couple of minutes, maybe. No more than that. Do you really think Jill and Adrian are at the house?'

'I don't know, but it's worth checking out, surely?'

'We're not *checking* anything, Violet. We're going to pass the keys on to the police. End of.'

They turned left after the church, onto the lane that ran behind it.

'If you park on the road, we can stay out of sight, behind the hedge,' Matthew said.

Violet did as he suggested, and then searched in her handbag for the keys. After what seemed like an age but was probably less than a minute, she felt an overwhelming urge to peer through the gates, to see whether Jill's Ford Fiesta was on the driveway.

'I won't be a second,' she said, making up her mind to get out of the car.

'What are you doing?' Matthew hissed, as she opened the driver's door.

'I want to check whether Jill's car's there,' she said, stepping onto the grass verge and being careful to close the car door as quietly as possible.

The rising sun had melted away most of the ground frost, but a few stubborn patches clung on in the shade. In a half stoop, Violet crept along the lane to the tall double gates, which stood open. There was no Fiesta on the driveway.

She turned, intending to return to her own car and report her findings to Matthew – but when she turned around, she collided with a tall figure in a padded coat.

Matthew.

'What the—' Violet placed a hand over her mouth to suppress a squeal of surprise. 'Bloody hell, Matthew. Are you trying to blow our cover?'

He pressed his lips together and laughed soundlessly.

'We're not MI5 operatives, Violet. And if anyone's blowing our cover, it's you. Come and sit in the car.'

'It doesn't look like they're there anyway,' she said, as they hurried over to the Toyota and got inside. 'There's no car.'

'Maybe it's in the garage,' Matthew said.

Violet looked at him, thinking through their next move.

'Plan B,' she said, as she turned the key in the ignition. 'I'm going to park on the driveway.'

'What? For God's sake, Violet, what are you doing?'

Ignoring his protests, she steered through the gate and along the driveway, pulling up directly in front of the garage.

'Care to explain yourself?' Matthew said. 'I thought we were supposed to stay hidden.'

'If Jill and Adrian aren't here, there's no harm done.'

'And if they are, and they see us?'

Violet shrugged. 'We'll play it cool . . . tell them we're here for another look around the house. By parking here, we're blocking off the garage.' She nodded towards the up-and-over door. 'Unfortunately, it doesn't have a side window, so we won't be able to see if the Fiesta's in there – but if it *is*, it won't be going anywhere now. Adrian won't be able to drive away, will he?'

They sat for half a minute, looking towards the house and checking for signs of life.

'How long before the police get here?' Matthew asked.

'Another ten minutes or so. Are you thinking what I'm thinking?'

'Probably not,' he said, flashing her a look of disapproval.

'We should go inside.'

'Don't even think about it,' Matthew said. 'We shouldn't even be on the driveway, never mind inside the house. Charlie Winterton specifically told you to wait on the road.'

'He did, but Jill could be in danger, and I'm more than willing to incur the wrath of DS Winterton, if it means keeping her safe. All we have to do is let ourselves in on the pretext that we've come for another viewing. If they are in there and Adrian has a genuine reason for driving Jill to the house, we won't have a problem. On the other hand, if he's brought her here to hurt her in some way, our presence will put paid to his plans.'

Matthew squirmed in the passenger seat. 'The police will be here in a few minutes. I think we should wait.'

'That's fine. If you don't want to come, I'll go in on my own. I'll leave the door on the latch in case you change your mind.'

'Violet! You're being very manipulative. You know full well I'm not going to let you go in there on your own. If we're right about Adrian, there's no telling what he's capable of. If he intends to hurt Jill, he won't hesitate to include you in his plans.'

'Come with me, then,' she said. 'Because I'm going into the house, Matthew, whether you approve or not.'

She slipped the key into the lock and opened the door as quietly as possible. Matthew followed her into the hallway, where they paused, listening for any kind of sound.

Putting a finger to his lips, he opened the door into the living room on the right.

Violet followed silently. The room was empty, as was the dining room and the kitchen. Just as they were beginning to think there was no one else in the house, they heard a low murmur of voices as they entered the panelled sitting room. The sound was coming from somewhere upstairs.

'Let me go first,' Matthew whispered. 'And if I tell you to run, you run like hell. Agreed?'

Violet nodded. She stayed a couple of steps behind him as they climbed the stairs. Halfway up, they heard the voices again, which seemed to be coming from the top floor.

They tiptoed along the landing and stood in front of the door that led to the attic. There was a key in the lock, but the door itself was ajar.

'The attic stairs are very creaky, remember?' Violet whispered. 'They'll hear us, if we go up there.'

The sound of muffled conversation came again, louder now.

Matthew leaned in and spoke in Violet's ear. 'What do you want to do?' he said, giving her the choice. 'From the sounds of it, they're having a normal, friendly chat. I suppose we could go up there and join them . . . act casually . . . pretend everything's fine, and tell them we've come back for another viewing. Or – and this is my preferred option – we get the hell out of here and wait for the police.'

'Tempted as I am to scarper, I think we should go up,' Violet said. 'Right now, Jill's obviously OK and quite safe. All we need to do is buy a few more minutes until the police get here.'

Matthew nodded. The door to the attic opened outwards, and he began to climb the stairs, making no effort to hide his presence. Violet followed, her ears peeled for anything out of the ordinary.

On the top-floor landing, they walked past the first room and the tiny bathroom and stood in the doorway at the end of the corridor, which opened into the largest attic room – the one with the kitchenette.

Jill was sitting on the dusty chaise longue, and Adrian was standing in front of her with his arms folded. His expression froze when Matthew and Violet walked into the room, and he gazed at them with a look of complete incredulity. Jill, on the other hand, turned and smiled. She looked relaxed and unsurprised.

'Here you are,' she said. 'At last. I was beginning to think you weren't going to show up.'

## Chapter 32

'You were expecting us?' Violet said, unable to disguise the note of suspicion in her voice.

'Of course we were,' Jill said. 'You texted Adrian and asked to meet us here. We're assuming it's something to do with this?'

She pointed up at the bowed ceiling and tilted her head, waiting for confirmation.

'I haven't sent any texts,' Violet said.

'Oh!' Jill pouted. 'So, what *are* you doing here then?'

'You gave me a spare key and said we could keep it over the weekend. We're here for another viewing. I did try to call you – several times, in fact – but your phone is switched off.'

Jill wagged a finger. 'My phone's at home. It was Adrian who received the text. You asked us to meet you here to discuss a problem in the attic.'

Matthew shook his head. 'I'm sorry, Jill, but we don't know what you're talking about. We don't have Adrian's number, so there's no way we could have sent him a text message.'

Jill regarded them quizzically. 'Show them the message, Adrian.'

Adrian seemed to be playing a game of statues – standing stiffly, as if by not moving, his presence would go unnoticed.

'If they said they didn't send it, I think we have to take them at their word,' he said, springing back to life suddenly. 'Obviously someone's been playing games. Come on, Jill. Let's go home and let Violet and Matthew finish their viewing.'

Violet considered keeping her own counsel and staying quiet about what she knew, but instinct told her that would be a grave mistake.

*It's now or never*, she thought. *We either let them walk away, or we can get to the truth of the matter.*

'I believe it's you who's been playing games,' she said, abandoning all pretence that she was there for a routine viewing of the house.

'I beg your pardon?' Adrian said.

'May I ask where you've been since yesterday afternoon?' Violet said, jumping straight in to keep them talking and delay their departure. 'Eric told me you went home because you didn't feel well, Jill. He's been trying to get hold of you to check you're OK. He's been worried about you.'

Jill looked embarrassed. 'I'm afraid I wasn't completely honest with Eric. Adrian and I have been away. We paid the deposit on the hotel yesterday, and Adrian surprised me with an overnight trip to Harrogate to celebrate. Obviously, I couldn't tell Eric where we were going, so I told him I didn't feel well.'

'Why haven't you been answering your phone?' said Matthew.

Jill smiled nonchalantly. 'We decided I should leave it at home. Adrian wanted me to relax and get away from it all.'

*Very convenient*, Violet thought, wondering if Jill's phone was now in Tamsin Buckland's possession. Had she gone to Overton Cottage yesterday afternoon to collect it, in case there were any security calls from the bank that needed to be dealt with?

'When did you get back to Merrywell?' Violet said.

'About twenty minutes ago. We would have stayed longer in Harrogate, but then Adrian got the text from you. We came straight here.'

Violet corrected her. 'The text *purporting* to be from me. May I see it?'

Reluctantly, Adrian pulled his phone from his pocket and showed her the message.

> Matthew and I would like to make you an offer on Rock House, but we have some concerns about a problem in the attic. Can you meet us there at 10 a.m. to discuss?

'That's not my telephone number,' Violet said. 'I didn't send this message.'

'Well, someone obviously did,' Jill said. 'Ring the number, Adrian. Find out who it was.'

Adrian made a great show of calling the number, which Violet assumed must belong to some kind of burner phone.

'It's saying: *The number you are calling is not available*,' he said. 'Like I say, someone's playing a prank.'

Violet sat on the chaise longue, next to Jill.

'Jill, yesterday you said you were putting down a holding deposit on the hotel. I take it this was all done through your solicitor?'

'Of course it was,' Jill said. 'We were hoping to exchange contracts at the same time, but some of the searches and enquiries haven't been completed yet. We've paid a deposit, but it's fully refundable should anything untoward crop up during the searches. The hotel is now officially off the market, and will be ours once we're able to complete on the contract.'

'And is that your understanding of the arrangement, Adrian?' Violet said.

'Yes, it is – although I fail to understand what any of this has to do with you. Why are you asking all these questions?'

'Because I don't believe a word you're saying,' Violet said, jumping in with both feet. She could see Matthew glancing at his watch, willing the police to arrive.

'What *is* your problem, Violet?' Jill said, as she stood up and linked arms with Adrian. 'I think you'd better go. If you and Matthew want to buy this house, then I'll sell it to you, but please don't expect me to continue with our friendship. I find your attitude offensive. You've obviously taken against Adrian for some reason. I'm not sure why that is, but I want you to know I won't hear a word said against him.'

Adrian looked down at the floor, refusing to meet Violet's gaze.

'I'm sorry to be the one to tell you this, Jill, but I believe you've been a victim of fraud.'

A look of intense fury blazed in Jill's eyes – but it was directed at Violet, not Adrian.

'The Brighouse Hotel isn't for sale, and Tammy Buckland isn't the owner,' Violet said, steeling herself to continue. 'Tammy is your sister, isn't she, Adrian? Or, should I say, Ed?'

Finally, Adrian's head shot up. He looked grim and angry, his mouth pressed into a hard line.

'That is a wicked thing to say,' Jill said, as she clung even tighter to Adrian's arm. 'Adrian's sister is dead. You know that, because I told you so myself. Why are you being so cruel? And what about you, Matthew? You're standing there with your arms folded, saying nothing. Don't you think it's about time you got Violet under control?'

'Controlling people isn't my style,' Matthew said. 'Violet is her own woman, and just because you don't like what she's saying doesn't mean it isn't true. You need to listen to her, Jill.'

Adrian snapped into action, tugging on Jill's hand. 'Come on, darlin'. Let's go. We don't have to stay here and listen to this rubbish.'

'This is my house,' Jill said, standing her ground. 'If anyone should go, it's this pair.'

'We'll leave if you want us to – but please be aware that the police have already apprehended your sister, Adrian,' Violet said, hoping the patrol car had finally managed to catch up with Tammy. 'And they're on their way to pick you up now.'

All the colour drained from Jill's face as the truth began to sink in. She pulled her hand from Adrian's grasp and turned to face him.

'What's this all about?' she said, her voice barely a whisper. 'Tell me. What have you done? I want the truth.'

Adrian blew air through his nostrils, but said nothing.

'You're not the first person he's duped,' Violet said. 'Remember Daniel Midship, the guy found in the alleyway?'

Jill gave an almost imperceptible nod.

'About three years ago, Adrian swindled Daniel's sister out of £10,000. He was operating as someone called Ed Hampton back then. He took Helen's money and did a runner, and she never heard from him again. We believe Daniel Midship must have seen Adrian – the man he knew as Ed Hampton – at the shopping village. Presumably, he managed to slip away the first time, but Daniel came back. Did he chase you into the alleyway, Adrian?'

He glared at her, brazenly silent.

'His sister is his partner in crime,' Violet said, addressing Jill directly. 'Despite everything Adrian has told you, she is still very much alive.'

Jill swallowed a sob, and her eyes filled with tears. Stumbling back, she stared at Adrian as if he were an alien lifeform.

As succinctly as possible, Violet explained what she had learned about Adrian and Tammy. Jill listened intently, becoming more and more distressed with each new revelation.

'What was the purpose of bringing Jill here today, Adrian?' Violet said, after she'd given Jill the bare facts. 'That text didn't come from me – so I'm assuming it was sent on a pay-as-you-go phone. Did you send it, or did it come from your sister? It was a ruse, wasn't it, to get Jill to Rock House. What were you planning to do? Tie her up? Hurt her? Or worse?'

Adrian broke his silence at last. When he spoke, it was to Jill.

'I would never have hurt you,' he said. 'All I was going to

do was lock you in here. I needed to buy some time, so that I could get away.'

Jill clapped a hand over her mouth. 'It's true, then?' she said, her voice barely a whisper. 'Violet's right?'

Adrian nodded once. 'I'm sorry,' he said. 'I was going to go downstairs on the pretext of checking where these two were, and on my way out, I planned to lock you in. No harm would have come to you, I swear. Someone would have found you eventually. Obviously, I wasn't expecting Violet and Matthew to actually turn up. You didn't tell me you'd given them the spare key.'

Jill's legs buckled, and she sank down onto the chaise longue.

'Where were you planning to go?' Violet said. 'Up the M6 to join your sister?'

Adrian folded his arms, looking furious but also fearful.

A text from Charlie Winterton pinged onto Violet's phone.

We're five minutes away. Tammy Buckland is in custody, and her car has been impounded. The CSIs are checking it over. There's damage to the front bonnet, so we're pretty sure we'll find forensic evidence to prove she ran down Zac Wallis.

Violet felt a flush of shame as she remembered the way she'd inspected Robert Dorman's van and had, fleetingly and very reluctantly, suspected him.

She returned the phone to her pocket, more confident now about facing up to Adrian.

'Are you willing to tell me what happened in the alley?' she said, pushing hard for the answers she was looking for. 'Was Daniel Midship's death an accident?'

The question seemed to drain Adrian of all strength and colour. He went over and sat on one of the chairs at the table in the corner, moving awkwardly under the sloping ceiling.

'I would never intentionally hurt anyone. Tammy . . . she's

different. She had a tough upbringing – we both did – but it hardened her much more than it did me.'

It was far from being an emphatic denial. Violet let him talk, sensing that the truth would need to be extracted at a speed of Adrian's choosing.

'You're right about Dan,' he said. 'He saw me, on Wednesday. I'd gone over to the shopping village to deliver a tray of canapés and finger food for a group that meets in one of the studio rooms. They normally get the café to do the catering for their meetings, but their gathering was doubling up as their Christmas party, so they wanted something special from the hotel. Just my luck . . . wrong time, wrong place. As I was crossing the courtyard on my way back to work, I happened to look up – and found myself locking eyes with Dan Midship. I couldn't quite believe it, but there he was, looking down at me from the top-floor window of the bookshop.

'I realised he'd recognised me, so I knew I had to get out of there, and fast. There wasn't time to reach my car without Dan seeing me, so while he was heading through the bookshop, I slipped into the plant room off the courtyard. I hid in there, in the dark, for over half an hour. When enough time had gone by for Dan to give up the chase, I stuck my head out of the door. There was no sign of him anywhere, so I kept a low profile and returned to the hotel. I thought I'd got away with it.'

'But he came back,' Violet said. 'On Friday.'

'Yes.' Adrian nodded. 'Although I've no idea how he knew I'd be there.'

'Were you wearing chef's whites when he saw you on Wednesday?'

'Under my coat, yeah. We're supposed to take them off before we leave the kitchen, but it was just a quick delivery trip, so I didn't think anyone would notice.'

'Daniel obviously noticed, and it was enough to alert him to the fact that you had a local connection,' Violet said. 'He must have come to Merrywell on the Friday to look for you.'

Adrian rested his elbows on the table and put his head in his hands. 'He should have stayed away. He'd be alive and well now, if he had.'

'What did you do to him?' Jill demanded, tears of disbelief streaming down her face.

'I went to the shopping village to walk you home,' Adrian said, a dash of the gallant gentleman still lingering in his words. 'I came in through the alleyway, and just as I was about to step into the courtyard, I saw him – Dan – outside the café. He shouted my name, my *real* name, so I turned and legged it through the alley. The problem was, he was only a few strides behind me. I knew if I ran out to the car park, he'd catch up with me.

'As I approached the end of the alley, I remembered that someone had left the chain barrier lying on the ground – I'd stepped round it as I walked in. Dan's footsteps were echoing behind me, so I made a split-second decision. I grabbed the end of the chain, ducked down in the dark at the side of the alley, and used it to trip him up. I only wanted to bring him down temporarily, long enough for me to make my escape. I pulled the chain towards me, keeping it low and taut. Dan was running when he tripped over it, so he went down fast – and as he fell, he hit his head on the bollard. At first, I assumed it had knocked him out, but as I stood up, ready to run away, I saw the wound on his head, and the blood. He wasn't moving, and I couldn't hear him breathing, so I switched on the torch on my phone and shone it into his face.

'I could see from his eyes that it was too late to do anything for him . . . He was dead. I staggered away, back to Overton Cottage, running in a blind panic. There was rust on my hands from the chain, so I washed them and got my breath back, and tried to calm down. I knew I had to carry on as normal and act as if nothing had happened.

'So, for the second time that evening, I set out for the shopping village. On the way, I bumped into Andrew Talbot, and we walked there together. We went through the front entrance and into the bookshop, which is when someone told us that a body had been found in the alleyway.'

'I remember you looked convincingly shocked,' Matthew said. 'You put on a good act – I'll give you that.'

'Trust me, there was no acting required,' Adrian said. 'I *was* shocked . . . I still couldn't believe Dan was dead. I didn't set out to hurt him, not seriously. I only wanted to slow him down. I never intended to kill him. You have to believe me, Jill.'

He held out his hands and looked at her imploringly.

'I don't have to do any such thing,' said Jill, who was weeping silently. 'Why should I believe you when everything you've ever said to me has been a lie?'

'Not everything.'

Adrian stood up and caught hold of her hands, but she snatched them away, out of his reach.

'I know I've hurt you, Jill, but no matter what you think of me, I do care about you. The last few weeks have been torture for me, knowing what I was about to do.'

'Torture?' Jill said, screaming at him. 'You don't know the meaning of the word. You've just ripped apart my hopes and dreams. My emotions are in shreds. If anyone's feeling tortured, it's me. You must have known what you were doing was wrong. You've stolen £50,000 of my money – my *brother's* money, actually. I am so, *so* angry – angrier than I've ever been in my life – but most of all I'm sad – ashamed and embarrassed and devastated that I've allowed someone to do this to me. I trusted you, Adrian. I *loved* you. And in return you've made me feel like the biggest, most gullible fool known to man.'

'I really am sorry,' Adrian said. 'You're right . . . what I did was wrong, and you didn't deserve it. I wish things could have been different between us, and I wish I *could* have made your dreams come true – but I'm not the man for you, Jill. I'm not worthy of you. I just hope that you do, eventually, find someone who is.'

Jill buried her face in her hands as her body was racked with sobs.

'Tell me about Zac Wallis?' Violet said, knowing the police would be less than a minute away and this would be her last chance to get the answers she was seeking. 'I assume he saw what happened with Dan and tried to blackmail you? Is that why you left him for dead on the road?'

'*I* didn't do that,' Adrian said. 'I've admitted I was there when Dan died, but that was a mistake . . . an accident. I would never purposely hurt anyone. I'm not a violent person. Besides, the four of us were together at Overton Cottage when Zac Wallis was injured. You know I had nothing to do with that.'

'That doesn't mean you can absolve yourself of blame,' Violet said. 'The police are examining your sister's car as we speak, and I'm sure they'll find the evidence they need to confirm that she was the one at the cross that night. So . . . yes, I know you weren't driving, Adrian, but you were still an accessory to her crime. Tammy must have told you what she was going to do to solve your blackmail problem.'

He shook his head. 'I swear to you, I had no idea. She told me she was going to pay him off.'

He made one last attempt to take hold of Jill's hand, but she batted him away.

'Please forgive me,' he said, sounding genuinely contrite. 'If I could take it all back, I would.'

And with that, he dashed past Matthew and ran out of the door. As his footsteps pounded along the corridor and down the creaky stairs, the wail of a siren sounded from somewhere in the distance.

'Don't worry,' Violet said. 'He won't get far.'

Jill stared at her, looking pale and dejected and bereft. 'That's a pity, because the more distance there is between that man and me, the better. I never want to see his face again as long as I live.'

Violet would have liked to have granted Jill her wish, but at some stage in the future, there would be a court case and, whether she liked it or not, Jill would have to face Adrian and Tammy once again. Hopefully, the last time would be when they were in the dock, being sentenced for their crimes.

Violet went to the Velux window, opened it and peered out, watching as two police cars sped down the driveway. Matthew had gone downstairs in pursuit of Adrian, leaving Violet and Jill alone in the attic room.

'I'm so sorry about all of this,' Violet said. 'I know how much Adrian meant to you. What he and Tammy have done is despicable. The good news is, the police have managed to intercept the money you transferred to the Tamed Forager account. It might take a while, but it sounds like you'll get it back.'

Jill laid her head on the back of the chaise longue, looking utterly broken.

'There's no need to apologise,' she said. 'I'm the one who should be asking for forgiveness. You tried to warn me, and if it wasn't for you, things could have turned out much worse than they already are.' She wiped her eyes. 'It's a relief about the money, obviously, but quite honestly, the trauma of a huge financial loss is nothing compared to the emotional agony I'm feeling right now.'

She sat up and wrapped her arms across her body, leaning forward as if holding in her pain.

'I'm a silly, stupid fool,' she said, spitting out the words. 'I thought Adrian and I had a connection. He was so sympathetic . . . so tuned in to how I was feeling about Steven. I thought he understood because he'd lost his own sibling – and now it turns out his sister is not only alive, but the mastermind behind a succession of frauds.'

'It does sound as though Tammy has been the ring leader in all of this,' Violet said. 'Who knows, without her corrupting influence, Adrian . . . Ed might have made a whole different life for himself. He might even have got that restaurant he talked about.'

'He is an excellent cook,' Jill said, trying (and failing) to muster a smile. 'That's the only good thing I can think of to say about him. I wonder if it was even true, what he told us about saving up for a restaurant?'

'I don't know, but even if it was, I suspect Tammy had other plans for him.'

Jill clutched her stomach and groaned, doubling over as if she'd been punched in the gut.

'He always sounded so sincere when he talked about how much he missed his sister. How could he have pretended she was dead? What kind of person would do that?'

'Maybe he got through it by playing a part, like an actor on the stage.'

'That's exactly what the last few months have been . . .' Jill said, her words fractured by tears. 'A fabrication. A fictional construct. I can't believe it. I honestly thought Adrian and I had something special, but everything about our relationship – our shared grief, our plans for the future – it was all a sham. All that's left are false memories. What am I supposed to do now?'

Violet's heart ached for Jill, and for all the people like her, but the most important thing Jill could do now was stay strong, and stay angry – at least until such time as Adrian and Tammy had been punished. After that, she could let go of the anger but always, *always*, stay strong.

'What you're going to do is carry on,' Violet said. 'You still have your job in the bookshop, and lots and lots of friends in the village. There are people in Merrywell who care about you and, although it might not seem like it right now, you will come through this, Jill – and you'll be a stronger, more resilient person because of it.'

'Will I?' she said, letting go of her emotions and allowing the tears to flow. 'I hope so because at the moment, I feel weak, and stupid and naïve. I've spent months trusting the wrong people at the expense of my real friends, including you. Will you ever forgive me?'

Violet opened her arms. 'I already have,' she said.

# Chapter 33

Adrian Billings exited Rock House through the back door, at the same time as the police were racing in through the front. He dashed across the garden, clambered over the stone boundary wall, and had managed to sprint into the adjacent field before PC Turner caught up with him, and arrested him. He was now on his way to the police station to be interviewed.

Violet and Jill encountered DS Winterton on the first-floor landing, as they made their way downstairs. After confirming that they were both unharmed, he instructed a detective constable to drive Jill home and take a statement from her.

'You can go home too, Violet,' Charlie said, sounding even more crabby than usual. 'I'll deal with you later.'

Several hours passed before he finally showed up at Greengage Cottage. Matthew had returned to work by then, but Rachel had returned from her shopping trip with Jacqueline, and she and Violet were in the living room, adding some newly acquired decorations to the Christmas tree. Carols were playing at low volume through a Bluetooth speaker, and the cat was having great fun chasing a stolen bauble around the carpet.

DS Winterton's arrival was heralded by the rat-a-tat-tat of the brass door-knocker.

'Come in, Charlie,' Violet said, smiling as she opened the door and invited him into the hallway. 'I was hoping you'd call by.'

'This isn't a social visit,' he said, looking exasperated. 'I'm here on official police business. You and I need to have a serious conversation.'

'Are you about to tell me off for going inside Rock House?' Violet said, turning down the corners of her mouth.

'This is no joke, Violet. I'm not kidding around. I told you to wait on the road.'

'I wanted to find out if they were at the house,' she said, in a feeble attempt to defend herself. 'There's no window in the garage, so I couldn't tell whether the car was parked inside it. There was no outward sign of anyone being in the house, but I was concerned about Jill, so I decided to go and look for her. I knew that if I found them, I could buy some time until you arrived.'

'You can't just barge in like that in these situations,' Charlie said. 'You had no idea what you were walking into, or what you might have been dealing with. As it turns out, you *did* buy some time, and there was no harm done – but things could have ended very differently. You might not be so lucky next time, which is why this mustn't happen again. I want your word on that. If you and I ever cross paths in the course of a future investigation, you follow my orders. Understood? If you can't agree to that, then you and I can no longer be friends.'

'Don't be like that,' Violet said, saddened at the thought of losing Charlie's friendship. 'I'm sorry I didn't do as you asked, and I promise to listen to you in the future.'

'Not good enough, I'm afraid. You always *listen* to me. What I want your reassurance on is that you'll *follow* my instructions – not just listen to them and then blatantly disregard them.'

'OK, I understand.' She gave him a penitent smile. 'Should the need arise for you to give me orders in the future, I promise to follow them. Although, quite honestly, I'm hoping for a crime-free Merrywell from now on.'

'Amen to that,' Charlie said. 'I think we can agree this village has had more than its share of trouble lately.'

Violet smiled, pleased that harmony appeared to have been restored.

'Why don't you take your coat off and go and sit in the living room?' she said. 'I'll introduce you to my mother, and I can warm up some mince pies, if you're hungry.'

'Go on then,' Charlie said, his eyes twinkling in anticipation. 'A mince pie would go down a treat – just so long as this doesn't turn into some kind of soirée. I've got work to do, so I can't stay long.'

'So, you're the detective my daughter's always going on about,' Rachel said, when Violet had made the introductions. 'I hope you're not planning to involve her in any more of your cases.'

'I'll try not to,' Charlie said, with a wry smile. 'But unfortunately, Violet does have a habit of being in the wrong place at the wrong time.'

Rachel gave a knowing smile as she volunteered to organise the mince pies and a pot of tea. While she was in the kitchen, Charlie offered to give Violet a brief update on the case.

'Thanks,' she said. 'I'd appreciate that. I do have a lot of unanswered questions.'

'So did we when we made the arrests, but I'm pleased to say that Ed Hampton . . . Adrian . . . is being very cooperative. "Singing like a canary" you might say – unlike his sister, who "no comment"ed her way through the entire first interview.

'Adrian has admitted to being a professional fraudster. He started his career as a chef, but his sister persuaded him to pursue what she thought would be a "more lucrative" line of work.'

'By which I assume she meant ripping people off?' Violet said.

'Yes. Tamsin Buckland is undoubtedly the brains behind

their increasingly bold schemes. Her brother is the good-looking charmer, whose job it is to wheedle his way into the affections of unsuspecting people. Adrian is adamant he's never hurt anyone physically, although he accepts he's broken quite a few hearts.

'He says that Tamsin told him to whisk Jill away on Saturday afternoon for a "relaxing, phone-free" stay in a fancy hotel. After Jill had transferred the £50k to the Tamed Forager account, Adrian drove them straight up to Harrogate. As soon as they'd gone, Tamsin let herself into Overton Cottage to collect Jill's phone and be on hand to answer any security calls from the bank.'

'I'd imagine it's routine to query such a large payment,' Violet said.

'It would be, ordinarily, but weeks ago, Adrian persuaded Jill to upgrade to a premier bank account, and set Tamed Forager up as a payee. Adrian told Jill he was dealing directly with the solicitors, and they wanted to pay the deposit from one bank account. He persuaded Jill that the best one to use would be his business account. It was all nonsense, of course. There were no solicitors.

'Jill was able to transfer the money using the faster payments system. Adrian had found out her passwords and had given them to Tamsin, so she could deal with any queries from the bank to confirm the payment was genuine.

'Tamsin is refusing to confirm any of this, but we have found a burner phone hidden in the boot of her car. In the recently deleted messages, we found a text sent to Zac Wallis, arranging to meet him at the cross to hand over five grand in hush money. We don't believe Tamsin had any intention of paying him and, once we've finished gathering evidence, we'll be charging her with attempted murder. Fortunately for Zac, he's a lot tougher than Tamsin gave him credit for. He's recovered well enough to tell us what he saw from the car park, and what happened at the cross.'

'Jill seems like a very switched-on person,' Violet said. 'How did they manage to convince her that Tammy was the owner of the hotel?'

'Adrian cloned the Brighouse Hotel website and recreated it using a .com domain name, as opposed to the actual .co.uk site. On the cloned site he removed the real owner's details and replaced them with Tammy's name and photograph. He then accessed Jill's phone and laptop to block the hotel's real website address, and got a small quantity of fake business cards printed, listing Tammy Buckland as the business owner. The cards also included the burner phone as the contact number, and the .com domain name as the hotel's website address. That way, when Jill logged in, they knew she'd see the things they wanted her to see.'

Violet nodded as she absorbed the information. 'Ironically, on the night Daniel Midship died, I remember Jill telling Eric that Adrian was "brilliant with computers". If she'd known he'd been using those skills to deceive her, I suspect she wouldn't have been quite so proud of his abilities. She even volunteered his services for downloading the CCTV footage for the police.'

'That was when Adrian spotted Eric's book of passwords,' Charlie said. 'After everyone else had left the bookshop, he waited with Jill while she completed her final check of the shop before locking up. While she was on the balcony, Adrian took the notebook from the drawer, found the login and password details for the security system, and snapped a photo on his phone. The next morning, he logged in remotely and deleted a couple of days' worth of footage from earlier in the week – including the file from Wednesday, which showed his movements in the courtyard prior to Dan leaving the bookshop. It would have been "game over" for him if we'd got our hands on that.'

'He must have been desperate to delete it,' Violet said. 'I wonder what he would have done if he hadn't sussed out Eric's notebook?'

'He might have tapped up Jill for the information – although that wouldn't have been easy without raising her suspicions. Adrian knew things were beginning to unravel, so he arranged an emergency meeting with Tammy to discuss bringing forward their plans. Time was running out for them, and they realised they'd have to settle for a lot less cash than they'd originally set their sights on.

'At least Jill will get her £50k back, and that's mainly down to you, Violet. If you hadn't tipped us off when you did, it would have been too late . . . the money would have disappeared into the ether.'

'I'm glad about the money,' Violet said. 'Jill must be relieved that it's been recovered, but it's going to be hard for her to get over such a terrible betrayal of trust.'

'For what it's worth, Adrian has expressed a great deal of remorse over his treatment of her.'

'That doesn't wash with me,' Violet said. 'If Adrian regrets anything, it's more likely to be that he's been caught. And anyway, even if he is genuinely sorry, I doubt whether Jill will forgive him. The only thing that might bring her some consolation is knowing he won't be tricking any more unsuspecting people.'

'I expect Dan Midship would have been happy to know that too,' Charlie said. 'I spoke to his daughter about an hour ago, to update her on developments.'

'How did she take the news?'

'She was relieved that we'd been able to make the arrests, and pleased that Adrian – or, as she called him, Ed – had finally got his comeuppance. Most of all though, she said she felt sad, because she'll never get to spend another Christmas with her dad.'

# Chapter 34

On Christmas Day, they decided to eat lunch at Matthew's house, around his large and very beautiful table – which, if everything went to plan, would soon grace a new dining room.

A few days earlier, Jill had confirmed that she was still keen to sell Rock House – and, in the new year, Violet and Matthew were going to put Greengage Cottage and Tanbeck House on the market and begin the process of moving in together.

Bustling around in Matthew's kitchen, Violet felt unexpectedly nervous about roasting a turkey in an unfamiliar oven – but thankfully, Matthew was pitching in, as was his mum, Joyce, who was currently peeling a huge bowlful of Brussel sprouts.

'Just think,' Joyce said. 'This will be your last Christmas in this house. It's going to be an exciting new year for you both.'

Matthew put his arm around Violet's waist. 'We hope so,' he said. 'We're certainly keeping everything crossed. If we do get Rock House, there'll be a lot of work to do. Painting and decorating. Building and installing kitchen units. Fitting at least one new bathroom. We won't have a spare minute to ourselves.'

'It'll be worth it, though,' Violet said. 'Rock House will look stunning by the time you and I have finished with it.'

'And we'll pitch in and help,' said Joyce. 'Brian's a dab hand with a paintbrush.'

As Violet smiled her thanks, a message from Molly popped onto her phone.

You'll never guess what!? xx

There was no need for her to guess. Violet already knew what Molly was bursting to tell her – but not wanting to spoil the moment, she sent a quick, two-word reply.

Do tell! x

Ten seconds later, the message Violet had been expecting arrived.

Robert has proposed!!!!! My Christmas present is a beautiful diamond solitaire ring. It's absolutely gorgeous! Apparently, that's where he was the day the *Antiques Emporium* was closed. He'd bought the ring online from an auction house in Leicester, and had to go over there to pick it up. He was desperate to keep the whole proposal thing a secret, so that he could surprise me on Christmas morning. He's admitted to misleading me about where he was that day. When I challenged him about it, he kept the story going – otherwise he would have ended up telling me everything!! Anyway . . . mystery solved. I'm so happy, Violet!! Robert loves me, and he wants to marry me! This is the best Christmas ever!! 😊 xx

Apart from the overuse of exclamation marks, Violet thought the message was one of the best things she'd read all year.

That's wonderful news, Molly. I take it you said 'yes'? xx

The reply was almost instantaneous.

Of course I did. Obvs. xx

Violet felt a surge of joy – for Molly and for Robert. When he'd told Violet about his plan to propose on Christmas morning, Robert's biggest fear had been that Molly would turn him down. Violet was relieved the secret was out at last, and the tension, suspense and misunderstanding Robert's white lie had caused was finally over. It was during his trip to Leicester to pick up the ring that his number plate had been damaged, but he'd only admitted that after he'd told Violet the full story.

The message she sent to Molly was heartfelt.

Congratulations to you both. That really is wonderful news. I can't wait to see you (and see this fabulous ring). Happy Christmas xxx

After a huge and very filling lunch, the younger members of the party joined forces to clear the table and load the dishwasher, while the older generation settled down to watch the King's Speech on television (or, in Brian's case, take an afternoon nap).

Later, after several rounds of laughter-inducing charades and a couple of hours of watching TV, they set off en masse for the Nashes' house, for an evening buffet and party.

Jill Atherstone was there when they arrived, having been taken under Fiona's wing for the duration of Christmas Day.

Eric and Fiona's house had a cluttered, lived-in look, but whoever was lucky enough to be invited there was guaranteed a warm welcome. As the Christmas music played and the drinks flowed, Violet managed to get Fiona on her own.

'How's Jill been today?' she asked.

'Quiet,' Fiona said, as she topped up their wine glasses. 'But that's understandable. She's really shaken by what's happened. It's knocked her confidence, but Jill is a resilient and resourceful soul. She'll bounce back, eventually.'

Violet cast her gaze around the huge and slightly chaotic living room in search of Jill. 'Where is she? I was hoping to talk to her.'

'I'm sure you'll get the chance later. Right now, she's in the conservatory with Jacqueline. I believe they're swapping notes about their recent experiences.'

'I suppose it's nice that they've got each other to talk to,' Violet said. 'It'll do them good to open up – and it's a lot easier to do that with someone who's been through a similar ordeal.'

At the other end of the room, Rachel and Amelia jumped to their feet – prompted by the opening bars of Slade's 'Merry Xmas Everybody'.

'Uh-oh,' Violet said. 'It looks like you're about to see my mother's dance moves. I have to warn you, it's not a pretty sight.'

Fiona laughed. 'As long as she's enjoying herself, I don't care.'

'What about Molly and Robert, then?' Violet said. 'It's great news, don't you think?'

'Yes, I'm really chuffed for them, and I understand you have some exciting news of your own. Jill tells me you're buying Rock House.'

Violet smiled. 'We are. If everything goes to plan it'll be "all change" in the new year.'

'I'm thrilled for you,' Fiona said. 'You and Matthew are made for each other.'

'Thanks, Fiona.' Violet raised her glass. 'Merry Christmas.'

Fiona peered over Violet's shoulder and laughed.

'Don't look now, but Rachel is boogeying her way over here. I think she's going to force us to dance.'

Violet put her glass down and stood up. 'Come on then, Fi. Let's give in to the inevitable and join them. It is Christmas, after all.'

# Epilogue

Violet had eaten too much and danced too much, and she'd had one more glass of wine than was good for her. At half past nine, she draped her coat over her shoulders and went outside, to stand alone in the Nashes' enormous garden.

A crescent moon hung in the clear night sky and the temperature was below freezing, but the cold air felt pure and fresh and exhilarating. Violet breathed it in, glad to temporarily escape the Nashes' centrally heated living room.

Gazing up at the stars, she thought about the events of the last few weeks, and gave silent thanks that she had been lucky enough to spend the day with her wonderful family and friends.

She recalled Daniel Midship's Christmas video, which was saved on her cloud storage account. Feeling an inexplicable urge to watch it again, she downloaded the file and pressed 'play'.

Daniel's smiling face filled the screen of her phone. Even though she'd seen the video several times already, she listened in rapt attention as Daniel recalled the magical Christmases he'd spent with his daughter when she was young enough to still believe in Santa Claus. His description of his beloved Lucy, clad in a fluffy red dressing gown and opening presents on Christmas morning, brought a lump to Violet's throat.

But it was the final minute of the video that brought tears to her eyes. Smiling dolefully at the camera, Daniel said:

*'Christmas was never quite as magical after Lucy stopped believing in Father Christmas. The joy of it . . . the sparkle . . . faded away. I guess that was inevitable. Kids grow up. Life changes. It's an unavoidable fact of life that nothing stays the same for long – which is why memories are so important. They can transport you to the past, if you let them.'*

His smile widened as he closed his eyes.

*'When I shut my eyes, I can still see Lucy's face lighting up as she opens her presents from Santa. I can see the smile on her face, and hear her squeals of excitement. That kind of Christmas magic is fleeting, never destined to last – but it is meant to be remembered, and savoured.'*

He opened his eyes and looked directly into the camera lens.

*'If you can't be with your family on Christmas Day, the next best thing is to call them up and tell them how much you love them. That's what I intend to do. That way, Lucy and I can reminisce about the good times we've spent together and look forward to the days that are yet to come.'*

'It's a real pity he never got to do that,' said Matthew, who had joined Violet in the garden as the last twenty seconds of the video played out. 'Listening to that makes me feel enormously grateful for everything we have.'

'Me too,' Violet said, as Matthew rested his chin on her head. 'It's a reminder to make the most of every single day, because none of us know what the future has in store.'

'We don't need a crystal ball to know what *our* future holds,' he said. 'It's going to involve a lot of DIY and hard work – at least in the short term.'

Violet put her phone into her pocket and turned to face him.

'When it comes to DIY, I can't think of anyone I'd rather have alongside me than you.'

Matthew laughed. 'Good, because it looks like this move

is definitely going ahead. I think I've found you a buyer for Greengage Cottage.'

'Really? Who?'

'Someone I was talking to a few minutes ago . . . someone who's toying with the idea of moving to Merrywell and thinks your house would be perfect.'

'Who?' Violet said again.

Matthew grinned. 'Your mum.'

Violet's eyes widened. 'What?! Seriously? I didn't think Mum would ever want to move house.'

'Well, you were wrong,' Matthew said. 'And I must admit, it'll be nice to have her close by. You'd like that, wouldn't you?'

'Of course I would,' Violet said. 'It means I'll be able to keep an eye on her, and make sure she's OK.'

'Actually, I think it's going to be the other way around. Rachel intends to keep an eye on *you*. She told me she's hoping to keep you away from Charlie Winterton and out of trouble. She said, and I quote, "When I move to Merrywell, I'll make sure Violet doesn't go looking for any more mysteries to solve."'

Violet threw back her head and laughed . . . and laughed, and laughed, and laughed.

# Murder in Merrywell

**Welcome to Merrywell. Population: small. Secrets: aplenty.**

Ex-journalist Violet Brewster is keen to make a good first impression in her new community, having just moved to the small village of Merrywell. When Violet hears about the mystery of Helen Slingsby, who disappeared from the village forty years earlier, she decides to help uncover what happened. But despite Violet's best efforts, she can find no trace of the missing woman.

As Violet talks to the other residents, it becomes apparent that something sinister is lurking beneath the village's idyllic exterior.

When a villager is found dead in their home, Violet becomes convinced that the murder is connected to Helen. Did Helen ever really leave Merrywell? Who in the village is hiding something? And can Violet finally solve this forty-year-old mystery before someone else gets hurt?

# Murder at the Book Festival

**When a body is found at the Merrywell Book Festival, amateur sleuth Violet Brewster must leave no page unturned to solve the mystery . . .**

The small and idyllic village of Merrywell is getting ready to host its first ever book festival, and Violet Brewster is delighted when she is asked to interview the star author.

Leonie Stanwick, now a bestselling romance author, is the featured guest of the festival. She was born in Merrywell, but abruptly left when she was 18 years old and never came back.

But the festival takes a dark turn when Leonie is found murdered; her return to the village had clearly shaken someone up. When a shocking secret about Leonie's past is revealed, Violet's suspicions must turn to her own neighbours. Who in the village was intent on making sure Leonie could never leave the village again?

# Murder at Maple Grange

**Maple Grange is the perfect place to retire for the residents of Merrywell. But when a murder investigation unfolds on its grounds, Violet Brewster must dust off her sleuthing skills once again!**

Violet Brewster has just finished a project at local retirement village Maple Grange, when she learns that one of the residents, Phyllis Gibson, has passed away suddenly.

Violet is surprised that Phyllis left her a beautiful jewellery box in her will. When she goes to collect it, Maureen Bond, Phyllis's best friend, tells Violet that Phyllis had become paranoid during her last days, and was convinced that someone was trying to kill her.

When Maureen is pushed off her balcony, it becomes clear that something ominous is happening at Maple Grange. Violet is certain that the clues lie within the jewellery box. As the dangerous occurrences continue, can Violet unlock its contents and uncover the killer, before someone else gets hurt?

# Acknowledgements

Many thanks to everyone involved in the editing, cover design, book production and sales at HQ Publishing, especially my brilliant editor, Sophia Allistone. Thank you, one and all – I really appreciate the work you do to make my books the best they can be.

Thanks also to my husband, who listened attentively to my initial ideas for this book, and helped me to thrash out some of the finer details of my latest murder. Thank you, Howard. Life is always lots of fun with you around. I feel blessed to travel alongside you on this wonderful journey called 'life'.

As an author, I continue to be grateful for the unwavering support I receive from my family, friends, fellow authors, reviewers and readers. My sincere thanks to you all. I hope you enjoy reading *A Christmas Murder in Merrywell*.

The truth is, I'm not a huge fan of Christmas, so writing a book set in the festive season was quite a challenge! It didn't help that I started the first chapter in late August, when it was warm and summery, and not in the least bit Christmasy. However, on the first day of September, our local Morrisons supermarket came to the rescue by stocking mince pies on their shelves. Early September is (in my opinion) much too early to sell mince pies (especially when they have a 'best before' date that expires weeks before Christmas) – but hoping that a warm mince pie might get me into the Christmas mood and help with the writing, I bought a box. Of course, I would have preferred some of Fiona Nash's mince pies, but beggars can't be choosers. Thankfully, by the time I was polishing the first draft of the book, it was December. Christmas trees and twinkling fairy lights were everywhere, which made it much easier to get into the 'spirit of the season' and set the right tone for the book.

Whatever time of year you are reading this, I thank you for choosing *A Christmas Murder in Merrywell*. Rest assured, there will be more to come from Violet Brewster in 2026.

Website: janebettany.co.uk
Facebook: facebook.com/JaneBettanyAuthor
Instagram: Instagram.com/bettanyjane
Threads: threads.net/@bettanyjane
BlueSky: janebettany.bsky.social

Dear Reader,

We hope you enjoyed reading this book. If you did, we'd be so appreciative if you left a review. It really helps us and the author to bring more books like this to you.

Here at HQ Digital we are dedicated to publishing fiction that will keep you turning the pages into the early hours. Don't want to miss a thing? To find out more about our books, promotions, discover exclusive content and enter competitions you can keep in touch in the following ways:

### JOIN OUR COMMUNITY:
Sign up to our new email newsletter: http://smarturl.it/SignUpHQ
Read our new blog www.hqstories.co.uk

𝕏 https://twitter.com/HQStories
f www.facebook.com/HQStories

### BUDDING WRITER?
We're also looking for authors to join the HQ Digital family!
Find out more here:

https://www.hqstories.co.uk/want-to-write-for-us/

Thanks for reading, from the HQ Digital team